honey

honey

Isabel Banta

CELADON
BOOKS

NEW YORK

HONEY. Copyright © 2024 by Isabel Banta. All rights reserved. Printed in the United States of America. For information, address Celadon Books, a division of Macmillan Publishers, 120 Broadway, New York, NY 10271.

Designed by Michelle McMillian

ISBN 9781250333469

For Collin. And, always, for my mom.

I already knew the story, knew that I was helping to build it with the kindling of my own body.

—Melissa Febos, *Girlhood*

2002

New York, NY

Let's begin with my body. Look to the corner of west Forty-Second and Eighth, where a girl is reaching for a magazine on a newsstand. Around her, skyscrapers beheaded by mist, the stink of a city weaning off summer.

Women are splayed out like bars of candy, ready to be unwrapped. The girl picks up the latest issue of *Rolling Stone*, recognizing me on the cover. I am draped in fabric the color of honey, of syrup, of ooze. She flips through the heavy paper and finds the article—"WE ARE ALL TRAPPED IN AMBER"—nestled between perfume and cigarette ads. Sonny said I owed everyone an explanation, and here it begins: "Amber Young licks her lips before she speaks. Now they are wet as sap. Her auburn hair is the color of redwoods, her eyes mahogany brown. She speaks so softly I have to lean in closer to hear her properly. This is what she wants, right? When she looks up at me through thick lashes, I can't help but wonder if the rumors are true. Did these eyes blink and, like a Trojan horse, cause the great city to come crashing down? The city, in this case, being the relationship between Gwen Morris and Wes Kingston?"

If the girl loiters too long, the man behind the counter might ask her if she wants to buy something. She'll return the magazine to the stack, the pages closing like legs. Or maybe she'll buy it.

When I imagine what this girl might presume about me, how I might flicker in the backdrop of her life, I want to suck up everything I've ever done, wipe away anything I've ever stained.

VERSE 1

1990–1992

1990–1991

Morristown, NJ

The night before the Christmas talent show, I can't sleep because of the crickets. Dozens have escaped from our bearded dragon's cage, and now they are singing. If not for the lines of snow on our windowpanes, it could be summer, the air thick with vibration and sound.

When we first moved here, my brother and I asked for a dog, not a lizard, but my mom said our apartment was too small. Where would it run? At first, I didn't understand—we drove by tidy houses with buzz-cut lawns and bicycles kicked over in driveways, sleek retrievers that chased us to the edges of their electric fences. But then our sedan slid into the lot behind our apartment complex, only a few doors down from the orthodontist's office where my mom works as a receptionist. I immediately understood what she meant. The stairwell was littered with cigarette butts, the halls moldy with neglect. There would be no space for an animal here. No space even to spread my arms out wide. To open my mouth and have something come out.

This is why I hide my voice away, I think. I have pushed all my urges down, past my ribs and into my gut, because I am afraid of the hair growing between my legs, the hard buds in my chest. When I asked about these changes, arriving too soon, my mom said, "You're becoming a woman," and I started to cry.

So the crickets keep me up. Might as well practice alongside them. I stand in front of my mirror, pretending my hairbrush is a microphone. I've chosen "Tell It to My Heart" by Taylor Dayne for the talent show, and when I let myself sing, I understand the purpose of gods. It is belief taking on shape. Something I can't name moves inside me; something finally magnetizes. I release all that is pent up, yearning to burst forth. From every corner of the apartment, crickets hum.

The next night, I walk onto the stage, a rickety old thing with a stack of dusty gym mats in the corner. A red curtain hanging over my head like a guillotine. Rows of parents and grandparents with itchy holiday sweaters and grocery store flowers. My mom, chewing her Nicorette gum, and Jack Nichols, sitting in the second row with Lindsey Butler and Rachel Morrow. Just last weekend, a group of us gathered in Lindsey's basement and pushed *The Silence of the Lambs* into the VHS player, but none of us actually watched; the television was only color and sound in the background. Inside me, a similar glint. First shaft of desire. All my shapeless lust thrust at Jack Nichols, warped, then returned to me. He is the boy at school everyone wants; a collision of eyes always follows him. So when the spinning bottle landed on me, and he took my hand and led me into the closet, all the other girls visibly withered, and I expanded. In the dark, we leaned toward each other. Warmth bloomed between my legs, but the swipe of his lips was like a credit card through a slot. Behind the door, I could hear the others breathing, someone stifling a laugh. And, after, Lindsey took me into the bathroom. Said, "You know why he likes you, right? He only likes you because you have big boobs."

I glanced down at my chest.

"Do you want to date him?" Lindsey asked. "Like, you have a crush on him?"

"Yes."

She exited the bathroom and returned a minute later, then told me she had spoken with Jack.

"He's not into you," she said. "Sorry." She tried not to laugh but a little escaped. She's not the type to push someone over, but she loves pointing when they're already sprawled on the ground.

This humiliation is still fresh. Now they will watch me perform. Good. I am desperate to prove them wrong.

I step into the spotlight, my small hands wrapped around the microphone. My heart punches my ribs. The audience is whispering. I want to drag their eyes to me and hold them all in place.

As I begin to sing, I don't know a talent agent named Angela Newton is somewhere in the back row. She's driven down from the city to watch her nephew perform magic tricks. Her sister promised her the show would be only an hour, but now it's stretching into the second, an endless train of tap dancers and baton twirlers and pitchy singers. Then the light travels from the stage to her eyes. There—who is that? She sees a girl wobbling on unsteady foal legs. She sees a girl who would burn the stage if she could, just to step beyond it. Reaching for a pen in the dregs of her purse, she circles my name in her program.

I remember this performance as if it is trapped in amber. Memories like this sink into the earth in perfect condition, fossilize, and become a life.

Days pass. The year curls up. Many months later, in October, the phone rings. My mom taps her fingers impatiently against her jeans. There is a lasagna in the oven, Anita Hill's testimony crackling on our small television.

She places a finger in one ear and leans into the phone. "Sorry, who am I speaking to?"

"Angela Newton," says the voice on the other end. "I'm with Newton and Croft Management. I've been trying to reach you for months. I've left messages. Didn't you get them? I'm calling because I want your daughter to audition for us."

"I'm sorry, what? Audition for what?"

"For representation."

"Representation for what? I didn't sign up to receive your calls or anything, did I?"

"I saw your daughter perform at her talent show back in December. I'd like to have her come to New York. It's just an audition, of course. I can't offer representation at this time, but I'd like to see her again."

1992

New York

After I am signed by Angela, my mom calls in sick to work and takes
me to auditions. Most are for acting, not singing, which is what I really
wish I could do. And they are all in Manhattan, an hour and a half
away on a good day, two hours in traffic.

At a tollbooth, she picks through her wallet, plucks out a dollar bill.
Then she curses, searching under the seat and inside the cup holder for
stray coins. When we are ground back into traffic, she says, "You know,
I have to pick up your brother from school right after this. Look." She
points to the lane going in the other direction. Cars inching forward,
like ants carrying heavy leaves. "That's our way home." She sighs. "Do
you have your headshots?"

I do. I pull the heavy manila folder out of my bag. The photos inside
are thick and glossy. The photographer who took them kept asking
me to try on different sweaters, and I pulled and pulled but there was
always a small gap in the curtain as I changed, his eyes always waiting
there.

Now I run my hands along the edge of the photographs. *Amber
Young*, it says. *Newton and Croft Management.*

We have trouble parking in the city, as always. There is the stench of fried food, piles of trash that shudder with rats. My mom curses again, turning onto a one-way street. "We'll have to use a garage," she says. What is left unsaid: we can't afford all these parking garages.

The car doors slap shut, and I fish my underwear out of my butt crack, straighten the long jean skirt so it rests below my knees. My mom licks her hand and flattens my flyaways with her spit. A swipe of lip gloss across my mouth, gooey and sweet, but I lick it off by the time we've found the audition location: an inconspicuous door next to a dollar pizza joint.

In the waiting room, girls fidget while their mothers flip through magazines: *Ladies' Home Journal*, *Redbook*, *McCall's*, the bibles of white suburban women. Michelle Pfeiffer on one cover. Strategically placed around her face, the headlines say: "What She Did to Become a Star," "The Sex Life of the American Wife," "AIDS & the Woman Next Door," "GREAT GUYS: What Turns Them On." Each daughter is a miniature of her mother, and I can see exactly how their noses will lengthen, their limbs will stretch. I think daughters must lie inside their mothers like Russian dolls. Stacked bowls, one on top of the other.

Instead of taking a magazine, my mom sets her purse down and pulls out a shiny copy of *Jewels* by Danielle Steel. Last week, I searched for a sex scene, eyes darting like hummingbirds to flowers, but then I heard the floorboards tremble and shoved the book back onto her nightstand.

They call names. My mom's eyes flit over the pages, I strum on a hangnail. Then, my name. It is time. I enter a white room, where a casting director and her assistant stare dully at me. The assistant reaches for my headshot, glances at it, then flings it onto a table already piled with stacks of girls, all of us white, slim, beaming. From the top of the pile, I grin in my green sweater, an adolescent gap between my teeth. My mouth and eyes too big for my face.

"Name, age." The casting director smacks on gum. It is the sound of wet batter being stirred. "Look into the camera, please."

I raise my voice two octaves. "My name is Amber Young, and I'm twelve years old."

"Great. Now, what I want you to do for me is to look here." She points to a piece of tape on the floor. "That's where the Easy-Bake Oven and Snack Center will be. Pretend you wanted it more than anything, and now you have it. You're totally shocked. You can't believe it. Okay? Can you do that for me?"

I kneel on the ground and cup my hands around the invisible Easy-Bake Oven. Crumbs from their lunch dig into my knees. I stroke the air and lean forward, widening my eyes. "Wow! An Easy-Bake Oven! This is so great!"

The casting director shakes her head, confused. "No, honey. Can you start again, but this time act *surprised*? Pretend your dad surprised you with it. You've been wanting it for Christmas, and you *finally* got one. Okay?"

"Wow! Dad, this is the best present ever. I've always wanted an Easy-Bake Oven!"

The casting director and her assistant exchange a glance. "Thank you, honey. That's enough."

Months later, the commercial comes on during an episode of *Beverly Hills, 90210.* I recognize a beautiful girl from the waiting room. She's ecstatic about the Easy-Bake Oven her dad got her; she wants it more than anything. She makes cupcakes and cookies and brownies that drip with molten chocolate. And I want to shove it all into my mouth at once. I imagine the softness of the cake, my teeth bursting the cherry on top of it, the rush of juice down my throat.

I feel like a fruit swinging from a tree. Plump and flush with color, waiting to be plucked.

The auditions sting for days afterward. They are scrapes all over my body. I leave school early most days, don't turn in my work on time, return with nothing. I float around inside myself. Before auditions, I watch the older girls in the waiting rooms. Some of them are so beautiful, I pray to trade faces with them at night.

I hold the hairbrush up to my mouth. My dad's old tape recorder is perched on my dresser. I rewind the tape. Begin again.

My brother, Greg, bangs against the wall. "Will you shut the hell up?"

"Um, no!" I scream back. Doesn't he understand? I can't stop. Because I can only find well-oiled gears in my lungs, I love this part of my body more than anything else. More than my thighs, my chest. My eyes, which jolt away like an engine each time I catch another man staring. But my lungs, my vocal cords? These haven't changed. They are dependable in a time of great betrayal.

My mom throws open the door. She is always upset after her shift. "What's with this noise?" she slurs. "What are you doing?"

"Making an audition tape."

Her eyes mark the clothes on the rug, a wet towel slung over my desk chair. She picks each of them up one by one, lets them fall and crumple again. "Do I look like a maid? Clean up."

I put everything in the hamper.

"This place is such a pigsty," she mumbles under her breath. The door slams. Then she knocks on Greg's door, and their voices seep through the walls. It's your fault dad left. Move out, then. I hate you. You're an asshole. Bitch. Your grades are shit. You're a terrible mother.

I take a deep breath and press record. When my voice shields me from the outside world, it is the strongest it will ever be. I sing myself into silver armor, into tough lichen that crawls on volcanic rock. This is the tape Angela will send to *Star Search*. Until we hear back, there's nothing to do but wait to be plucked from a pile.

Later, Greg sits on my bed, pink and bristling from their argument. "I'm leaving here and never coming back," he says. "I'm going to go to college across the country, in California or New Mexico or Arizona."

"Will you look up Dad?"

He laughs. This makes me feel stupid for even suggesting it.

"Maybe living with him would be better than this," I say.

"Yeah," agrees Greg. "Maybe."

Greg and I have never been very close; we both retreat behind closed doors. At seventeen, he has been cultivating a type of manhood I don't particularly like, moving in a throng of boys from the liquor store to the park. If our mom is out drinking, he brings girls home. Some are perky and athletic, others inky-haired and pierced. Each has made a clear choice about how to present herself. Most are prickly around him—cruelty that is just flirtation—but I can tell this is for their own protection; they really want him to slash through this front, to find what is soft. Greg is too dumb to understand this.

Sometimes I can hear him having sex with them. On these nights, I fall asleep listening to my mom's Walkman, the volume on full blast.

Out of habit, I press the button to hear our messages as I search the cabinet for bread and peanut butter. It's Angela. She's heard from *Star Search* casting about my tape, and she's screaming into our answering machine.

Orlando is sticky. Bogs spread in my armpits. We stay in a hotel with itchy peach sheets, a pool full of floating, washed-up flies. One morning, I ride the coasters at Disney alone, since my mom says she's used her vacation time from work for the trip and wants to lay out on the beach. When I return at midday, I find her snoring and reeking of liquor. I practice my songs in front of the bathroom mirror while she sleeps, using her hair dryer as my microphone.

Backstage at the Disney-MGM Studios, they have a buffet of chicken wings and other fried foods. A production assistant guides us through cinder block hallways to a green room, where I'm deposited in a makeup chair. There are jewel-toned eyeshadow palettes, wands and brushes and powders, the same objects my mom hoards. But her palettes are cheap and flimsy—pharmacy-bought. I close my eyes and enjoy myself as a mask of womanhood hardens on top of my face. I'm wearing my favorite overalls over a baby tee, a red flannel tied around my waist, messy plum polish on my nails. I tried to paint them on the plane ride *Star Search* paid for, but I screwed them up during turbulence.

A middle-aged man, a comic, comes up behind me. We both watch my reflection changing in the mirror. "You must be in a dance group," he says. "You look like a dancer."

I shake my head and tell him I'm a Junior Vocalist. A singer. Strange to say this out loud. To declare myself.

"I bet your voice is real sweet," he says, but his voice doesn't match the look in his eyes. He's one of those men who flatter and console but have hidden shards behind a soft exterior. And his gaze is so righteous, so claiming, it feels like I should step out of my skin and hand it over as a gift.

He slinks away as soon as my mom arrives, pausing only to shake her hand.

"Good luck!" she calls to him, but she makes a face as soon as he's gone. Fixing her hair in the mirror, she says, "I've found out who you're challenging." I follow her gaze—who?

He looks older than me, but not by much. A makeup artist is patting foundation under his eyes, and he chews on his full bottom lip. He has dark, slick hair. Loads of zits on his cheeks, a whole mountain range of red. He would be a troublemaker at school—one of the boys with impish smiles who light firecrackers in the parking lot and dare one another to jump over the sparks, who carry pocketknives just to show off, not intending to ever use them.

Our eyes meet in his mirror, and I quickly look away.

I feel like I've been strapped into a roller coaster. The metal handlebars are pressing too deep into my skin, and I want their grip to release me. But the car is already vibrating; it is about to shoot into the sky, and there is nothing I can do now. How else do you become somebody? How else are you finally chosen?

. . .

"To find our next challenger, we traveled all the way to New Jersey," says Ed McMahon. "Here's Amber Young!"

The theater is starred with thousands of eyes. They blink at me, expectant. Cameras tilt and flow in my direction as I step onto the stage. My mom is in the wings, her lips pursed. And my competition, Wes Kingston, watches me from a monitor. His mother's hand grips his shoulder, digs in.

I have never sung in front of so many people, and I feel like a nude statue in a museum, assessments coming from all angles, but I'm on a pedestal, too. The light is streaming down from above. I love this more than anything—to watch mouths fall open in delight, to hear a chorus of cheers and whoops whenever I hit a high note.

Then it is my turn to watch. As soon as Wes starts to sing, I know it is over and done with. He knows how to work the crowd; he's probably been doing it for years. His performance is much more rehearsed than mine. I had thought, naively, that if I just showed up and sang my little heart out, I could win, that I needed no flourishes, no choreography, only my voice.

After Ed McMahon reveals the scores, 3.75 stars to 3.25, I am led offstage. There, I fold into a corner. My body cannot hold itself up; my weight sags. Hot tears flow down my cheeks. I wasn't good enough—what a mortifying thing to discover about yourself.

There's a gentle tap on my shoulder. I turn around.

"You were amazing," Wes tells me.

I blink up at him.

"Really," he insists. "I thought you'd beat me. When you started to sing, I thought I was done for."

It is a kind thing to say. It makes me cry even harder. "Thanks."

He kicks the wall with his white sneaker, scuffing the front. "I'll probably lose in the next round, anyway."

I use my sleeve to collect more tears.

"I just wanted to tell you. You should have won."

When he's gone, and the color of this memory fades, I will still remember the texture of his voice, his kindness, how his head appeared before me like a satellite reflecting the sun.

My mom says the auditions need to end. Maybe I'm not cut out for this. What she won't admit: my breasts are too big for kid parts now. I have a woman's body.

Besides, she says, I haven't gotten a single part. Remember how much I cried when I didn't get the McDonald's commercial? Or the off-Broadway musical? After two callbacks, too. What a waste of time. And we don't have the money for dance lessons, voice lessons, theater camps, all these tollbooths and parking garages in the city. Don't I know what I've taken from her? She never sees her friends, never does absolutely anything for herself—and all for nothing.

So I agree to quit, and she makes the call. This time, I don't listen to her on the phone with Angela. I only hear the click of the receiver, which means it's done.

Most singers say they loved performing as a kid. There are grainy VHS tapes of them wearing feather boas, sashaying around the living room with their siblings. Gwen was like that, and so was Wes, but I didn't like to perform. I liked to be loved.

But now? I think these two things might stem from the same want: to be inflated. To have hot air blown into you by another person's lips. For helium to lift your bones until you're caught in whetted branches.

PRE-CHORUS

1997–1999

1997

New York

Angela's office is still in Midtown. On my walk over from Penn Station, people weave around one another like hands braiding hair. Taxis honk and loiter and fume. I don't remember much about the agency, and for some reason, I am expecting an impressive reception area, a man at the front desk leading me to an elevator, which will shoot up like a missile. Through the glass windows, there will be a spread of buildings all the way to the Twin Towers, car-bombed four years ago.

Instead, the office is in a run-down building with chipped paint on the stairwell. The waiting room smells like an ashtray. Files are thrown around in haphazard piles. The receptionist stares blankly at me, then says Angela will be with me in just a minute, she's on the phone with a client right now, but why don't I take a seat? I flip through an issue of *YM* as I wait.

When I'm called in, Angela is still on the phone. She holds up a finger for me, pointing toward the peeling leather chair in front of her desk. After she smacks the phone into the receiver, she says, "Hi, honey, sorry about that." She cranes her neck toward the waiting room. Frowns. "Is your mom with you? Does she want to come in?"

"She doesn't know I'm here."

Her eyes trail over my face, the very same beam that settled on me when I was ten and marked me forever. I wonder what she was hoping to see in me, what she sees now, what the difference is between these two things. Something was building before, each atom accumulating kinetic energy, but now there is only wasted potential. Now I am sixteen, almost seventeen, and this age is a hinge; I could swing forward or backward.

"You've dyed your hair," she observes.

"Oh, no, I haven't. It just got darker over time." When I was younger, it was more auburn, streaked with sun each summer. Now all the red undertones have faded. Now it is the same shade of brown as my mother's.

"Very pretty."

I take a strand between my fingers and comb it. "Thanks."

"Are all the boys nuts over you? Do you have a boyfriend?"

I laugh. "Um, no."

"I remember when I first met you, you know," she says. "So much talent. It was almost falling out of you."

Yes. She understands. But when we first met, I was so porous, so easily wounded, a sponge for failure. But nothing will happen to me unless I ask for it. Unless I lean forward here, at her desk, and say, "That's why I'm here. I want to audition again. I made a mistake—quitting, you know. I shouldn't have done it. I didn't really want to."

She frowns. "You can't go out for the same roles, sweetie. It's different now."

Together, we glance down at my body. I wish I could spread my life out before her so she can understand the ways in which it has diverged from my hopes.

"I don't think I can take you on again," she says.

"I don't want to act. I want to sing." Naive again, I think singing must have nothing to do with looks, that all that's needed is a capable voice.

She leans back in her chair. "You want to sing," she repeats.

I nod. I want to sing, yes, but it's more than that: I also want to be heard. I want specific people to listen.

"Well, I haven't heard you sing in years."

"Here," I say. I hand her the tapes I've stuffed into my bag. "I've gotten better."

She taps a fingernail on her desk. "Why did you quit, Amber?"

"My mom wanted me to. She thought it was pointless. And it just hurt too much." Doesn't she remember calling us after every audition? I would rush to the phone, and Angela would break the news: the part had gone to someone else. There are just so many talented girls, she would say. Amber needs more training. Amber is too young. Too old. Too enthusiastic. Too shy. She doesn't have the right look.

Now she nods. "Most of the kids we take on get nothing," she says. "One commercial, maybe. And their whole lives, someone—their parents, a teacher, maybe, but someone—has been telling them they're special. This business is especially cruel to them. Especially brutal."

"But no one has ever told me that," I say. It's just the opposite. Years ago, no one chose me after hundreds of auditions, but I am still desperate for praise, hoping someone important will say, "Yes, *you* are the one we want." And in that moment, I will finally change from a gaseous to a solid thing.

Angela considers me, crossing her arms. "Well, I'll listen. If these are any good, I'll give them to a former colleague of mine. I think he knows some people in A&R at the labels. He might be able to advise you."

She slips the tapes inside her desk.

This is how my voice makes its way to my manager Sandy Anderson, though I will always call him Sonny. He's worked for various talent agencies—briefly with Angela—but now he is hoping to manage musicians and bands independently. I am his first and only client. Sonny has ruddy, sunburned skin that never peels, no matter what season it is. A brassy laugh that can shake a room. "You know what success looks like, Amber honey?" he'll say. "You'll only know when we get there. It's something that can only be felt."

But before my tapes reach Sonny, nothing happens. I slip back into junior year. Parties held in basements, weekends of loose, humiliating emotion that we contain again by school on Monday. Tests slid onto my desk, mediocre grades circled in definitive red. Unlocking the apartment door each night to find it dark. But when my mom is gone, I know I can blast my favorite albums as loudly as I want to. I slide the CDs out of my backpack and into the player in our living room. They spin and spin, and so time passes. So music moves across me, the water carving into my stone, until I am widened and deepened by other voices.

In May, Lindsey drives Rachel and me to the shore in her new car. We are friends because older boys pay attention to me: this is valuable currency to these girls, so I am now rich. "Dreams" by the Cranberries is playing. I lean my head against the window, closing my eyes, the highway thumping below the tires. It's true—*I want more, impossible to ignore.* Sometimes a song sounds exactly the way you want your life to feel. Sometimes it makes you believe you can change it.

We carry the warm beer we bought at a 7-Eleven to the sea. Dune grass rocks in the wind; a raccoon scavenges for turtle eggs. When Lindsey and Rachel begin gossiping about the slut list found in the bottom of a desk (*Number two: Amber Young*), I walk along the shore and skip rocks. Each slap: *more, more, more.*

Afterward, we get ready at Lindsey's for a school dance. We're always there, since her house is the largest, but tonight she wasn't invited and has been sulking about staying in. She's flipping through a CD—*Jagged Little Pill*—never waiting long enough to listen to the entirety of a song before she begins the next.

Lindsey has begun to smoke, but really she just likes to hold the cigarette between her index and pointer fingers, inhaling once or twice before stamping it out. Now she takes a single drag and leans out the window, lazily watching the smoke escape.

"Here," she says, holding it to me. I take it. "Are you going to wear that again?"

I glance down at my outfit, the leather jacket and tight black dress. The pins in my hair nip at my skull. She likes to remind herself that I don't have a lot of clothing. "Didn't you wear that exact same thing on Monday?" she will say on Friday. I space outfits at least three days apart, hoping no one will notice, but she always does.

Ash falls on her rug. I say yes. I forgot I wore it last weekend.

I can see her eyes inhale this answer, but she chooses not to press further. She knows she can, and I'll let her, which is enough.

I lean over her shoulder to check her driveway. There is a charge of expectation, a current traveling through the circuit of my body. To-night, something will happen. We all keep glancing outside, waiting for a flash of metal, and then there's the car pulling up, packed with senior boys, their hands stretched out the windows, "Bop Gun (One Nation)" oozing from the radio.

In the car, Rachel sits shotgun next to her date. The other three seniors are squished into the back, thigh against thigh. My date, Nathan, pulls me onto his lap because there aren't enough seats. His cheeks and neck are flushed. He smells like beer, body odor, sweat—all beneath cologne. It is like a pile of leaves covering up dog shit.

Rachel's date, Colby, takes his hand off the steering wheel to pass Nathan a bottle of liquor. He chugs it for a few seconds, then holds it out in front of me, eyebrows raised. A challenge. I take the bottle between my hands and raise it to my lips, desperate to prove myself to him. The vodka burns my mouth and throat. My entire face clenches.

Nathan's hand brushes my leg. "Bad?"

"Awful."

"Here, I brought us chasers." He reaches under the seat, fumbling around for something: a pack of apple juices, the same brand my mom used to buy me when I was little. Each box has a clear straw in plastic wrapping, a body of red-and-green cardboard.

I poke the straw through the top and suck out the juice, which is warm from sitting in the car for days.

"Better?" Nathan asks. He pushes my hair behind my ear. The alcohol has started to settle in my chest. It is far easier to lift a hand now, to laugh at Nathan's jokes. The night whips by, fences and houses blurring like insect wings.

We're at the dance for only an hour, maybe two. The gym is hung with white and silver streamers and a table is laid out with pretzels, chips, sherbet punch. Hands dig through bowls. Plastic cups are tossed by the trash. On the dance floor, girls sway to "Rhythm Is a Dancer" by Snap! in tight rings, looking over their shoulders self-consciously. We sit at a corner table and pour alcohol into our cups under the vinyl tablecloth.

"You're chill," observes Colby. "You're not like the girls in our grade."

"How?" asks Rachel.

"They don't put out," says Colby, but then Nathan smacks him on the arm, as if he's revealed a terrible secret: we are just a calculation they've made. Which girls have the highest probability to lead to sex?

Later that night, Nathan hoists me onto his bathroom sink and I wrap my legs around his waist. Nathan says if we're quiet, no one will hear us.

When his fingers struggle with my bra, I hop down from the sink and show him what to do. "There," I say, and suddenly I am undone. He pulls me through the door, revealing his sparse, clinical bedroom. It is devoid of any personality. Who is Nathan Ross? I know so little. A senior, popular, admired by the other boys for his height. Now he's lying on the bed beneath me, cupping my breasts in his hands. "Jesus," he says. He presses them together and then releases, so they swing apart.

"Nathan."

"Yeah?"

"I've never had sex before."

He shrugs. "No worries."

I realize then how little I mean to him. But something has already been set in motion, lights whirring, and it never occurs to me that I can change my mind. What would he say if I did? I wait for the stab, the bulldoze. But he is small. It is a shock at first, but then he is inside me and there is no pain like my friends or magazines said there would be, but no pleasure either. He doesn't really know what he is doing; neither do I. He probably believes he can start a flame just by striking me again and again. All I can think is, *I am having sex, this is sex, I am having it, I am having it now.* I explore the strange machinery of my body, and I pull all the levers inside myself in order to please him. When he gasps and collapses against my chest, I remind myself to moan.

"Did you come?" he asks.

I tell him I did, and he nods, pleased with himself.

Everyone says there is a boundary crossed, a before and an after. I have become something new. When exactly did it happen? Was it when he used his tongue, which felt like a wet fish flopping on land, or when he entered me? Or was it all over years ago, when I first surveyed myself, moving across my own terrain? All I know is tonight Nathan Ross caused no landslides, no floods.

A week later, I am watching *Daria*, a new show on MTV. My mom walks in front of the television, scowling at the cartoon. "I hate this crap," she says. "Someone on the phone for you."

I jump up and race over to the landline.

Before I press the phone to my ear, I close my eyes and take a breath. I tell myself it could be anyone—Lindsey, Rachel, a telemarketer. But my heart is an insistent fist pounding on a door.

"Hello?" I breathe.

"This Amber Young?" The voice on the other end has a Long Island accent and is midchew.

"Yes, this is she."

"It's Sandy Anderson from Anderson Management. Honey, I've got to tell you, this is the best tape I've listened to in a long time."

"Really?"

He laughs. "Don't bullshit me with that false humility, hon. You know you can sing."

"Loads of people can sing." I am not bullshitting him, not even close. Many people have talent like mine. The tragedy is wasting it.

Sonny then says my tape is in the hands of an A&R representative at Siren. Artists and Repertoire, he clarifies. These are the people in the music business who weave careers together. They scout the artists, choose the songwriters and producers, craft the albums.

"He's looking for the last member of a girl group. He'll need a demo tape of the four of you."

"But I don't have a demo tape."

"Well, you'll go to New York to audition for the label first. You'll record one there."

"Today?"

"Next week."

"I have school."

Sonny laughs. "What's school for if you want to sing? Are you going to ace choir?" And the line goes dead.

Early morning. I'm woken by a crash from the kitchen. It's my mom, collapsed on the floor. Her taupe lipstick is smeared across her face. There's an open cut on her forehead. A wine bottle leans reverently against the back of the couch, which divides our tiny kitchen from the living room.

We are alone now—Greg is in Arizona, the lizard is dead, and she has no one left but me. I pour the wine down the sink. I lean over her and rub antibiotic ointment over her cut, then tuck her into bed on her side so she won't choke on her own vomit. As I close the door, I tell her I love her, even though I know she can't hear me. The apartment makes its sounds: the radiator mumbles; the floorboards creak under my feet. I try to fall asleep again, because this is just another day, and my mom will sober up and brighten, like the light gathering strength underneath my blinds.

Later that morning, I laze in our bathtub, running my hands through the lukewarm water. I'm supposed to get on the train in thirty minutes for the audition. The futures before me: senior year with Lindsey and Rachel, or the possibility of a different life. A life that holds a charge. My mom wants me to think practically—to consider college, a career—and chasing your own talent to its conclusion is anything but practical. It's a kind of relentless insanity. It's believing in something higher and unknowable—a god—while everyone around you is shaking their heads in confusion. "I just don't see it," they say, again and again, until you wonder if you are deluded in your fanaticism. Am I deluded?

I submerge myself. The water zips shut. Now, I think, some path will clear for me. But I don't consider how to cut down a forest, what I need to slash and burn.

I want this moment—the before—to stretch on forever. Now. No, *now*. My head breaks the surface.

In a glass room, a dozen silver-haired men sit at a cold table and watch me sing. They have hungry eyes. These men want another song, so I clear my throat and sing something else a cappella. My voice is the only sound in the room other than the clicking of pens, the shuffling of papers, my own needy, insistent pulse. Sonny taps his fingertips against his knee. My mom's lips are a thin line, and her purse has tipped over, the contents scattered on the floor. At first, I am conscious of my pitch, the slight crack in my voice on a belt. One man winces slightly. Then I rein in my voice, corralling it, and I can tell they like this better. Their approval is a guidepost, and they clearly want me to contain myself. Fine. In their eyes, I can see myself reflected: someone elastic, someone they can press on.

Outside, skyscrapers like stalagmites are spread across the horizon. This is the nicest building I have ever been inside, and I know I'm shaking. The building is, too: this high up, we are swaying and groaning in the wind.

After I finish, I dig my nails into my palms.

"Let's get her in a room with the other girls," the head of the label says. His eyebrows are much lighter than his hair. "We'll put her up in a hotel, and tomorrow we'll see."

I glance at Sonny. Does this mean no school tomorrow? There's a history final I haven't studied for. Rachel was going to lend me her notes. But the label head is purposefully vague. No promises, of course. Don't get your hopes up. He pushes a smile onto his face and asks what grade I'm in. He has a daughter, he says, just about my age.

After small talk lobbied back and forth, one of the younger men ushers us from the room. "I'm Simon," he says, shaking our hands. He has a thin face and rheumy eyes, the look of someone who never calls in sick but should. "I'm the A&R rep who saw your tape."

"So why did you pick her?" my mom asks. She hasn't had time to put her things back in her purse, so she shoves it all in as we walk.

Simon slows to accommodate her, wrongly assuming she is the stage parent he needs to impress, the battery powering all my ambition. "I was listening to so many tapes, from managers and agents and what have you," he says. The elevator dings; we step inside. My stomach flips with the swiftness of the drop. "This guy—" And he claps his hand on Sonny's shoulder. "He sent Amber's in and I just—well, the girl she'd be replacing couldn't even hit some of those notes."

"Why did this girl drop out?" I ask. I can't picture anyone not wanting this the way I do.

"She was a bit difficult, and she had a problem being part of a group." He says this very quickly, hardly pausing for breath. Then he smiles at me, because he senses what all the other men in that room have already sniffed out: I'm the opposite. I will do anything, whatever they want me to do, and that's why I'm perfect.

We weave through rows of cubicles to another set of elevators. He says, "We'll have you back here tomorrow. My assistant will take care of everything. Leslie, can you come here?" He waves a girl over from her desk. "Leslie can help you. The thing is, we're trying to rush this,

Ms. Young, to be completely frank with you. We need to be on top of trends, you know? The kids want to see groups. They want different characters they can identify with. And I think they'll aspire to be just like your daughter."

"Who will?" my mom asks.

Simon smiles. "Other girls."

When I lie in the hotel bed that night, I toss and turn because of the pressure of my heart against my pillow. Bugs crawling through my body, the labor of my breath. My mom's luxurious snores from the bed beside mine. Outside, an urban cacophony—sirens, shouts, honks, a peal of laughter. Layer upon layer of sound, rising and collapsing, and it sounds just like voices.

I meet Gwen Morris for the first time in the recording studio bathroom. There is a sudden bang, then the door opens and swings on its hinge. Flip-flops against the tiles. A tap turning and water spurting out of the sink. Through the slit in the stall, I see her for the first time, but only in fragments. A slice of pale thigh, strands of dark hair.

Staring at her reflection, she bends over and smacks her lips. Then she tugs on her eyelashes and starts pulling out clumps of mascara, rubbing the black goo on the sink's edge. Her lips part in concentration, and a pink tongue flickers inside her mouth.

I make a sound and her eyes jump to my stall. I startle, quickly wipe and flush, then shimmy my underwear up my thighs and unlock the door.

"Sorry," I murmur. I don't know what else to say to her. She is the most beautiful girl I have ever seen. Her face is a golden ratio. She has no sunspots or freckles, just a dark mole above her left eyebrow. Her eyes are resort-water blue, and she has thin, Linda Evangelista limbs. As I pump soap out of the dispenser, I stand on my tiptoes to lengthen my reflection beside hers. My beauty takes more convincing than hers does. All my features are larger.

"Hi," she says, a little reluctantly. "I'm Gwen."

I introduce myself.

"Pretty name," she says. "I've always wanted a name like that."

"Um, no, you don't. It sounds like a stripper's name."

"Let's see how you dance, then." When she smiles at me, I notice her teeth are covered in streaks of plaque. An imperfection. It soothes me somewhat.

In the vocal booth, the four of us are lined up in front of music stands. Gwen Morris, Claudia Jeong, Rhiannon Walsh, me. The producers and Simon sit behind the mixing board in the control room, arms crossed over their chests. Only Gwen doesn't show her nerves. The rest of us fidget and pick at ourselves.

"Let's just sing something you all know," says Simon. "The national anthem. Let's just see how it sounds. Okay? Great." He claps his hands together.

Before we begin, before it all begins, Rhiannon leans over to whisper in my ear: "They expect us to know the words to the fucking national anthem?"

I swallow a laugh. We suck air into our lungs. Our voices are tentative at first, then full. Rhiannon hums most of the words, while the rest of us grasp at lyrics. When we've hit the final note, the four of us look at one another and begin to laugh. I think we are all eager to be a part of something. Until this moment, we were alone as the world began to look at us differently, catching another glance over its shoulder.

"We've got something here," Simon says, clapping. "We've got something. Again, girls. Let's go again."

1997

Los Angeles, CA

Los Angeles is long days of dry heat. Falling into bed at night, exhausted from hours of choreography and voice lessons. Siren sending black cars to take us everywhere, making us believe we are special. Claudia turning up the radio whenever Missy Elliott's "The Rain (Supa Dupa Fly)" comes on, the sun drilling us through the windshield, the freeway blasting hot air into the car. The feeling, however fleeting, that we are watching our lives kindle. As we plunge into the hotel pool, as our bikinis soak through the shirts we throw over them, stamping new moons onto our chests, it is all golden.

My mom takes a few days off work to fly with me to California, but she quickly returns to New Jersey, trusting Sonny to chaperone me for the rest of the time. After she's gone, Simon, our A&R guy, hosts a dinner at an Italian place on the strip. All the other mothers are there. Mrs. Morris, a small blond woman, won't shut up about Gwen's accomplishments, boasting as if they are hers, like she is really pulling the levers inside her daughter like a forklift. "Gwen could have been *anything*," she tells us. "She was good at everything she tried. She was known around town for all her talent. Gosh, she won everything. She could have been a soccer player if she wanted. She won beauty pageants all over the state."

Simon interrupts her, raising his glass. "To the girls. To Cloud9." Mrs. Morris's eyes widen, as if she's been stopped up midpour, and all the things she hasn't said yet are pushing against her face.

The light from the chandelier refracts off our glasses. There is a stillness, a hallowed silence. Everything is just starting for us, this night seems to say. The noise is not far off. It's all accumulating, and soon we won't be able to hear beyond it. But first, the label will listen to our demos, then decide if they want to sign us as a foursome. I ask Sonny what this means—Simon called it a development deal.

Sonny says, "It means they have thirty days to decide whether they want to invest in you, and if not, it's over. We go back home with nothing."

Our choreographer moves me from the front to the back during dance rehearsal, saying I'm not putting my hands in the right places. I watch Gwen, her thong just visible above the line of her sweatpants. Her limbs are fluid, effortless. Mine don't move the way hers do, no matter how hard I try.

Sonny is watching us from one of the folding chairs beside the mirror. These chairs have also hosted label executives in recent days. Simon, too. They are all wondering the same thing: Do we bet on these girls? Are they a good investment?

When we break for water, Sonny holds up a CD. "Do you all know what this is?"

"Oh my god," breathes Claudia. She reaches for it. Rips away the clear wrapping. The cover art shows five boys standing on a hill. They wear long black trench coats, and their faces are raised to the sky. Lightning forks in the distance, forming the album title: *Lightning in a Bottle*. Below that, in golden block letters: ETA.

"Have you heard 'The One I Want'?" Sonny asks. We all nod. It's been on the radio every day; Rhiannon always turns the station when she hears it in the car. The beat is incessant, like a buzzing fly: *It's obvious to me / Should be obvious to you / You're the one I want / What more can I do? / Girl, I'll plead / I'll be your fool.*

"This is their full album," says Sonny, pointing to the CD. "This is what we want to capture."

Claudia smirks. "What? Lightning in a bottle?" She has lime-green eye shadow on today, but her sweat has caused it to smudge.

Sonny shakes his head. "No."

What, then? What do we need?

Discipline, it turns out. He tells us ETA was put together by one of the band member's mothers. She found them by scoping out talent competitions, hoping to find boys the same age as her son. They were eventually signed by SMG, one of Siren's competitors, over two years ago. Two years, no hit singles. Lackluster sales. Again and again, the label threatened to drop them. Now, sudden success. Sonny narrows his eyes and says we might have to be patient. We'll need to have grit. I watch Gwen absorb this information. I can tell her ambition is a battering ram; she wants to break through already, same as me.

It is late at night, past two a.m. I'm still in the studio practicing our routine. I watch my reflection in the mirror and clench my fists in frustration. Lift my shirt and wipe the sweat off my face.

As I dance, I count off to myself, and a shadow lengthens across the studio. Gwen's reflection is a pale specter in the mirror, watching me silently. Once she's seen enough, she tosses her flip-flops in a corner, then gets into position in front of me.

"When we sing *You remind me of summer heat*, that's when you should start the spin. You keep watching your reflection. Don't watch yourself. You'll always be a step off if you do that."

"But I'm terrible."

"You're not. You're just a beat behind. And you have the best voice out of all of us."

"Don't lie." I'm afraid her kindness is just a deposit for future gain.

But maybe what she's saying is free. I don't understand it: she doesn't need to put others down to hoist herself up.

"I'm not," she insists. "I swear. Let's start from the top. You've got it."

Again, her kindness. I try it for myself. "You're the best dancer, you know."

"Yeah, I do know." It's knowledge that has sunk so deep within her, she doesn't try to deny it. I admire her directness.

"I know, too. That I'm the best singer."

She smiles and tells me that's good. She begins counting us off. "And one, two, three, and four . . ." She spins around to adjust my arm, then back to the mirror.

This is Gwen—not the way the media will portray her, both of us, as if all we are is one face of a prism. She is beautiful and kind and determined—all the things they will want her to be—but she is the contradictions they fear from her, too. To me, she will forever be dawn blooming outside the window, coaching me through the routine for hours, until I finally get it right.

This time feels sacred. Not like high school and the friendships I valued for reasons unknown to me now. Lindsey and Rachel haven't answered my calls for days. When they do pick up, they tell me who slept with who behind the basketball bleachers, how they drove to the shore and lit a bonfire on the beach. Strange to realize I don't care about these old dramas. The Cloud9 girls see the world the way I do, hunger for all the things I'm starving for. Here I am a part of something warm and intimate, a community felt in the body.

One afternoon, the four of us push the twin beds together in Gwen's hotel room.

"Gwen, you haven't told us anything about your boyfriend yet," Rhiannon says. She's covered in so many freckles, it is as if a pointillist painter has worked with golden flecks over a canvas of skin. Leaning back on her hands, she blows her choppy bangs out of her eyes.

"I mean, he was only my boyfriend back home," Gwen says defensively. "We broke up when I came here."

"But you had sex," Rhiannon says.

"I gave him a blow job, but we didn't have sex. It's different."

Rhiannon raises an eyebrow. "Are you secretly a slut? You totally are, aren't you?"

This word: slut. A knife scraped along flesh. My mother uses this word to describe other women, but I've never heard Rhiannon use it. I think we all first picked up on these words from our mothers: slut and bitch and whore, even prude. They taste bitter on the tongue, but sweet on release, as long as we aren't the ones they describe. Rhiannon has probably called me these names behind my back, but I don't know which ones; the way she turns people and definitions around in her hands is unclear to me. In her mind, there seems to be a perfect amount of sex to have that doesn't label you as one thing or another, but she can't determine exactly what that is. It appears to vary from person to person. I wish there were a universal answer, so I'd know what to do.

I press my knees to my chest and sink my toes into the sheets. A better version of myself might stick up for Gwen, but I say nothing.

Claudia says, "Giving head is a subset of sex. It's, like, under the same umbrella."

I nod, thinking of the rings around a tree, how sex and my own understanding of it have expanded outward over time. When I was younger, I thought you could have a baby when you ingested someone else's DNA—hair, nails, even flakes of skin. Once, I swallowed a hair on a piece of pizza and became convinced that I was pregnant by the big, ursine man who worked at the pizzeria.

Rhiannon then asks us all what we've done.

Claudia says only making out. Gwen snaps, "I already told you." I say I've had sex, just once. I am proud to have information to share, as if this makes me worldly, a real woman, but I am also careful to avoid the carnality of it. My unfamiliarity with Nathan's body, his unfamiliarity with mine, the way his dick sagged afterward, as if all the ropes inside it had been loosened.

Rhiannon says she's done everything, but she particularly loves giving head.

"What's it like? What do you even do?" Claudia asks her.

Rhiannon holds up a finger, kicks up her sheets. She returns with two bananas, a grapefruit, a knife. She takes the banana first. "So, this is him." She licks it from base to tip. Her mouth bobs up and down like a buoy. "It's like this. This is how I've always done it."

"But what if you bite down by accident?" Claudia asks. "What if your teeth—"

"You *won't* if you use your lips. Like this." Rhiannon shoves it farther down her throat, then retracts it. She places the banana beside her, picking up the grapefruit. Then she slices through the grapefruit's rind and pith. "And when he's going down on you, it's like this." She runs her tongue across the center. "It will feel nicer closer to the top." She moves her way up, circling around and around, her tongue like a sputtering flame. Eventually, she throws the grapefruit back onto the bed.

"I'm not eating that, by the way," says Claudia. Clear juice leaks from the ragged grapefruit, staining the sheets.

We have a bad rehearsal. When Gwen runs out of the practice room, the rest of us stretch at the ballet bar, rolling our tight muscles. Rhiannon turns to me. "She's being too difficult."

Is she? I also think the songs we're recording are tired and mediocre, but I'm afraid to push for fear it will all topple, my one opportunity razed to rubble and powder. I contain myself within the label's fist because I remember what Sonny said about going home with nothing. We have only two weeks until they decide to sign us or not, and Gwen is integral to this choice.

"I'll talk to her," I say.

Rhiannon nods.

I find Gwen out in the hallway by an empty vending machine. She's curled over her knees, and I can see she is drawing borders around herself the way I do. What is she really thinking, feeling?

"Rhiannon send you?" she asks.

"Uh-huh."

I sit beside her, trying to be still, because she might spook. I need her. She is the tempest, and we are flags lucky enough to be caught in it, all blowing in the same direction as she is.

"What's wrong?" I ask casually.

"If Allegra changes the routine back, I'm going to lose my mind." Gwen hates Allegra, the choreographer hired by Siren, and undermines her in the few off-hours we have, rearranging the hotel room so she has the floor space to teach us. "My ideas are better. They just are. We need to at least have interesting choreography, so no one will pay attention to what we're singing."

I lean my head against the wall. Close my eyes. "Do you want to be here?"

"I just want control," she says. "I want to make decisions without anyone second-guessing me. You know?" She raises her arm above her head and then lets it drop on her lap. "That's my brain telling my body what to do. It sends a signal, and then my body reacts. It only takes a second. *That's* what I want."

"Maybe after we're signed, we'll work with better people."

She scoffs. "Maybe. Maybe not. But I don't want to go back to Arizona. My town. Nothing happens there. Every so often, we have these massive dust storms called haboobs. When they move in, everything gets dark, like nighttime. I don't want dust storms to be the only interesting thing that ever happens to me." She rests her cheek on her fist. "I'm scared of saying anything, because what if they don't sign us and I have to go back? What if I have to finish high school? And that's the problem—I can't move my own hand."

"Would you go to college?"

She shakes her head.

Only months ago, I thought of my life as a dulled edge. A path to community college, like Greg. "Maybe I would," I say, even though she didn't ask. "I don't know what else I would do, if this doesn't work out."

"Stop saying that. It's going to work out." She stands, pulling me to my feet. "Let's go practice. I can't think when I'm sitting still."

Sometimes I watch Gwen, and I know who she will become. There is no doubt. She is sixteen years old, but she already walks a long, resolute path with only one destination: herself, her life, the one she was born to inhabit.

One night, we stay up late watching *The Price Is Right* in her hotel room. She screams at the television. "Seven hundred and thirty dollars? For that?" Turning to me, she says, "We have the strangest game shows. Who came up with this? Do you ever think about that?"

I shrug.

"Were you ever on *Star Search*?"

"Yeah."

"Same."

"Did you win?"

She shakes her head.

"Same!"

This reframes my own past failure as something we both had to overcome, which makes me feel better about it.

Sometime before we fall asleep, but after the television is turned off, we keep talking. It is the whispery part of a sleepover, when eyelids are heavy but we battle to hold them up, because this is when intimacy is really braided between girls.

I tell her all about the first time I had sex, speaking softly into the darkness. For a while, she's quiet. Then she says he sounds like a piece of shit.

"Maybe. I don't know. It might be my fault. I imagined it differently, so it was always going to disappoint me."

"How did you imagine it?" she whispers back.

"With someone I was in love with. And I thought it would be hot or something. There would be all this buildup and we wouldn't be able to stand it any longer."

"Hmm. I've honestly never imagined it. What's the point? It's a waste of time to think about something like that, if life is going to go differently."

I glance at her, the blue light from the television outlining her profile. Her hair, curling at the ends like an Ionic column. She is everything I hope to be when I finally become myself. When I shape a room instead of drift through it. Even though she is a year younger than I am, the world doesn't swipe at her the way it does at me. Everything I read, listen to, experience, is a new cut, but she discovered her taste and morals long ago, and they have already scabbed over, solidified.

We are opening for ETA at SeaWorld San Diego. When we are led past the ticket booths to the roped-off area where the audience is gathering, I gasp. It feels too massive for us. The fans are feral; I can feel the want steaming off their skin. Elbows thrust into chests as they press forward, all these limbs like a giant pile of pick-up sticks. Since a rare show of rain is expected, a tarp has been placed over the makeshift stage. Most of the crowd is outside its bounds, so once the storm begins, wet marker dribbles down poster boards, all that devotion now illegible.

I would be one of these girls in another life. Fantasizing about these boys, not wanting sex so much as wanting to be chosen. It is human nature to fall deeply when there is a wide distance to overcome. The gap itself is the attraction: the space between stage and crowd, where a warm hand just might hoist you up.

When Gwen notices the audience, her eyes widen, too, and she frantically rubs the back of her hand across her lips. She's stained them with a Baby Bottle Pop.

"Still blue," says Claudia.

"ETA will think she's sexy anyway." Rhiannon dances around Gwen, cupping her face. "Who is this gorgeous creature?"

"Shut up," says Gwen, pushing her away. Still, she flushes.

"And we can't forget about these," Rhiannon says, pointing to my breasts.

I instinctively cross my arms over them.

Sonny calls for us, and we follow. We check one another's teeth for food, then readjust our tube tops and capris. While we wait for the sky to clear, we are introduced to the ETA boys under the awning of the food court, where our teams have taken over several tables. Their manager, Mike Esposito, shakes Sonny's hand. He is a smarmy type, small and oily, wearing an old wifebeater that doesn't cover his nipples. The boys glance up from their food to greet us, but they all seem agitated—by the rain or by Mike, it's hard to tell. I sit at a nearby table with Claudia, studying the boys from this safe distance. By all standards, they are attractive. Alex Kowalczyk is the oldest and the most confident. His legs and arms are spread wide, taking up most of the space at the table. His mother, Hanna, is the comanager of ETA, along with Mike, and she is the one who auditioned all the other members. Beside him is Ty Jefferson, the prettiest among them. He is Black, tall, and curly-haired, with graceful limbs and incredibly long eyelashes. He trails a fry through his neighbor's ketchup, steals the chicken tenders off everyone else's plates. Slowly, eyes shining, he licks the oil from his fingers. Then there are Cam and Gabe Barone, the blond, blue-eyed cousins. Cam is small and baby-faced, while Gabe is a bit leaner, like a stray dog sitting beside a well-fed one of the same breed.

The last band member is looking everywhere besides me, as if I am the glare in his windshield. This face. I recognize it. Sometimes memory is a hand underneath water, and only vague shapes remain. He is one of those shapes for me, and eventually the past sharpens, becomes clear. My heart does not skip—no, it lunges. It is the boy from *Star Search*, Wes Kingston.

Everything about him has deepened. He is taller, fuller. Lean muscles have risen beneath his tight sweater. And as my gaze sweeps over him, everything inside me says yes over and over. The wide shoulders. The cluster of dark hairs beneath his collarbone, the thick eyebrows.

"By the way," he is saying to Gwen, stroking his uneven stubble. "This is a joke. I lost a bet, so now I have to grow a mustache."

His voice is a shovel—it picks up something heavy when he speaks.

I squeeze into the picnic table beside Gwen, and she gestures to Wes with her chin. "He lost a bet," she repeats, even though I already heard.

"What bet?"

Wes scratches his cheek. Ty leans over, interested by fresh conversation. He slaps Wes's shoulder and speaks for him. "The bet was who could go the longest without shaving. Wes lost easy, because he's a very pretty boy and cares about his appearance more than the rest of us. So now he must suffer."

"The rest of you don't look like you can even grow a mustache," I admit.

Wes's eyes finally jump from Gwen to me, and his entire face opens up in delicious recognition. "I finally figured it out. I *knew* it."

Ty glances between us. "Figured what out?"

Wes shakes his head. "*Star Search*. Yeah, I knew it. That's wild." He draws a line in the air with his finger, connecting us. "We competed against each other on *Star Search*, like, a million years ago."

"He won," I explain.

He shakes his head. "I shouldn't have. I remember being so shocked when I did, because you were so good."

We are all silent. My body is boiling underneath heat. I open my mouth to say something, but before I can, Sonny claps his hands and gestures to the microphones, the stage. We say goodbye to the boys and file out, up slippery steps, the rain beating down harder, faster, a reminder we are not welcome. Since we are the opener, our set is only two songs, both painstakingly choreographed, but in the rain our movements will be blunted.

From beneath the awning, Wes's eyes cut through the rain. It takes only a few terrible moments for me to realize it is Gwen he is staring at, not me. While she waits for her verse, she licks a sheen of spit across her lips. Then she inhales and begins to sing, tipping her head back to expose a long, pale throat. Her voice conjures a woman twice her age; I can picture her leaning out a window, stamping a cigarette out in an ashtray, an angry ocean swell in the distance.

But during the bridge, I sing a harmony a third above the melody. Throughout the chorus, I am waiting for this moment. Waiting to be watched. There is something both perverse and pleasurable in it, as I feel the eyes sliding from her to me, as I wait for one pair of eyes in particular. Because seeing Wes again makes me realize how often I have returned to Orlando, to that moment, and stroked it for comfort. The girl who cried backstage is still staring up at him. She exists layers down inside of me, shaking with emotion, all her hope renewed.

ETA moves in unison like mechanical parts. Gwen says they all look the same to her.

Offended, Claudia makes a face. "Only the cousins look alike. The two blond ones—Cam and Gabe." And between them all, there are further nuances, if Gwen bothered to look closer. Cam is a good dancer. Precise, like she is. Ty is even better. Alex is clearly the one the label is setting up as the leader, since he is always in the center, but Wes's tenor powers their verses. I can't help but gape at his control, the way he flexes his voice like a muscle.

"There's a third blond one," Gwen complains.

"Yeah, Alex," Claudia says. "He has the hat on."

"See! They all blend together."

I don't really notice these similarities. Instead, I'm interested in the differences between our groups. How they perform in long-sleeved turtlenecks, covered up like presents for girls to unwrap, while our paper is already discarded on the floor. How they excite this crowd, stoke this ferocity, and we don't. Their performance makes me want to scream, it makes me want to jump up and down, it makes me want to tear their posters out of magazines, it makes me want to die. Our music doesn't even make me feel alive. And for the first time, this is clear to me. I turn to Gwen. I watch her watching them, and I know she has realized the exact same thing.

After the show, Wes asks Gwen if she wants to see the jellyfish. Gwen shoots me a desperate look, and I know she doesn't want to be alone with him, so I tag along, aware Wes prefers her. They are tall enough to look each other in the eyes as they talk, but I am forced to crane my neck. I feel like a valley between their mountains.

The jellyfish room is circular so visitors can view the cylindrical tank from all angles. Inside, it is dim. Undulating blue and green lights. Jellyfish stingers drag slowly through the water. I walk up to the tank and press my hands against the glass. Wes and Gwen move to the other side, and through the water, their bodies seem to congeal. He never talks without gesticulating, and I can see the arcs his hands are making. Then his head pokes out. "Amber," he says, waving me over. "Look at this one."

I circle the glass to where two jellyfish are floating on top of each other. They bob with total ease, stingers interlaced. Wes sticks his nose up to the tank.

"So, what have you been doing for all these years?" he asks. Only his eyes turn toward me.

"High school."

"Seriously? How was that?"

"Well, I'm here, so it clearly wasn't great."

"It's good. That you're here. I'm glad, because if you had ended up an accountant or something, and no offense to accountants, that would have been such a waste."

My face is hot and shiny. "My dad is actually an accountant."

He pauses to see if he's somehow offended me and then, seeing he hasn't, asks, "Who do you get your voice from, then? Your mom?"

"Nobody." The truth is my dad was always singing, or so my mom says. I was too young to remember. But part of me wonders if she hates my voice because it is also his.

Wes pushes off from the glass and turns back to Gwen, guiding her to the next exhibit, where a sea turtle bobs in a flurry of quicksilver fish. He is pointing, leaning down to whisper something, too soft for me to hear. His gaze is sweeping across her like a lighthouse beam, and she is the ship he is guiding home.

1997

Los Angeles

The folding chairs in our rehearsal rooms host more executives, a rotation of suits. Their eyes follow along as we practice routine after routine. Presumably, they listen to our demos in a sterile boardroom and watch tapes of us performing at SeaWorld, but they also need to inspect their products in person for any dents.

Two days before our thirty-day trial is up, Simon gathers us together. We blink at him, wringing our hands. Sweat cools on our backs. After a few moments of silence, Rhiannon snaps, "Just tell us, Simon."

He holds up a patient hand, wiping his nose with his sleeve. Siren likes our sound, he says slowly, but they aren't convinced we have an album here.

Rhiannon moves her hand to her hip. "What does that mean?"

"They don't see hits in this batch of demos. They want an extension."

"How long?"

"Another month or so. Not to worry."

Claudia exhales, relieved. We all exchange glances. I am the only one who notices the falseness of Gwen's smile. And that's when I know: she's leaving, but she hasn't worked up the courage to say so.

Or she has plenty of courage, but little thought for the rest of us. Suddenly, I am full of rage—not at her, but at myself, for being foolish, for thinking success would happen to me in one powerful stroke, like a spell cast over my life.

I visit Gwen at the hair salon later that afternoon. She has gotten permission to dye her hair Pepto pink, and it takes five hours for the double process. She swivels in the chair while the stylist wraps her strands in tinfoil. Of course, this will be her signature look for years to come. Thousands of girls will buy pink hair dye at the pharmacy to look just like her. They will cut out her face from magazines, and in each photograph she will look ethereal, alien, a fairy or a sprite from some star-dusted planet.

We stare at each other in silence. I want her to tell me, but I don't want to ask her to tell me. I want us to be the kind of friends who can pass information unprompted, sensing the other's needs.

"I gave Wes Kingston my number." She fiddles with her hands in her lap. "Well, Sonny gave it to Mike, who is going to give it to him."

I shrug, trying to force passivity. The truth is they are two of the most beautiful people I've ever seen. I can picture them moving together so easily.

"I don't want to date anyone, though," she continues. "Too much going on."

I'm impatient now. I decide to just ask her outright. "So you're not going to stay with us, are you?"

She looks down at her hands.

"Why not?" I press.

The stylist leads her to the dryer. I follow.

Her eyes are teary. She is not a pretty crier—and it is one of the things I picture when I try to thaw my envy. She uses the back of her hand to scrape at her eyes.

"My mom thinks I should audition for labels as a solo artist. Mike Esposito said he can set them up for me. He's my manager now."

I bite the inside of my cheek. She watches me. Then she says something that changes my life, a push with both her palms, hard against my back. "You should go solo, too, Amber."

"Yeah, right."

"I mean it. Why not?"

What she is saying is I don't reach out and take things for myself. Never have. What am I compared to her? What is my dullness next to her shine?

"Why not?" she repeats. "Why do you even want to be in a group?"

"Because it's being offered to me."

Her hands are in the tinfoil. She checks the color, then folds her hair away again. "I've never pictured myself in a group. I just feel like I'm so close to what I *really* want, I can't settle for a lesser version of it. Does that make sense?"

It does. But can she detect my fear, like some animals can?

"Also, Simon was being so vague. A few months? This album isn't happening, Amber."

I taste blood in my mouth from my ripped cheek. "When are you going to tell Rhiannon and Claudia?"

"As soon as I sign my contract. We have another meeting with SMG tomorrow."

"I thought you said Mike could set up the meetings for you, not that he already had."

The foil is framing her face in a silver crown. She blinks away more emotion. Her jaw is set. "Do you hate me?"

I shake my head. I mean it. How could I hate her? I'm jealous of her. I wish I had the nerve to do it first. These are emotions with very different colors.

She wipes her eyes again. "Good. But what about you?"

"What about me?"

"What do you want?"

"Nothing."

"Don't lie."

I shake my head. "I'm going to stay in Cloud9. I don't want anything else."

"You do."

"Gwen."

Her eyes narrow. "Amber."

So, I concede. Such relief. Because the depth of what I want feels like a trench I am afraid to dive into, cold and bottomless. I name my desires for her. First, I tell her, I want to be a solo artist. A real force in this industry. What else? For my dad to hear me on the radio and regret leaving me behind. What else? To create music that makes me feel alive. What else? My name on an album cover.

What else? There's always something if I search for it. Maybe I will never be sated. What else, what else? Wes Kingston. But I don't say this one out loud, and his name passes though me.

Rhiannon is pacing back and forth across the dance studio, flaring and spitting heat. She was named after the Fleetwood Mac song, but maybe she imagines she is the queen from the Welsh story. The mythic woman. The white horse. She believes in her own greatness, even with little evidence to support it. She can confuse feeling hurt with permission to be cruel.

"Fuck her," she says. "She's fake, she lies all the time. I'm sick of it. She told me her ex-boyfriend is named Brian, but then she told Claudia his name is Ben." Here she gestures to Claudia, who nods. "I don't think she's ever had a boyfriend, honestly. Remember when we played never-have-I-ever? She said she'd hooked up with someone in the ocean on some vacation. Bet she made that up, too."

Claudia frowns. "But *why* would she lie?"

"Because she hasn't done shit, Claudia." Rhiannon tucks her hair behind her ear and waits for our reaction. We are both silent. Given nothing, she steamrolls on. "And Mike Esposito is so in love with her. He's managing her now. Did I tell you that?"

The skin of Claudia's forehead contracts like an accordion. "What if no one wants us without her?"

"They're just going to find someone to replace her. Everyone is replaceable," says Rhiannon. Finding no other pathway, she directs her frustration at me. "Are you going to say anything? You're just standing there."

"I'm thinking."

"Okay, whatever. You were like—" She widens her eyes, tilts her head, and opens her mouth a little, mimicking my vacant expression. "Do you ever form an opinion?"

Laughing to herself, she begins stretching. I stare at my blotted reflection in the dirty mirror. *Everyone is replaceable.* I am standing in a mold where a thousand other girls could be. Siren executives have told us this plenty of times. My body is another girl's body. My hips, her hips. My eyes, her eyes. But a mold is just an object held in a suspended moment. I want friction. Movement. To begin here and end all the way over there.

I call my mom, which is a mistake.

"What is Sonny's interest in this?" she asks. "What do we really know about him?"

"He'll take care of me. We're going to audition for labels like Gwen did."

She sighs. "I shouldn't have left. You won't go to college, and now you turn down a potential record deal to chase nothing? That's thoughtless. You're not Gwen. Her mother is irresponsible, in my opinion. You really think another label will sign you as a solo artist? You're asking for too much. Gwen? Fine. She's a separate case, a different kind of girl. You're not that. Why don't you come home, Amber? It's time."

She thinks I'm meant to have an ordinary life—and for my mom, this is a good thing, a natural thing. She is from a time when seat belts were a suggestion, and the looseness of the late sixties and early seventies was a boomerang for her morals, shooting her back in the other direction. After she got pregnant, dropped out of college, and had my brother and then me, she decided to rewrite her life and cling to some sort of dignity. So when I first told my mother I was no longer a virgin, she grabbed me by the arm and led me into her room. The floor was littered with her clothes. Ivory sheets stained with faded brown patches from before menopause. The heady scent of her oud perfume.

"I don't want to hear about it ever again," she said. Her jaw twitched. "Do you think I bragged about having sex in high school? No. I didn't. All your friends are sluts, Amber. Now you want to be like them? They're the fast crowd. You think I don't know that? I know what's going on. You come home reeking of cigarettes. You come home wearing that. You think I wore that?" Her eyes swept over my fishnet tights, a brand of shame. I felt a new hatred for my body. Realized that it was never mine; it had always been hers.

Now she says, "Put Sonny on. I want to speak with him."

I hand Sonny the phone. "Donna," he says, scratching his head. "We really do think this is the way to go. Don't scream at me, Donna. Amber made the decision. If you want my advice—I know you don't. Fine. I'll listen." He cracks his knuckles. "If you want my advice, Donna, I think the advance will be much higher for Amber as a solo artist. I see an opening for her. SMG just signed Gwen, and—"

He closes his eyes, pacing around the hotel room. When he slams the phone into the receiver, he shakes his head. "What a goddamn piece of work. Your mother is something else. She's already halfway through a bottle, I can tell."

"Don't worry about it. If she actually cared, she wouldn't have left me."

To cool off, Sonny drives us to McDonald's. We order burgers and fries and McFlurrys. The food is spread out in my lap, the massive shake in the cup holder. Sonny talks as he chews. "Cloud9 is a sinking ship," he says, fishing through the bag for a fry. "So we'll do auditions with Epic and Columbia and Lolli." He takes another bite of his burger, throws the fry into his mouth beside it. "Mike knows what he's doing. That girl is going to sell millions of records."

There is money in his eyes, coins that wink in the light as he stacks them.

"Sonny," I say.

"What, hon?" He licks grease from his thumb.

"Do you really think so?"

He nods. "Course she will. But you can, too. We just need to make a new demo and get you into the right rooms again. I'll make the calls; you'll do the rest. Look at you. It's a no-brainer."

Outside, a steady stream of hot metal. A homeless man with a gray beard holds up a cardboard sign in the parking lot. The flat buildings bake like sheet pans; the sky is a cloudless blue. A slant of sun filters through the dash and honeys my skin. I turn to Sonny and say, "Rhiannon and Claudia will hate me."

"They'll hate her more."

"Why?"

"Because she left first. And she's going to be everywhere first."

This isn't true, of course—in 1998, Monica Lewinsky is everywhere first.

I watch Bill Clinton's speech as he stands at the podium in a red tie and speaks to the American people. "I did not have sexual relations with that woman, Ms. Lewinsky," he says. That woman. The "Ms. Lewinsky" only tacked on seconds later, an afterthought.

Lolli is our fifth and final audition. While the executives deliberate, Sonny and I walk laps around the block, telling them we have somewhere else to be. "To show we're in demand," explains Sonny.

A statue of Atlas lifts up the world. A church with thick wooden doors advertises a congregation potluck. Sonny smokes on the steps. I step inside, for no reason other than to have quiet while I wait. Heads are bowed over pews. Votive candles flicker, sparked from whispered prayers. I do not believe in any god, but I want to believe in myself, to believe that pockets of silence might exist for me to fill them. I sit. I look up. And it is very beautiful, it really is, even if it is not for me. I can't help but feel moved in a space like this: the grandeur of it just lifts you. And when I return to Sonny, he's standing on the steps and smiling.

CLOUD9

This article is a stub. You can help by expanding it.

Cloud9 was a girl group formed in 1997 by **Siren Records** and disbanded in 2001. Original members were **Gwen Morris**, **Amber Young**, Rhiannon Walsh, and **Claudia Jeong**. After Morris and Young left the group, they were replaced with Janice Lacy and Maisie Borello. A fifth member, Casey Dane, was added in 1999.

DISCOGRAPHY

Singles
- "That Summer Feeling" (1998)
- "Bop" (1999)

Albums
- *Cloud9* (2000)

BUBBLEGUM

Gwen Morris   Track 4 on *Bubblegum*

Produced by
Axel Holm

October 30, 1998

[Intro]
Hate to burst your bubble, baby

[Verse 1]
Did you think this would be forever?
Sorry but it's now or never
Got to have those hard conversations
And now's the time

[Pre-chorus]
The taste is getting stale
You used to be fresh on my tongue
But for a while now
I've been feeling it's all wrong

[Chorus]
Won't let you pop my bubble
'Cause you're losing flavor, baby
Just like bubblegum
You're losing my favors, baby
Just like bubblegum

[Verse 2]
Did you think you'd get into me?
Like a lover
And now I know I should find another
Been thinking long and hard
You made me feel so crazy

Genius Annotation
3 contributors
She was just starting a relationship with ETA's **Wes Kingston**, who symbolizes something new and fresh for her.

Genius Annotation
3 contributors
Pop my bubble is a play on "pop my cherry."

Now I'm playing my cards

[Pre-chorus]
The taste is getting stale
You used to be fresh on my tongue
But for a while now
I've been feeling it's all wrong

[Chorus]
Won't let you pop my bubble
'Cause you're losing flavor, baby
Just like bubblegum
You're losing my favors, baby
Just like bubblegum

[Bridge]
Toss you in the trash (Oh, no)
Toss you in the trash (Oh, no)

[Chorus]
Won't let you pop my bubble
'Cause you're losing flavor, baby
Just like bubblegum
You're losing my favors, baby
Just like bubblegum

[Chorus]
Won't let you pop my bubble
'Cause you're losing flavor, baby
Just like bubblegum
You're losing my favors, baby
Just like bubblegum

ABOUT

Genius Annotation   **3 contributors**

"Bubblegum" is the lead single from Gwen Morris's debut album of the
same name (1999). It was a global sensation upon its release, with the
single ultimately selling over 12 million copies. The music video, featuring
a pink-haired Morris in a candy store, was a hit on MTV's *TRL* and became
synonymous with the teen pop era.

What have the artists said about the song?

"To me, the song is about choosing yourself. It's about recognizing your
own needs. I mean, the fact that it's become such a breakup anthem . . .
it's amazing that it's empowering people." —Morris on *The Rosie O'Donnell
Show*, 1999

CHORUS
1999–2000

1999

New York

After my record deal is signed, my new A&R guy at Lolli, Patrick Mackey, invites us to the Midtown office to discuss the direction of my first album.

He begins, "So, you've had sex."

I exchange a glance with Sonny. I nod, confused. I've already confessed this. I was afraid to, but Sonny said it was something my new team should know.

Pat scratches an itch on his neck. Hesitates for only a moment. "Exactly. We're thinking it's the only other way to swing. Savannah Sinclair is a virgin. Gwen Morris is right there on the edge. They don't have sex; you do. It's one or the other. You've had it, and you're not ashamed. Right?"

My body tenses. There are many flags planted in famous bodies. But there is also a part of me that relishes the impalement. Each time, it is a strange thrill. This makes me uneasy, because I cannot reconcile these contradictory desires: to push it in further, to rip it out.

Gwen chews a wad of gum, thrusts her hand into a jar of gummy bears. A candy choker is cinched around her throat.

I cannot take my eyes off her as she dances. The power of her body, the intensity of her gaze. I know she must have perfected the choreography during weeks of rehearsals, but it seems as if she was born for this video, for this moment, sprung fully formed from the head of some god.

When I call her cell, she picks up on the third ring. "Did you see it?" she asks breathlessly.

"Of course. It's everywhere."

"What do you think?"

"You're amazing."

"Now they're looping me in with Savannah Sinclair, as if we're the same person."

"You're totally different. She's—" And I want to say less beautiful, less talented. But this isn't the truth. Savannah Sinclair has a four-octave vocal range. Her riffs are ribbons of sound twirling through air. "Play with Me," her debut single, was number one on the *Billboard* Hot 100 for weeks, until Gwen knocked her off. The video premiered on MTV a few months ago: miniature Savannah, shimmying through a dollhouse. Cleavage locked away, stockings to her knees, blush slapped on her cheeks. A golden cross swaying on her neck like a wagging finger.

We can't help but turn against one another—it is easy to do. We are racehorses: whoever starts in front can always fall behind. Of course, I don't know this yet. My turn hasn't come. For now, all I can do is assure Gwen she is enough.

I hear her shout encouragement to a choreographer or background dancer. A stranger to me. "Sorry. Fuck. I feel like I've been cursing way more now, since Mike says I can't. Or maybe I'm just paying closer attention to everything I say. If I curse in an interview, everyone will freak out. I never cursed before, did I?"

"Not really," I say.

"No, that was always you. Or Rhiannon. Have you talked to her?"

"Nope." We haven't spoken in over a year.

"Same."

"So are you really dating Wes Kingston?"

"Who said that?"

All I can hear is my own pulse. "The world."

"I don't know if I am."

"How can you not know?"

"I guess if people talk, that's fine. You know? The album is coming out soon." She lowers her voice. "We went for a drive in Los Angeles. We kissed once."

"What was it like?"

"It was like nothing."

I understand.

"Anyway, I'll call you later, okay? I gotta go." The line goes dead. Her mall tour continues. She has described it as a front-row look at the backwaters of America. At each venue, there is a stage, two background dancers. Her tracks are beamed through the mall, drawing in shoppers. She performs a set of four or five songs, depending on the day, then signs autographs. These malls, she has told me, could all be cousins. But now? Her music video is on MTV. Her single is number one. Malls will become real stages.

Each morning, I am picked up from my hotel suite and driven to studios around the city. Inevitably, I hear "Bubblegum" during the ride, sometimes twice if there's traffic. I also bought her CD, of course, one of the last copies on a display with her face on it at Tower Records. On the cover, her head is angled to the side in mock confusion, a pink bubble rising out of her lips.

In the vocal booth, my cheeks flush with heat as I sing about a sexuality I don't know how to wield. Andy Sacks, one of my producers, asks if I'll come out to the control room. He's short, freckly. His pale eyes are always flickering over my chest.

"I still don't know about that line," I say.

He puts his hands on his hips, plainly frustrated. "The one you mentioned yesterday?"

I nod. It is *I'm so wet / Can't control the sweat.* I try to convince Andy that this is too pointed, that subtlety can be even more suggestive.

He scratches his stubble. After some back and forth, we settle on *Let's sweat, baby / Draw it out of me* instead. I twist my voice until he likes the shape.

"You have a boyfriend?" he asks.

"No."

"Well, pretend like you're singing in an imaginary boyfriend's ear. Or someone you're really, really into. Okay?"

I nod and return to the vocal booth, pulling my headphones back on. This I can do, and I know exactly who I'll think of. The sun circles the window, offering and then denying light. We are still recording when the garbage truck labors down the street in the morning, crushing trash. So go the weeks I spend recording my first album. I had a vague idea of writing a few songs myself, but I don't dare suggest this to anyone, since clearly no one expects me to write my own material. At least the world isn't sharp yet. Studios are wombs: here creativity is gestating, here it is soft and dark. During this time, I don't speak to many people other than my producers and engineers, Pat, and Sonny. I am eighteen in a world of older men. Of executives like Lyle Michaels, the head of Lolli, who stops by the studio every so often to listen to me sing. After Savannah's and Gwen's successes, he wants to put everything into my album—marketing dollars, promotion, a tour supporting a big name in the summer. You will be *this*, he says, and who am I to argue? I don't have a compelling counteroffer.

Gwen is on my television. Seeing her there, bite-size and shimmering, I consider calling, but she rarely picks up these days. Our friendship has risen and waned; it's been months since we've spoken. She's standing next to Carson Daly, answering fan questions before a live performance on *TRL*. I don't know the answers to many of them, which embarrasses me. Maybe we were only thrust together due to circumstance, clinging to each other in a transitional time, the way I imagine college roommates might.

"What is your favorite song to sing?" a fan asks.

"Oh, definitely 'Let's Take a Drive.' That song just reminds me of driving around with my friends." She nods and entwines her fingers together.

Another asks, "What about Wes Kingston? Is he just a friend?"

She laughs. "He's a sweetheart."

Sweetheart is a word with no pulse. Still, she keeps using it to describe Wes.

"What do you miss most about Arizona?"

She considers. This answer I think I know: She misses the endless sky, roads that stretch through rust-red desert. Maybe her grandfather's skinny old horse, which lives on a ranch outside the sprawl of Tucson. A family cat. But she says none of these things. "Usual stuff. My friends from school. Playing soccer. I was an honor roll student. I sang in the school choir. I was super normal."

I find this hilarious, almost offensive. Gwen Morris is not normal. She is energy, thrust, all forward momentum.

Carson says, "Your number-one request today, 'Bubblegum,' is next!" Screams drown him out. I change the channel.

The "Sweat" video soundstage is designed to look like a gym. There are ellipticals, yoga mats, muscly men pumping weights. I jog on a treadmill, my breasts bound by a tangerine sports bra. The director follows them with his eyes. He twists to glance at the monitor, then back to me.

I watch the playback, crossing my arms. Sonny leans over my shoulder to watch, too. There is a strange dissonance: myself, there, the coiled-up power of my voice, and the way I feel. "Don't I look a little confused here, Sonny?" I ask, pointing to my face. "I look like I have no idea what's going on. What is she thinking?" I rub my finger over my face on the monitor.

When I faint on cue, the actor playing my love interest runs over and squirts water over my chest. Originally, he was supposed to give me mouth-to-mouth, but I pull the director aside. My chest is where their eyes go anyway. Why not light a bonfire on it?

The actor's face reminds me of a chair: square and functional. During a break, he tells me his name is Drew. He's twenty-five, new to Los Angeles, working at a bar on weekends and living with six room-mates in a seedy part of downtown. He says the city reminds him of grime collecting under a dresser, only revealed once you move it to a new corner.

I imagine having sex with him. While I wait for the album release, I fill every empty space inside myself with other people. Wes King-ston, this actor, strangers I pass on the street, characters I've seen on-screen. When these unbidden thoughts arrive, I darken the rooms in my mind like I'm letting down the curtains. There, I can want all the things I am ashamed to want, explore every sensation I haven't expe-rienced. There, shapes form stranger shapes.

"Is my hand good here?" Drew asks now. His calluses brush my waist.

"That's fine."

The track begins to play again. Dancers gyrate on the ellipticals, and I lip-synch over my own voice. Lights descend from above. I stare directly into the camera lens, and it unfurls like a dark flower.

Men will confess they've jerked off to me in this video. Sometimes they are sheepish and embarrassed, describing teenage lust. Sometimes they are boastful and territorial, as if their eyes can still push me into bed. I never know what to do when they tell me this.

Gwen calls. I can't believe it. She says, "I'm on the bus right now, so I might break up a bit if we go into a tunnel."

In the background, I hear the steady groan of an engine, the suction of an open window.

"That's fine. I don't have much time anyway." I'm refilling my water bottle in the bathroom sink of the studio. I lean toward the mirror and pluck out stray eyebrow hairs with my fingers. We are both silent for a few moments. I'm not sure we remember how to talk to each other.

"I'm so tired," I eventually say.

"Yeah, I'm so fucking tired, too. I might collapse right here, honestly." She tells me she rehearsed for the tour nonstop for three weeks and now she can't fall asleep at night. She gets an hour at most. Her dancers like to drink on their bus after shows, but she can't manage it. She's too exhausted. Now she's turned down too many invitations, so they all avoid her.

"They probably think you don't want to be friends with them."

"But I do."

"They're just intimidated by you. You have to initiate."

She's quiet for a moment. "It's my face. It's my face that's the problem. I'm serious. I remember, when we were together in Los Angeles, people would come up to us all the time to ask for directions. No one ever comes up to me when I'm alone, but with you, they always do. There's something about your face. You have a very friendly face."

"Everyone always tells me I look like someone they know, but they can't remember who. They always ask if we've met before."

Through the phone, I can hear the bus pull into a gas station, her murmuring to someone beside her. "Anyway, it's fine. My face naturally repels people and it's fine." She sounds so sad as she says this. Her beauty is remote, something to observe from a safe distance, as if she's surrounded by sensors and bulletproof glass. "So, I was shooting this cover."

"What cover?"

"*Rolling Stone.*"

"Oh, shit."

"I know." She describes the set for me. A photographer who looks like a hawk, always swooping down to adjust her. A bathtub swaying with gallons of milk and floating Lucky Charms marshmallows. She looks naked inside it, but the opaque waterline is just above her breasts.

She's instructed to place one thigh on the rim, so she does it. There's no one there but the photographer and Mike, who loves the shot, says it's provocative.

"Of course, I wanted to look beautiful," she says. "I really, really wanted to look beautiful. Now I'm not sure how I feel."

I tell her it's okay. I probably would have posed nude in the bathtub if the photographer had asked me, and this thought is woven with strands of pride and shame. I have trouble separating them—they are too tightly bound. I'm uncomfortable with the attention I receive from older men, but I've also been taught to anticipate it. And how can one look be two different temperatures at once? I can see this is what she's struggling with, too.

"Anyway, let's talk about you," she says.

"Why? There's not much, compared to you."

"Stop it."

"Well, Lolli wants this song called 'Sweat' to be the first single. We shot the video last week." What else is there to say? "Have you watched anything good?"

"No, I have no time. The dancers were watching an episode of *Buffy* and I caught a little of that. You know what I think sometimes? I think it's like we're living in a tunnel. Like the world is happening around us, and we're moving, too, but separated from it all by these thick walls. What do people even like these days? You know? What's even happening?"

"You are what's happening."

She takes a while to respond. I wonder if she's looking out the window. She'll be on a highway now, somewhere on the northeastern coast, maybe even close to where I grew up—gray beaches, sharks circling beneath clueless seals.

"Maybe," she says reluctantly. "There must be other things."

The *Rolling Stone* cover is kerosene. The bathtub, the milky thigh. She's asked about it in every interview. I will eventually be asked similar, recycled questions: Do you think you set the right example? Is this what a role model does? Do you feel responsible? Don't you want to be good? Aren't beauty and goodness synonymous? Aren't we conditioned to believe this?

On that cover, Gwen looks like she has sex. She hasn't. But she is captured in a moment, her head tilted, eyes bright, thinking something that must be so delicious, so erotic, it lights her on fire. America is depraved and crazed, so it can't get enough. It digs its teeth into her.

1999

Los Angeles

A parking lot again, this time Taco Bell. Sonny is chewing a burrito with his mouth open. There's a piece of lettuce stuck between his left canine and incisor. When he swallows, he has news for me. "You're opening for ETA's next leg. Starting in Phoenix next month."

He pauses for a beat, glancing at me folded into the passenger seat, feet up on the dash. Suddenly the car is far too small. I will see Wes Kingston again. In the past year, he has become a haze of a person, made of heat and air. I try to play it cool with Sonny, but he must know what this is doing to me, how it moves through my blood.

"Do you have any idea what goes into a tour like this?" he asks.

I shake my head. So he tells me. Depending on the venue, I'll be performing from a side stage, the main stage if we're lucky. I will sing as the audience files in, while they wait in line for concessions or the bathroom. "It's good exposure for the album," he assures me. A thin slice of chicken falls into his lap. "All those girls in the audience, they want to be sexy, like you. They want those boys to see them as women." He wipes his mouth and looks over at me. "You didn't eat anything."

"Wasn't hungry."

He reaches into my bag. White paper crumples under his hand. "Great."

A hair stylist pulls at my scalp. Beside her, a makeup artist drags foundation across my forehead with a soft brush, erasing all the irritable red puberty. I watch his progress in the mirror, thinking about sixth grade, when a boy said I was ugly. When you are young, these comments stay with you, like footprints left in drying concrete.

It is easy to slice myself up. Lips: thick slugs. Eyes: too far apart. An open, unremarkable face, every emotion beating across it. As Gwen said, it is a friendly face: it will reflect desire back at you.

The makeup artist is now dusting bronzer along my cheekbones, telling me about a man he recently flew to Miami to see, when a production assistant enters the greenroom. "Are we ready?" she asks. She's holding a clipboard in one hand. "Here's your earpiece. You can follow me. Just this way. When you're announced, walk stage left."

Sonny guides me by the shoulder. I can feel the heat of his palm, always damp even in the cold. I'm deposited with another member of the production crew to wait. I peek around the corner. The *TRL* stage seems larger on television. There are fluorescent lights overhead. Floor-to-ceiling glass windows looking out onto Times Square, the hive of teenagers cheering from below.

A voice saying, "Gwen Morris again in her *fifth* week at number one, and we'll see that video in just a minute.... But first, Amber Young and 'Sweat,' the debut single from her upcoming album. We're excited for this. Who loved that video? Any fans here? Good, because here she is, Amber Young!" The audience applauds. My heartbeat accelerates, my stomach drops. The crowd is elevated above me, and they scream as I wave to them. Some stretch out their hands toward me, but I don't think they know who I am. They are just performing excitement.

I stand on the blue studio floor, right in front of the windows overlooking Times Square. Everything feels exposed. I'm in low-rise jeans and a bandeau top, revealing my freshly pierced belly-button, but I'm also naked. When I was a kid, all I wanted was to be seen. Now, so many eyes. Too many—innumerable. I will be beamed into countless homes, where teenagers will shrug off their backpacks and turn on MTV after school. For the first time, I wonder if I've asked for too much. But this is what I love most: to close my eyes, cleaving myself apart from the world, just before I begin. To hear the audience's pulse. To gather my voice as the cameras and eyes swivel toward me. My two dancers unlock their bodies. God, I love this. I'm so in love.

A voice mail from Gwen: "Now we're really playing phone tag. I'm calling you from Amsterdam. Well, just outside it, in farmland. In the actual city there were bridges and cobblestones. Didn't see much of it, to be honest. I wanted to go see the red-light district, but there was no time. So, Tammy—have I mentioned her? She's one of my dancers. She was able to go while I was doing interviews and told me about it. She fed a coin into a slot and began to watch a peep show, just like she was buying a gumball from a machine. There were girls in windows, lined up and down the street, waving to her through the glass, and she told me they were very beautiful. I feel as though all these cities are completely closed off to me. I'm backstage, or onstage, or on a bus. I did press with some European outlets. A man asked me, 'What do you like in the bedroom?' and I wanted to say, 'Fucking sleeping for once.' Because I haven't been able to sleep at all, Amber. I keep thinking something is wrong with my body. I'm afraid my muscles will abandon me. I won't be able to swallow or blink, stuff like that. Even worse: I won't be able to sing, and all this will end. The best part about being a hypochondriac is since you constantly think you're on the verge of death, you don't worry when you're not doing much living. I sound like an asshole. Don't feel sorry for me. Anyway, I should go. Call me back when you can."

But I don't have time. I'm in and out of black cars with Sonny. Pulling headphones on at every radio station that will have me. Performing

"Sweat" on every talk show the label can book. Relentless vulnerability: love me, love me, love me. I finally have a moment during a long car ride to a radio station. "I was really hoping you'd pick up because I have a lot to tell you," I say, after I get her voice mail. "I'm touring with ETA this summer. What am I supposed to say to Wes? Does he know you're not dating, or does he think you are? Anyway, I went out with the actor I was telling you about. Drew from the 'Sweat' video. So, we go to this sushi place. The first thing, *the first thing*, he does is tell me how hot I looked in the video. I wanted to die, I thought about leaving, but I was also thinking, this is my first night off in a *year*. I should enjoy myself and try to have a conversation. So I ask him what kind of acting he wants to do, and he says serious acting. He starts shitting on music videos and how much he hates working on them. Then he asks if I want to give him a blow job in the bathroom. So that was my night off. I'm sorry about the hypochondria. When I was younger, I thought my boobs were cancerous because of how fast they were growing. Okay— I've got to go, but please tell me about Wes when you can."

And when I'm in an interview, she leaves another voice mail. Her voice is soft, breathy. She doesn't want to be overheard. "So. Wes. I think he knows we're not really dating. We only hung out once. He drove me around." I know exactly what she's talking about because I've seen the photographs. "It smelled awful in that car. His mom has a little dog and I think it took a shit in there and they didn't clean it up. We mostly sat in silence. There was nothing to talk about. Do you know when you're with a person and you can admit they are conventionally attractive, but you feel absolutely nothing for them? Like, he's attractive for sure. I can acknowledge that. He's nice, I guess. He's fine. He asked me if I had ever been in love. I said no. Then I asked him if he had, and he also said no. I felt sad for both of us. Mostly for him, because he's spent so much time with the other boys, and I don't think he knows how to talk to women. He acted as if I wasn't a real person. I think that's the problem: I'm the only currency he has. And I've been wondering how much love, I mean in *our* lives specifically, is just there for people to talk about? So we can prove our desirability and worth to them? Tammy says I need to shut the hell up. She wants to say hi. Wait, come back. Say hi."

From farther away: "Hi, Amber!"

"That was her. We are on our way to McDonald's. They have so many McDonald's here, and the menu is all the same no matter where you go. Yes, it is, Tammy. I swear. It's the exact same. It always tastes just like America. Okay, we're going now. Bye again."

Chew on This!
We Get to Know New Star Gwen Morris

Gwen Morris is just seventeen years old, but she's already an overnight sensation (and just *might* be dating our favorite boy-bander). How does one so young have so much confidence? Her debut single, "Bubblegum," off her first album, is a smash hit. She's embarking on a national tour. She's not surprised by any of it—in fact, this was her goal from the start.

Q: What is the first thing you bought once you became famous?
A: I bought myself a car, and I can't even drive it! I don't have a license. I'm on the road so much, living on a tour bus.

Q: Are you planning to get one?
A: Eventually. I don't have time to learn right now. Someday.

Q: Do you have any preshow rituals?
A: I love to huddle with my dancers. We hype each other up.

Q: What do you look for in a guy?
A: Someone who can keep up with me!

Q: Could Wes Kingston be the one to do that?
A: [laughs] Yeah, maybe.

Q: Is that a yes?
A: He's sweet.

Q: How do you feel being compared to Savannah Sinclair?
A: You know, we're really different artists. She's more of a ballad singer than I am, and her songs are more sugary than mine. I think I have more of an edge. And I can't hit a lot of her notes, frankly. I'm a big fan of hers, and I think she's really cool.

Q: Do you feel pressure to be a role model for young girls?

A: I think the best kind of role model I can be is showing girls how to be confident. Go after what you want. I try to do that every day.

Q: So, what do you want?

A: A Grammy.

Q: What's coming up for you?

A: I'm touring for this album. All I can do is keep working really hard and hope for the best. But I have a good feeling about what's coming up.

1999

Phoenix, AZ

We drive to Phoenix in a van. The paint is peeling, like blisters hanging off worn-down skin. We squeeze in together: Sonny in front; me; my two dancers, Gloria and Jay; then the three members of my band in the back. They all auditioned for me but were ultimately chosen and hired by Sonny, who said he had years of experience making these decisions, whereas I had none. All of them are also in their mid- to late twenties, a decade of touring between them. What do they think of this little creaking van advertising a teenager?

Outside Los Angeles, the route is bumper-to-bumper traffic, then dirt and heat. Shapes rise up from the earth, fists punching the sky. Everything grows craggy and red. When we hear "Play with Me," we all sing along. It is cloying but catchy—and I find myself staring into the rearview mirror, lip-synching the song as if I am Savannah in her music video. Sonny reaches forward to change the station, twisting the dial to find hard rock.

I press my fingers against the window, reading billboards that say JESUS CAN SAVE YOU, ARE YOU GOING TO HEAVEN OR HELL? HARRY'S

GIRLS ADULT BAR AND XXX CLUB, NEXT EXIT. HOT GIRLS, CHEAP LIQUOR. Cows kicking up loose dirt, packed in feedlots, one step away from the slaughterhouse. Eventually, the rough land softens into suburbia. When we finally pull into the stadium lot, slowing down for the turn, the clusters of girls are waiting. They snap to attention. Most are wearing ETA tour merchandise. Some are accompanied by weary parents. When they realize we aren't ETA's tour bus, they start to fall back, visibly disappointed. Like them, I am full of opposing selves. We are all in that moment when everything is extremity.

The amphitheater is a behemoth of steel and iron. Inside, ETA's tour manager, Bill, shuffles us through a labyrinth of white hallways. He is methodical and unsmiling. "Your sound check is at five," he says. "Doors are at five thirty. Then you're on at eight thirty. Got it? The boys are about to go to their meet and greet, so say a quick hello."

He waves to their security, turns a doorknob, and we are thrust into the green room. Cam, one of the blond cousins, rides a Razor scooter, weaving around clothing racks and a table loaded with chips and crudités. He perpetually looks like he's chasing fireflies in the dark, his attention snapping from one source of light to another. The other four boys are slung over couches. They glance at the door, vaguely interested in whoever or whatever has entered the room. Slowly, their awareness sweeps forward, and they perk up.

"You boys remember Amber, don't you?" Sonny puts his hands on his hips. They cast glances at one another, as if together they might draw up some lost memory. Then, to my surprise, Wes says, "Of course."

"What? How do you know her?" Alex asks, shifting onto his elbow. His hand brushes against Wes's chin, and at the contact Wes stirs.

"She was in Cloud9, asshole," Wes says. Then, to me, "I remember. Jellyfish tank."

"Cloud9," repeats Alex, letting the name slowly melt in his mouth. "Gwen Morris's old group. Right?"

I nod. I am only someone in relation to her, of course. But maybe a little of her dust will shake onto me just by association.

Cam continues scootering. Wes and Alex close their eyes, hands clasped over their chests. Ty says, "Hey, Amber, look how ticklish Gabriel is." Gabe starts to shuffle away from him on the couch, holding up a finger of warning.

"Come here, Gabriel." Ty crawls after him. A pillow is thrown; a potato chip bounces off Ty's head.

"Don't ever tell him your weaknesses," Gabe says gravely, huddled in a ball to protect his stomach. Once Ty's interest in this wanes, he beckons me over to the couch. I cross my thighs over each other because my skirt is so short. Ty leans forward conspiratorially, his breath sweet and minty. "Tell me about yourself."

"Me?"

He throws a chip on his tongue. "Uh-huh."

I think of a few things to say, then pull them back. I settle on, "I'm from New Jersey."

"Did you like growing up there?"

"Not really. I always imagined leaving. Where are you from?"

"Houston. But I left when I was thirteen." And he describes the beginning of ETA, how their personalities coalesced and hardened together, like sedimentary rock. A few times, Wes glances at us, coupled together in the corner of the room.

When their tour manager arrives to herd them out the door, Ty hugs me and wishes me luck with my first show. Cam scooters out, followed by Alex and Gabe. But Wes stays behind to clean up after the others. I can't decide if it's because he's thoughtful or because he might want to be alone with me.

"You look different," I say.

"Really? How?" Wes tosses a cup in an arc and misses the trash. His ears redden as he walks over and places it in the can.

"I think it's the hair."

He raises his hand to it.

"That's what's different. The frosted tips."

"Oh, right. Sexy?" A thick eyebrow lifts. "Or no?"

I pretend to study him. "I think I like your dark hair better."

"Shit, okay. That's what everyone is saying. And moms aren't hitting on me as much."

"How terrible."

Our smiles cross in midair. I want to tease him about this further, but I can't think of what else to say. Maybe by acknowledging his appeal to other women, I can somehow loop myself into this mass. He might be trying to do the same—telling me these mothers find him attractive, probing to see whether I do, too.

"Yeah, well, my self-esteem really depends on it," he says. He talks very quickly, as if his words are playing a game of tag. "You're different, too. You were quieter then. How old are you now?"

"Eighteen. Almost nineteen. I will be. In July."

"We'll have to throw you a birthday party."

"Okay." I laugh. "I'm trying to be more fun."

His eyebrow lifts again, beckoning me to elaborate, so I do. "Sonny is probably my best friend." I don't dare mention Gwen again, because I am afraid of his reaction, whether it be practiced nonchalance or a flash of interest. "And he's a fifty-something-year-old man. Give or take a few years."

"So, you don't hang out with anyone your age."

"Nope, not really. Never."

"Yeah? What's that like?"

"I know a lot about poker."

Older men are simple enough; their desires are not complex shapes. Sonny, for example, has porn magazines stashed in his car, which I catch him staring at from time to time, but he's never been in a relationship. He says everyone is too needy. Really, he's obsessed with money. He enjoys discussing how much things cost; it brings him real pleasure.

And Lyle Michaels, the CEO of Lolli, wants to believe attention is given to him due to charisma or attractiveness, not because of his obvious status or wealth. He doesn't look in mirrors because of it; he just allows other people to be his reflection.

But Wes—what moves him? I can't tell.

He asks if I really like poker, and I say I do.

"We have a game going on the bus. You could stop by."

We stare at each other for a few seconds. Now he really looks at me, not across me on the way to someone else. I twist around to reach for a water bottle and knock over the trash can instead. A landslide of plates, grimy napkins, and a torn condom wrapper. The heap of their day, the same detritus they leave in each city they travel through. I point to the condom wrapper. "Yours?"

He smiles, and I don't know what this means. Instead of elaborating, he leans down to help me pick up the spillage. We collect plastic plates smeared with red ketchup and barbecue sauce from their lunch.

When everything has been picked up, we are still kneeling on the floor, neither of us making any motion to stand. "Are you nervous?" he asks.

"What do you mean?"

"Are you nervous for the show?"

I had almost forgotten. I can't stop staring at his hands, his mouth. Where could he put such things? So many places. "Yeah. But I'm trying not to think about it. If I think about it, I'll get nauseous."

"Just pretend like you're dying, and you'll be born again the next day. Empty yourself out, give them everything you've got. There's nothing to lose because tomorrow will be a completely new group of people. Okay?"

"Okay, thank you."

He turns to the door. Someone has returned to collect him. I can see only his profile as he says, "Don't worry, by the way. We'll be your friends."

. . .

I stand on a rickety stage near the gates of the amphitheater. Because the sun is still out, I pour ice water down my neck, but it spills down my white crop top. The idea of my nipples is revealed through the fabric. I'm told to borrow Gloria's bra, but the cups are too small, and the straps dig into my flesh, so I perform braless, in the wet shirt.

The fans do not pay me much attention anyway. I am merely a passage to the main event. A mouth. For now, I have the freedom to perform without the scrutiny that will come later. No one is watching closely. The girls talk among themselves and clutch their posters: MARRY ME ALEX, I LOVE ETA, WHAT'S THE ETA FOR OUR WEDDING, CAM? One poster is Gwen's face, a slash of red marker across it, cutting her from forehead to chin. I begin tallying which of the boys they favor. I count eleven posters for Cam, eight for Wes, a handful for Alex. The rest for the entire group.

The sun begins to set, the stage darkened by loosening shadows. "Thank you all for coming," I say, taking a swig of water. "This next song is my first single. You may have heard it."

A few more people trickle by my stage on their way to the main amphitheater. The crowd is always at low tide, never expanding much. By the time I'm done, only five people remain: a young girl with her mother, arguing under their breath, and a group of friends in ETA T-shirts, chewing on fries and sipping milkshakes from the concession stand. Yet their indifference makes me ruthless. I am greedy for their eyes. It is a scream of a performance, and afterward, still breathing heavily, I stare at my face in the bathroom mirror, splash cold water onto it, and smile.

When I emerge from the bathroom, Sonny pulls me aside. Beyond the hall, I hear the pulse of the main stage.

"Listen," Sonny says. "You looked burned-out up there."

"I wasn't," I insist, still breathing hard from the adrenaline and the light. Did he watch the same show? Did he see me up there? How I left everything I had on the stage, emptying myself out completely, like Wes said to? "I just got a cramp at one point, but it only lasted a few minutes."

Sonny twists the stud in his ear. "Maybe we should change the routine. If it's too much. It's just a thought. I'll talk to Gloria and Jay about it." Then he says: "Maybe it would be easier, maybe you wouldn't cramp up, if you were more in shape. You know?" His words are palm-shaped and red, and I stumble back.

1999

Lubbock, TX

I'm invited on their tour bus to play poker.

The Texas plains are starved and yellow. A selfish sun grips the entire sky. At a rusted gas station on the side of the highway, I board their bus with a packet of Twizzlers and a Pepsi. As soon as I climb the steps, their stench is all-encompassing—body odor covering everything like settled dust. They are sitting at a rickety table in the back of the bus, past the row of bunk beds, scanning their cards. Ty raises his hand and beckons me to join them.

He makes room for me beside him, patting the red leather seat. "You can play with me until we start a new game."

Wes looks up from his hand. "It'll be quick."

I smile at him; he glances down again. "Why? Should I pick a new team member?"

"You definitely should," says Alex. "Ty gets too confident. Look at this kid. He's all in, but he's probably got nothing." He gestures to the pile in the center of the table. They don't have chips, so they've used coins and paper clips instead.

Ty puts his arm around my shoulder and points at Alex. "I beat y'all yesterday."

I ask if he'll be devastated to lose all his paper clips.

He nods solemnly. "Yeah. I stole them all from Jim."

The other boys laugh into their hands.

"Jim?"

"He's our production manager," explains Wes, rearranging the cards in his hand. "Funny guy."

"Definitely strange," says Ty. "But we love him."

Wes bites his lip as he draws. Their hands fly in arcs over the table.

Sudden movement: the door to the bathroom opens. Ty visibly brightens. "Gabriel! How was it?"

Gabe shakes his head. "Don't go in there for a while." He squeezes in beside me. Eventually, he turns to me, quickly bored with the game. His voice is tentative, unsure of itself. He always talks the least in interviews, so I'm surprised he's saying anything to me now. "How long are you opening for us?"

"Oh, just until July. Late July."

He nods. "Then your album comes out?"

"Supposedly. I'm not sure. Lolli might delay it to November. Sometimes they're worried I sound too much like Savannah or Gwen, and then other times that I don't sound enough like them. They change their minds about it, so the release gets pushed." I shrug, as if this is nothing to me and not my entire life.

"Damn," he says. Then, shyly: "Your music video was pretty good."

"Yeah?"

"Wes was watching it in his hotel room. We caught him."

Wes, who has until this point been focused on the table, glances our way. He's set off a flare of annoyance. "*TRL* was already on," he says. "I wasn't searching for it or anything."

My video was number eight this week, the highest it's ever been.

Ty holds his palm up. "You looked hot. We all said you did. Wes especially." Ty points a finger at him. "Don't look at me like that, you *did* say that."

Pleasure floods my body. "So what was your favorite part?" I ask Wes. Now he's not so frightening; something has been unlaced between us.

Indifferently, he says, "Definitely the scene with the water bottle." His eyes meet mine and we are both held there until I blink.

"Yeah, you would say that."

Color rises on his cheeks, and he pushes his hair back behind his ears. "That's not the reason. I like it because it's the part where you sing, what is it?" He mimics my voice. "*Now I'm melting duh duh duh.* Whatever that line is."

"Now I'm melted on the floor."

"Yeah. That one."

Ty looks between us. "That's not really a standout lyric."

Wes shakes his head and throws his cards down. "Call."

I have never seen male friendship up close like this. One look will trigger furious laughter. They banter and tussle. Touch as familiarly as lovers do. A hand resting on a shoulder or around a waist, hair casually ruffled. I can't help but seek their approval, and I am proud whenever they want me with them. Wes and I don't speak much—maybe he's avoiding me, sensing that our attraction to each other has been thrown open and can't be closed again. I begin to anticipate this space between us. It grows heavy, as if it's been drenched. And I twirl the small, meaningless exchanges we do have around in my mind for days.

Bonner Springs, Kansas. My nineteenth birthday. Thinking I am turning eighteen, Mike makes a comment about all the men who will be grateful I'm finally legal, which I ignore but Sonny laughs at.

"She's been legal for a year," Sonny says.

"All that opportunity," says Mike. "I had no idea!"

Mike is a fly you can't maneuver out of your window, no matter how hard you flap your arms to guide him. His passes at me have become routine, a daily chore.

We celebrate on their bus with an ice-cream cake. I study my own hands as they greedily wield the fork. It is mechanical: lift, swallow, set down. Sonny, Mike, and the boys are on their second or third pieces, licking chocolate off their fingers. But each bite is heavy on my tongue. I'm handed shots of vodka, of tequila, of rum. There is a city of alcohol on the table, towers of glass bottles. The boys are blasting Top 40. Smoke from their cigarettes tickles the bus windows. Light scatters through my bloodstream, through every limb, and I hide in the back of the bus, searching for a place to lie down. I climb into the bunk that smells best, the blanket full of fast-food wrappers and crumbs. I close my eyes. Waves crash against my eyelids, then roll away.

"You all good?"

I open an eye. Wes has pulled aside the curtain that gives each bunk privacy.

"Just feeling shitty." I push myself up. He settles in the bunk across from me, brow furrowed. He looks like a heartbeat, pumping in and out of focus.

He points to the bed I'm sleeping in. "That's mine, by the way."

"It smells good."

"Don't smell my bed."

"I already am."

He reaches over the aisle to shove my foot. There is so much charge between us then, I turn away.

"If you're feeling sick, I can go."

I glance over at him. "No. Stay."

"Okay." His head falls back onto the pillow. "We can talk about something until you feel better."

"I guess you can tell me about Gwen now. She doesn't say anything about you."

He begins to pick at a callus on his palm. "She doesn't?" Since he is looking down, I study him openly, rejoicing in the opportunity: Grecian nose, stubble, a strand of bleached hair cupping his cheek. The frosted tips are starting to grow out, revealing the dark roots.

"I don't think you really know her," I say.

"Never said I did."

"But you were into her."

He blinks. "At first. I mean, yeah, she's hot. But we don't have much in common. I never saw her laugh."

"She laughs if you get to know her."

"Well, I never really *got to know her*. Or maybe she doesn't think I'm funny."

"Could be that."

He smiles. "Look, they ask me, all of us, who we're dating in interviews. Constantly. Like, oh yeah, when I'm on a thirty-city national tour, I have time for a girlfriend. Are they joking? Everything in my real life ended when I was fourteen years old. You'll learn that soon enough. So I'm fine with whatever the press has created between us. Doesn't matter much to me."

"I'd probably date someone for publicity, too, if I was told to."

"Would you?"

"I guess. I mean, if it would really benefit my career, sure. Maybe I don't have any principles. When I was younger, it mattered more to me if my friends saw I was with someone than if I was actually with someone. Maybe that's sad of me to say."

A beat of silence. Then: "Were you raised Christian?"

"Random."

"No, I have a point, I swear." He rolls onto his side. "When I was a kid, I thought if no one saw you kiss in the church on your wedding day, then the marriage didn't count. That's why you had to have a witness." He breaks off, swats his hair from his eye. "What you said just reminded me of that. How people say if a tree falls and no one sees it, did it really fall? Same with our relationships. If no one else sees it, then it's not real."

"You mean if no one hears it. That's how it goes."

"Whichever."

"Yeah. I wonder if two people can really be happy if there's no one else to see it. If they can just exist together, truly happy."

"Mmm. Exactly. We can't think like that, it's not even something we can consider, given the circumstances. Someone is always going to see us." He pauses. "Do you think differently about me now?"

I shake my head. "A lot of people are raised Christian. I'm agnostic, I think, and we never went to mass or anything when I was growing up. But I actually walked into this church when I was waiting to hear back from Lolli. Waiting to know if they wanted to sign me or not. I don't know why. I sat there, and I looked up at the ceiling, and it was beautiful. The candles. Everything. And afterward, I found out I had a record deal."

He smiles again. "I'm probably agnostic, too, honestly, but don't tell anyone." He plucks a silver chain from underneath his shirt, and there's a little cross dangling from it. A part of my eye is reflected in the metal. He quickly makes a face and tucks it away again.

"I just don't get how we could know for certain," I say. "I don't think it's possible."

"Yeah, that's how I feel. But the preacher from our church has bestselling books. Literally, my mom—have you met my mom? She's on tour sometimes. Anyway, she got super into this guy, this preacher. She listens to him on the radio all the time. He has a real thick accent, a sound like two rocks rubbing together. Growing up, I thought he was God, until I found out he wasn't. I just thought if God had a voice, it would sound like that."

"I thought if God had a voice, it would sound like Whitney Houston. Or Joni Mitchell."

"Or you."

"Shut up. Don't compare me to them. There is no comparison."

"I'm serious. You should have beat me."

I stare at him. From this angle, all his sharp features are softened. "Yeah, maybe I should have."

We fall asleep talking. When dawn touches the windows, I turn over, a little frantic, unsure where I am. Then I remember. In the front of the bus, I can see the other boys peacefully slumped on benches. Wes is curled up in the bunk beside mine. Each breath pushes a strand of his hair up and down. His face is slack and creaseless.

Why are some people like floaters in your vision, still there no matter which way you turn? Why do certain people scald you? Every time I glance over at him, it feels like placing my hand on a stove and finding it's already on, jerking back in pain, and there's no reason I can give for such a violent reaction.

I have a voice mail from Gwen. I press my phone between Wes's pillow and my ear to listen, turning away from him.

"It is three a.m. here in Myrtle Beach," she says. "So that means it's earlier for you. Is it two a.m. in Texas? The time I'm living in doesn't exist for you yet. And maybe what happened to me tonight is forever lost between our time zones, and it will stay there, gone forever. Anyway, happy late birthday. Call me back when you can."

Years later, she will tell me about this night. A pirate-themed club in Myrtle Beach, with Tammy. On the dance floor, the lights tremble over every face. Tammy takes her hand, and it's wet from the rim of her drink. Gwen has had just enough alcohol to loosen herself. She sucks in a breath. They move closer together and suddenly Gwen is very afraid. Will she be recognized here? No. There are so many bodies, it is difficult to know where one begins and the other ends, where she begins and Tammy ends. And these bodies are so unabashed, so joyous, she can slip among them unnoticed.

Tammy pulls her in. It has not always been this way between them. For weeks on tour, Gwen didn't look up. Tammy walked by her, back and forth, and she refused to look up. Now, before shows, the dancers and crew form a circle, bowing their heads to pray together. She holds Tammy's hand and runs her index finger along Tammy's thumb, back and forth. Gwen has never prayed, doesn't believe in any kind of god, but she does this each night so she can take Tammy's hand in front of everyone.

In the club, the world is somehow still, and this moment is suspended. All the feeling inside Gwen is curious, sniffing the air and trembling now that it is allowed to wander. So, she takes Tammy's face into her hands and pulls her close. They collide angrily. She drags her teeth along her jaw, she nips at her earlobes. She's furious because she wants this night to stretch out endlessly, and she knows it will have to end.

And after, when they stumble out of the club and into the balmy air, she remembers my birthday.

1999

Washington, DC

We find the VHS tape in Alex's backpack. We are looking for snacks, but Ty feels something large and rectangular instead. He pulls it out. The cardboard slip has a woman with huge breasts, brown areolas the size of sand dollars, a tartan skirt.

"What is it?" asks Wes, reaching over Ty's shoulder for it.

"It's porn," I say. It is strange to see evidence of their sexuality like this. Usually it's glossed over.

Alex is asleep in his bunk, a bag of chips half-eaten in his lap. Wes's and Ty's eyes meet. "Let's put it back," Wes says, zipping the backpack closed. We deliver it to Alex's bunk and filter over to the front seats.

Wes turns to me. "Have you ever?"

"What? Watched porn?"

He nods.

"No." It's the truth. But I wonder if my answer should have been yes. If porn should have taught me how to have sex like it has for most boys my age.

Ty smiles. "Have you ever heard Alex on the phone with his girlfriend? It's like—" He looks behind him just to ensure no one else is listening. The three of us lean our heads closer together. Wes's small hoop earring catches in my hair. "It's like, 'Savannah, you're such a good girl. You make me so hard.' Stuff like that. He's so loud. Doesn't even try to whisper it. I think he wants us to hear him, honestly. I'm always his roommate in hotel rooms. Unfortunately."

"Savannah? As in Savannah Sinclair?" I pull away from them and lean back against the headrest.

"There's only one Savannah," says Ty.

"Doesn't she say she's a—everyone says she's a virgin. Don't they? I mean, doesn't *she* say that?"

"They haven't done anything," Ty confirms. "As far as I know. He would tell us immediately. But on the phone, they find ways. Clearly."

All I know about Savannah is what everyone else does: she sprang up from somewhere deep in the Bible Belt. A cream soda blonde. Strong, angular features, like the model Gisele Bündchen's. She prays before bed every night. Thanked God in her acceptance speech for Best New Artist at the Grammys. But no matter how many interviews of hers I listen to, she remains enigmatic, unbreachable; she unlocks herself only for certain people. This comforts me, since fame is being spread out on an operating table, cold silver twisting and prodding. Organs once folded behind thick walls of skin now exposed to light.

Still, I was taught that life is full of tolls, talent and beauty the only payment. And if the world has finite resources, then what is taken by others is forever lost to me. So when I watch Savannah or Gwen on television or hear them cycled on Top 40, my envy flares. I can't help it.

"Where are you now?" Gwen asks.

"We're near DC."

"I'm in Nashville."

"That's pretty close."

"I wonder if this is the closest we've been to each other all year."

"Might be." I glance out the window of the van, at the rock formations guarded by nets on the side of the highway bend. Where is she, out there? She's told me her shows are getting bigger and bigger, a progression of stages that she has trouble comprehending.

"I wanted to ask you about something," she says. "So Tammy and I saw a mother with two kids on the side of the road. She was pulled over and they were screaming in the back seat. Tammy said she never wants to have kids. Like, she knows in her soul that she doesn't. She's certain. But I've always been certain I *do* want them. I used to have a baby doll I'd carry around everywhere until it was so dirty my mom threw it out. So Tammy and I were wondering if everyone feels that way definitively. One way or the other. Like, if you lined up every person on the planet, would they say, 'Yes, I've dreamed of having children since I was little,' or 'No, I've never pictured myself as a parent'? Maybe most people fall somewhere in between, given the circumstances of their lives."

"Yeah, I think I'm somewhere in the middle," I say. "I don't actively fantasize about having a kid. And if I don't have one, if for whatever reason that doesn't work out, then I'd be fine with it. It would depend on how stable I feel. I don't know. I'm worried I wouldn't be a good mother."

"I wouldn't be fine with it," Gwen says. "Maybe that's just a problem with me. Maybe it's my personality—I very urgently want to pass down my genes to someone else."

"They are superior genes."

Gwen laughs.

"I think the main thing that appeals to me about having a kid is the reason I shouldn't do it."

She asks, "What's that?"

For a moment, I'm ashamed. It feels very wrong to reveal this about myself, for some reason. "Well, I think it's forced love, in a way. It's like, you bring this being into the world and it's dependent on you. It's helpless. It's going to love you for that reason. No matter how much you hate your parents, there's always love. I love my mom. I also hate her. Same with my dad, even though he left when I was a baby and I've barely spoken five words to him my entire life. And that's really appealing. You know another person in the world will have a connection to you, no matter what you do."

"Do you think anything could ever sever that?"

"Fuck no. My dad has a new family. A new wife, two boys. He left, and I still wait for him to call."

"Has he?"

"No."

"Well, maybe he's seen you on TV."

"Doubt it. Wouldn't he call if he did? Wouldn't he want something from me?"

"I don't know."

"Do you see what I mean, though?"

"I don't know," she repeats. "Maybe I just want to give myself completely to someone else because I'm afraid I'm selfish. Mike wants me to say I'm a normal girl. But I'm not, I never was. I always felt I had to prove I was better."

I remember having this exact same thought watching her on *TRL*. "Maybe you're being hard on yourself."

"You are, too. You don't see yourself at all."

"Because I look to everyone else for approval," I say. "Sonny says so. But where else is there to look? You can't be a singer unless someone is listening."

"Yes, you can."

I ask how.

"Don't you sing to yourself in the shower?"

"Yeah."

"Well, there you go." Then she asks if I'll do something for her, and I say I will.

"Record yourself singing. Play it back. Pretend it's not your own voice but someone else's, and assess it that way. Promise? Axel told me to try it, and it really helped me feel better about myself."

"Who's Axel?"

"Axel Holm. One of my producers."

"Okay, fine. But it probably won't help me see myself any differently. Do you ever feel like everything you say is stupid? The other day, MTV was here to film this behind-the-scenes video. Cameras followed the boys around. I said something—what did I say? I think the cameraman asked me, 'What's it like on tour?' Something like that. I said, 'The food is really good.' I really wanted to show this random cameraman I was eating. For some reason, it was so important to me." The van changes lanes. I wait for a moment as we race past a truck carrying stacks of cars. "Sometimes I feel like I walk around with this haze in front of my eyes. I keep waiting for the day when I'll wake up and it'll be clear, and I'll know exactly what to do and what to say."

On the other end, she sighs. I hear police sirens. The yap of a small dog. She must have opened the hotel window. I picture her reaching out, the wind running through her fingers, the sweet lick of freedom.

"I feel like that, too. That exact same feeling," she says.

I record myself, like Gwen said. Play it back. It takes effort to separate myself from the voice I'm listening to. What does it sound like, truly? When it's controlled and on pitch, it's like canyon rock, the layers stacked in thick, colorful bands. Sometimes it is soft and breathy, other times a hard, impressive punch. Sometimes it breaks a little, then recovers momentum. Maybe it's not as gorgeous as Savannah Sinclair's, but despite every internal protest, I know we can both be talented.

The next day, I'm on the treadmill in the hotel gym.

"Hon?"

It's Sonny. He has his pager in one hand and his cell phone in the other. "Looking great, sweetie. Lyle and Pat are on the phone." He returns his wet mouth to the receiver. "Yeah, yeah, she's right here."

They tell me they've set a date for the album release. In the fall, I will go on a national radio tour, then to New York, then Toronto, then London. And on a Tuesday in November, I will be born. After we hang up, I tick like a bomb, crying happy tears into Sonny's chest, because now I know when I will finally detonate.

I push through the double doors and into the hallway. At the craft services table, I hold up my badge so they will let me take food. I grab a napkin, two carrots, a stick of celery.

Ty and Wes are sprawled on the couch in their greenroom, eyes closed. They nap in any space they can find: an hour on the bus between cities, five minutes between meet and greets and sound check. One of their security guards is reading a magazine in a folding chair.

"So we want to go see some monuments tonight," Ty says, yawning. He uncurls his fists, then flexes all his fingers.

"When?" A carrot snaps between my teeth. I wait for a moment as I chew. "After the show?"

Ty nods.

"But won't we be pulling out?" By this, I mean the fourteen trucks carrying arena equipment and the buses carrying people.

Ty laughs, and Wes murmurs something to him about being immature, then shakes his head. "Not until late. We might have an hour or two. And we're only driving to Maryland."

"Didn't you already see the monuments on your eighth-grade field trip?" I remember matching green T-shirts and worn sneakers. A boy who vomited up macaroni, the stink lasting the entire drive home. On the bus, the cool place to sit was in the back row near the bathroom, and when our teacher's head was turned, couples would squeeze inside to hook up, the floor vibrating beneath them.

"No," says Ty.

"Nope," says Wes.

That night, for the first time, Wes and Ty watch me perform from the wings. I've moved up to the main stage for some performances. A banner with my name hangs down from a beam, quietly billowing in the wind. As the sky deepens from purple to black, I begin my set. Before, the girls in the audience were uncertain of me; some threw their empty water bottles. Hair elastics. A shoe. Others chanted "What's the ETA?" followed by three rapid claps. I don't think they understand their own collective power: to the labels, these girls are as influential as a pantheon of gods. I'm terrified to stand before them. But tonight, they are starting to bob their heads, a collective yes. The crew, carrying equipment and sputtering walkie-talkies, pauses for a moment to listen. Mike gives Sonny a thumbs-up. Wes and Ty exchange glances in the dark. My silhouette is framed by light. I perform a routine of hip isolations and dizzying body rolls, just praying I look like Gwen.

When my set is almost over, I reach for my water bottle. I feel a little faint, but I can't stop now. "Thank you all for coming. This has been so fun. I know you all want the main event." The chanting, screaming, crying builds. "I know you all want ETA, right? I have one last song for you. This one is called 'Sweat,' and it's my first single."

The reaction of the girls in the crowd surprises me. They are roaring. As music swells from the speakers, they recognize my song. The waves of validation batter me. For once I think: I might be gorgeous, might have talent, this all might be mine.

Illuminated statues cast long shadows on the silvered grass. We carry a pack of beer and a few Red Bulls. "Now this dude," says Ty, standing before a carved face, "definitely shouldn't have a gun."

"What war is he from?" Gabe asks.

"Hmm, can't read it," says Ty. "Don't think it says."

Wes and I walk a few feet behind them. He hands me one of the warm beer cans and says, "It was on the bus for a while. Sorry."

It sprays my cheek when I open it. He reaches forward to wipe it off, then licks his finger. "Yummy."

I slap his hand away. The night is muggy and damp. We struggle for breath, pausing to sip our beers, fingers slippery from the condensation on the cans.

Absentmindedly, Wes starts to walk ahead of me, toward the reflecting pool. He always moves like he knows exactly where he is going. The dyed strands in his hair are gilded by the moonlight. He lifts his hand to brush low-hanging leaves. Sometimes he tugs on them roughly, and they snap off. Because of the immensity held between us, I can tell we are alone.

"You killed it tonight," he says. "This is what the crowd was like." He presses his hands to his cheeks and raises his voice a decibel. "*Oh my god, it's Amber Young. Oh my god.*"

I look down at my feet; my face is hot. He must sense my embarrassment, and the joy behind the embarrassment, because his hands fall to his sides and suddenly he looks very serious. "It was cool to watch you."

"Did you ever get a feeling you were going to make it before it happened? Did you ever know for sure?"

"What do you mean by 'make it'?"

I frown. "I guess however you define it."

He scratches his head. Pulls me toward the pool's edge. We kneel beside it, and I touch my palm to the surface of the inky water. So does he, and the ripples we create collide together, then collapse. The water stills again.

We lean back on our palms and turn to each other.

"I'll never be satisfied," he says, shaking his head. "I'll always want the next thing. The next album to be better. To work with different producers. Whatever. So I don't really reflect on whether I've 'made it' or not. You can't get too comfortable."

He picks up his beer and takes a long, deep drink.

"I have this idea that when I can buy my mom a house," I say, "then I'll be successful, I'll have finally made it."

"I thought you hated your mom."

"Well, I think it's my way of getting back at her. It's kind of a fuck-you. I remember when we passed big houses in our town, she'd always say, 'Those people have more money than God.' She was so jealous. It's the life she always wanted for herself. So one day I'm going buy her one of those houses, and I hope it makes her happy."

He uncrosses his feet. A couple passes behind us and we don't say anything else until their footsteps fade away.

"What about your dad?" he asks.

"He left when I was a baby."

"I guess both our dads are pieces of shit."

"Yours, too?"

"Oh, yeah. He took me and my mom off his health insurance plan during the divorce, right before my mom ended up getting cancer. She lived, it's fine," he adds quickly. "But I remember her crying on the phone and I didn't understand she was trying to cover her treatment costs out of pocket. Which is impossible, obviously. Given how much it was. I was six or seven. Everything I was doing—the auditions, all the commercials I booked—was to bring money in for her treatment. I got my first paycheck for a commercial at seven years old, and it was for a couple hundred bucks. And I thought I could use it for something for myself. Then she told me about her bills and I felt like the worst person in the world."

"And you were only seven?"

"Yeah, I was."

I tell him I'm sorry. I didn't know.

"She's fine now," he says. "It's all good."

"What kind of cancer?"

"Ovarian."

"That's what my grandma died from."

"Oh, I'm sorry."

I laugh. "I don't know why I said that. It's fine, I barely knew her. Not to be morbid, but cancer is probably how I'm going to go. It runs in the family."

He takes another sip of beer. "Well, I think we really are going to have some sort of apocalypse next year. That's what everyone is saying. Maybe nuclear disaster. Or we'll be overtaken by all our garbage. We won't be able to live on the planet anymore. Does what we're doing, making music, even matter in that case? If the world is really going to end in a few months?"

"I think it matters a lot. I think it's all we have. It's proof of what we are able to do."

"If the only evidence of human civilization turns out to be an ETA song, that would be hilarious."

"No, it would be telling. It would say a lot about us."

He waves this off, but I can tell he liked hearing it. He rips out blades of grass and sprinkles them onto my knee, where they fall in a delicate pile. We're silent for a few moments as he does this. It feels like he's touching me.

"Wait," I say, reaching for his knee. I place my fingers on his knee-cap and slowly spread them open. It is the motion of a bomb explod-ing, or a jellyfish propelling itself toward the surface. "I heard this feels a bit like an orgasm."

"Does it?" He reaches forward and does the same thing to my other knee, the one without the grass. It is definitely a brush of a deeper feeling.

Suddenly, I'm nervous to be alone with him. Unsure, a preteen girl again in a dark closet with Jack Nichols, Lindsey and Rachel giggling just outside the door. My emotions are so huge, and words are so small—how could all this desire possibly fit through my mouth?

"Where are Gabe and Ty?" I ask.

He glances around and says he has no idea, but we should find them. He holds out his hand, pulls me to my feet. The pile of grass topples from my knee. Cicadas moan from the trees.

Looking down at me, he starts to smile. "You're short," he observes. He places his palm on the top of my head, presses down slightly. Everything is tensed and coiled, ready to spring, an animal hiding in the brush.

We search every monument nearby. Ty and Gabe are not at the Lincoln Memorial, but one of the girls sitting on the steps recognizes

Wes. He quickly pulls me away. By now we are laughing, weaving between trees, Wes singing, *Oh where, oh where has my little Ty gone, oh where, oh where could he be?*

Above us, the clouds disperse and reveal the full breadth of sky. Unable to find Ty or Gabe, and assuming they've already headed back, we set out for the buses.

1999

New York

We pull up to a club Alex has heard about. At the door, he throws out the name of the promoter he knows. The bouncer melts away to ask around inside, telling us to wait in line until he returns. Alex drinks from his flask and chats up two pretty girls, inviting them to join us. I can tell he's not really interested in either of them but likes playing with the strings of their attention. They brazenly inspect me, their gaze lingering for too long on my chest, then flicking back up to my face. I'm wearing a spaghetti-strap top, leather pants, a chain belt. My eyes are dusted in silvery shadow. Now I wish I had on anything else.

Alex's promoter rushes out, apologizing profusely. The rest of the line parts for us easily now, as if we are the prow of a boat.

At our table, huddled together and waiting for drinks, we play fuck-marry-kill. Ty says, "Okay, Amber: Brad Pitt, Leo DiCaprio, Keanu Reeves."

"No, not Keanu. Do Luke Perry," argues Alex.

"That's easy. Kill Luke. Fuck Brad. Marry Leo."

Wes frowns. We continue to play. I'm handed a gin and tonic. When I finish it: another. Cam tells a story about how, when he and

Gabe were younger, they were indistinguishable, and one time his own mother took Gabe home from a family gathering thinking he was Cam.

"No way she did that," says Alex, holding his hand up for another drink. He's bitten his straw until it looks like sheet metal.

"She did," confirms Gabe. "You would think our own mothers would be able to tell us apart. We look nothing alike."

I study them. They are both blond and blue-eyed, but the resemblance does end there. Gabe's face is thin, skeletal. His bottom teeth are crooked, crossing over each other—which is extremely sexy, many fans say. I don't really see it, but it's a reminder of how subjective attraction is.

"Anyway," Gabe says, throwing a half-bitten lime slice back into his shot glass. "Cheers to mommy issues."

"Cheers," says Ty, holding up his glass. I meet it with mine.

Gabe pushes Ty's arm away. "No, not you. You have daddy issues." He clinks his glass with mine instead.

"Do not," protests Ty. "That's Wes, not me."

"I have both," I say pleasantly, which makes everyone laugh, Wes most of all.

Ty gathers everyone and leads us to the middle of the floor to dance. I've improved in rehearsal; my body has been trained and sharpened over this past year. I sway back and forth, sipping my drink and thinking of my mother, stashing her wine bottles inside cabinets and behind curtains. Maybe I understand why: there is pleasure in submersion. Somehow the alcohol and the noise quiet my mind. I notice everything. How Ty and Gabe are always communicating—something radiates from Gabe and is received by Ty, a current traveling along telephone lines. How Wes pulls on my attention wherever he moves, as if my body is a compass and his is north. Now he is somewhere to the right, whispering something into a girl's ear. I run my fingers through my hair.

Ty leans forward and his breath is hot on my ear. "I know what's up."

"Huh?" I shout against the music, playing dumb. He draws a line in the air, linking me and Wes. I shake my head. Ty licks his lips and says nothing else. He spins me around and the strobe lights migrate to us. We are illuminated. Passed over. Our drinks spill out onto the sticky floor. Wes is across from me now, still speaking animatedly to the girl from the line, and the electronic music moves through me, fills me up, makes me bold. I want to make Wes feel what I've been feeling for years: that internal wrench when he looks at anyone else but me. I'm a black hole—I'll pull in whoever is closest to me. So I approach a man, all packed muscle.

"Hey," I say, and I know my desperation is leaking out, but men go to bars searching for exactly this. They are looking for a little spillage, a wet trail they can follow.

"Hey," he says, and it is easy, so terribly easy, to stand on my toes and smash our faces together. The man's lips are surprisingly soft. His tongue runs along my teeth. Large hands wrap around my ass and squeeze. Our mouths stir together, exchanging spit. Is this enjoyable? I can't decide. When the man turns me around, I can feel the hard press of him against me. Wes's eyes meet mine as the man is kissing my neck, as I grind myself back against him. His hands stroke my thigh, a step below pleasant but close enough. No one can see anything other than faces breaching the crowd, so I let him touch me. Who cares? Wes doesn't care, Wes doesn't want me; I could fuck this man in a bathroom stall, and it wouldn't matter. "You're gorgeous," he whispers. "You're gorgeous, honey," and this is what pulls me out of myself, because he sounds just like Sonny.

I open my eyes to see if the boys are still watching, but they are all gone. I turn and smile at this stranger. My lipstick is on his neck.

I squeeze his craggy shoulder. "I need another drink. I'll be right back, okay?"

I find the ETA boys and the two girls in a back corner. When I sidle up to them, Alex salutes me with his beer.

"How was that?" Ty asks.

I shrug, wiping my mouth with the back of my hand. "Unbelievable.

Sparks flew." I scan the crowd, unable to stop myself, but Wes has apparently gone to order us all more drinks. Ty says he's getting me a gin and tonic.

"Oh, I think I want something different. I'll go find him. He went to the bar?"

Ty nods. The crowd is so tightly packed now, it's difficult to push my way through. I apologize each time I force myself past someone. Far to the right, I can see Wes leaning over the bar, which is lined with taps and grasping hands.

I collapse against him. "What did you get me?"

"Gin and tonic."

"Perfect, thanks."

Silence on his end. I wonder if he's annoyed at me. Part of me hopes he is, since that would mean he cares. But he turns to me as if nothing has happened. "Want to explore the other room?"

"What about the drinks?"

"Here's yours," he says, handing the glass to me. "I'll give the boys theirs. Wait here."

I sip on my drink until he returns wearing a pink cowboy hat. "Someone just gave this to me," he says, laughing. "It'll look better on you." He positions it on my head, adjusting my hair. The rim is soaked with his sweat.

"What do you think?"

He nods. "I like it." And when he holds his hand out behind him, I take it. We entwine our fingers together. He pulls me to the other room, and the entire time I wonder if my body will crack open and all my happiness will fall out. We lean against a wall together, almost touching.

I stir the straw in my drink. The club spins around in the same direction.

"So, who was that?" He means the guy on the dance floor.

"No one."

"Oh, him. Yeah. He's great."

"I was just having fun." What I am trying to communicate is: other men are attracted me, so you could be, too. "I think I'm very drunk."

"Do you want to go?"

"Maybe sitting down would be good."

We squeeze into a booth already full of girls. They glance at him whenever they think he isn't looking. It is a given that most people know who he is, but we still move through the club with the illusion of anonymity. When he shifts against me to reposition himself, I lean my head against the cushion. The heat of his thigh on mine. His smell. I could luxuriate in this feeling for hours.

He is staring down at me, smiling. "You know what you could say? 'Thanks, Wes. You're a wonderful friend, looking after me like this.'"

Friend. That word is a pebble in my shoe. I open one eye and his figure is hazy. I don't want to say that at all; if I could, I'd tell him all the things I've noticed about him over the past few months, the things I don't dare speak aloud. The ease with which he holds himself. How he burns through a room. There is something effortless about him. Everyone knows it: the screaming girls, their mothers. Light reflects off others and is all absorbed by him.

Once, he told me the story of how he was first discovered. When his mom brought him to Los Angeles for pilot season, they were living in an apartment listed on the internet for a slashed price. There was thick grout in the tub and mysterious bloodstains on the wooden floors. He liked to sing to himself in the shower—his only happiness in that place. Then the ordained knock on the door: an A&R rep who had heard him through the thin walls. His boyfriend lived next door, and whenever he came over, they would both push their ears against the plaster to listen to Wes sing. Such things don't happen to ordinary people.

Now he's taken the cowboy hat from my head and placed it beside him so he can push my damp hair back behind my ears.

"Thank you for taking care of me," I finally say. "You're a really great friend."

"Do you want water? Wait here. I'll get you water."

I fall into his empty space. Glowing shapes as small as ants float across the dark planes of my eyelids. When Wes returns, my eyes are still closed. He runs his finger softly against my cheek and places the glass of water in my hand.

When I'm ready, we dance again. If his hand finds my waist, if our fingers brush against each other, so what? These moments are lost, dissolved. We throw these touches into the current and let them sink. And I submerge myself completely, the club lapping and steaming around me.

Which ETA member should you date?
J-14, 1999

If you answered mostly a's, you belong with Ty. His jokes will keep you laughing all day long, and you can visit comedy clubs and go on romantic dinner dates together. The conversation will always flow!

If you answered mostly b's, you should date Cam. Just because he's the youngest of the ETA boys doesn't mean he's the most innocent! Cam loves to get outdoors and is looking for a girl who will hike, bike, and camp with him.

If you answered mostly c's, you should be with Wes. His beautiful voice will sing you sweet melodies all day long. Wes wants a confident girl who will try new things with him. Could that be you?

If you answered mostly d's, your soulmate is Gabe! He's sweet, sensitive, a modern Shakespeare—what's not to love? If you want love poems and serenades, Gabe is your man.

If you answered mostly e's, your boyfriend should be Alex. He's charming, outgoing, and a little dangerous. He even has his own motorcycle! His dream date is sitting courtside at a basketball game.

1999

Wantagh, NY

The Jones Beach Amphitheater stands beside a polluted bay. On a stretch of asphalt, cars speed along, sand shuddering in the wakes of tires. Our van slows for speed bumps. I can already see the girls in the parking lot. Swarming together in excited clumps, flies around sugar.

There is nothing that sets us apart other than circumstance. These past few weeks, I have learned more about Wes by reading about him in the magazines I buy in mini-marts along the highway. I have learned that his star sign is Leo, which tells me lots of things. He's afraid of heights and forks. Why forks? He says he stabbed himself accidentally in the hand during dinner when he was a kid. Through this research, I am circling around some deeper truth about his personality. Maybe what I want more than anything is his nature defined in clear language, as compressed as a horoscope. It's all very banal and obvious: he is a real person, ugly and selfish at times, just like every other human being on the planet, but I don't want to know this yet. I want the ephemera, the wisps of a person that make them palatable.

I read about myself, too. I've done plenty of interviews over the summer. A few were placed by Lolli's in-house publicist, Cara. Other articles about me are in response to the "Sweat" video. Headlines like "SEXY AND SPICY: Inside Amber Young's Video," "AMBER YOUNG'S HOT SUMMER FLING: On Tour with ETA." I don't read all of them, only a small fraction. But now that I've been introduced in teen magazines, the persona is being steadily built. Lolli's Pygmalion statue has a naughty smile. She's a guy's girl, one who roughhouses and hangs with the boys on tour while maintaining her sex appeal. She calls them her brothers, her friends, but they all secretly want to fuck her. Her neuroticism is reframed as aloofness.

A question: Am I who other people say I am, or am I who I say I am? Lolli's version of me would take Wes's face in her hands. She won't be rejected—she can't even conceive of that kind of terror.

The five boys are clipped into harnesses because during one song, they fall to the stage on wires. Ty is up front, correcting the others. After their rehearsal is over, he waves me over. Sweat runs down his nose. He folds over and takes a sip from his water bottle. A cool breeze skims across the water and touches us.

"I'm done with Alex. *Done*. We have to rehearse this part again and again because it went wrong in Maryland. Guess whose fault that was?"

We both glance over at Alex. He's ignoring the choreographer speaking to him, twirling a toothpick around in his mouth. His hair is in cornrows, even though he's blond and Polish. Ty shakes his head, turning away. I wonder if the fissure between them will widen and become large enough to fall into.

That night, for the first time, most of the crowd knows the words to "Sweat." But the sun hangs low and cruel. During the second-to-last song of my set, I start to cramp up, clutching my ribs. The world spins. How much have I eaten? I can't remember. The heat has taken advantage of my emptiness. I sway on stage, blinking up at unyielding light. Darkness falls like a blade.

Sonny tells everyone it was the sun that made me pass out. I lie on the couch in the greenroom, a pack of frozen peas on my forehead.

"Who thought an amphitheater tour was a good idea in this weather?" he complains.

I am afraid he will understand what really happened. But men only notice the result, never the progression of hunger. In his eyes, my metabolism is a miracle. I eat oily fries, breaded chicken fingers, hot dogs, and it all seems to disappear inside my body as if tucked away in a drawer. A miracle! But when he's gone, I pick at baby carrots and cheese cubes. I run and run and run, and the destination is his praise.

Mike offers to fetch me some food. I ask what it is today, the hunger a knife in my stomach. He says they have barbecue ribs, corn, mashed potatoes.

"Yes, please. All of it."

When he returns, we're alone. Sonny is out in the hallway on a call. Mike hands me the plastic plate, sitting beside me on the couch. I shift away slightly, undetected by him. He thinks he has his own charisma, since he's surrounded by so many talented people.

"Are you wearing a thong?"

"Not right now. No."

He bites down on his own sandwich. "Huh. When I was watching you perform, I was wondering if you were."

"I'm not."

He nods. "That's what I thought. It's hard to tell sometimes, though." He snakes forward to take another bite, chewing and smiling at me with his mouth open.

I don't raise my head, trying to avoid his eyes and the thick tone he's shifted to. And I'm relieved when the boys return, sweaty and exhilarated from their performance.

"What happened?" Ty sits beside me on the couch and pulls my feet onto his lap. As Wes hands his jacket to a wardrobe assistant, he glances over at us.

"I fainted," I say quietly. "But it's no big deal. I'll be fine for tomorrow. I was just in the sun for too long."

"It was fucking hot out, wasn't it?" says Ty.

"Are you okay?" asks Wes.

"Fine."

Fans filter out of the amphitheater and into the parking lot, gushing about the show. Flickering red taillights wait to turn onto the highway. The crew begins to disassemble the stage and load it onto the trucks, until the amphitheater is bare.

A knock on my door. Wes's knuckles against the wood, and his voice whispering my name.

We are at a Marriott in Maine. It is one of the last stops on this leg of the tour. On the other side of the room, I can just make out the shape of Gloria's body beneath the covers, her silk hair wrap, the undulation of her chest. I wonder if I will wake her if I change—I'm wearing Greg's old T-shirt and mesh soccer shorts—but then I hear Wes step away, so I run to the door, wrench it open. It bangs against the wall. Behind me, Gloria turns over onto her back.

I whisper his name into the hall, which smells like cigarettes smoked years ago. Wes's retreating figure pauses by the elevator. He's wearing an oversize Old Navy hoodie and track pants. His hair is tousled, as if he's just had sex.

"What time is it?"

He smiles. "It's a little after eleven. Sorry, were you already asleep?"

"Not yet."

"I wanted to check out the pool."

"Isn't it closed?"

He shrugs. "We could try it." And he tugs on the elastic of his pants to reveal swim trunks.

I ask him to wait and slip back inside my room. Quietly, I search for a swimsuit in the piles of clothes I've left on the floor, then realize I didn't even think to pack one. I settle for a bra and my underwear instead.

In the elevator, through the lobby, we're quiet. There's only the sound of our sandals smacking against the hard floors. On the lowest level, the moist air builds and thickens. Wes pulls on the door and overhead lights snap on. He turns back to me, raising an eyebrow.

"Guess it's open," he says softly.

Our shadows beam across the turquoise water, textured with ribbons of yellow light. The tile floor is slick. Towels are stacked neatly on top of each other above the garbage can, still hot from the belly of the dryer.

Wes dips a toe into the water, and after declaring it warm enough to swim, he takes his shirt off, then his pants. I look down, embarrassed. Hearing a splash, I glance up again. He's dunked under. Seconds later he emerges, shaking out his hair, whipping water toward me. Maybe this is my problem: I don't want just any man, I want the most beautiful man I've ever seen. His gaze really is a lighthouse, a searching, hot beam. Under it, I'm drawn in. Under it, I'm always onstage.

He takes beers out of his backpack and pops a can, leaving it by the rim of the pool. Then he grabs my arm, pulling on me gently. Come in, he says.

I shake my head, swirling my feet through the water. "I have this song in my head. It goes like this." And I hum it for him.

As he listens, I draw shapes on my thigh with water, because I don't want to look at him, I can't. He reaches forward to wipe a diamond off my leg.

"What if you went to one of your producers with the melody?"

"Is that what you do?"

"Yeah, sometimes. Maybe it could be something."

I have never thought about it seriously before, only toyed with it. Voicing my ideas. Control. Raising my arm and lowering it, like Gwen said. Because now, I sing about sex in the form of various euphemisms, and this doesn't feel wrong to me, necessarily, because I do think about sex a lot. I just want it from my perspective, not theirs. I want it to feel like this.

"What's the overall vibe of the album?" he asks.

I tell him. *In Your Eyes* is trying to be many things at once. It's trying to seduce. It's playing against what Savannah and Gwen have already accomplished; at the same time, it's trying to mimic their success. It's withholding; it's giving too much. It doesn't know what it is, or what it should be. It is a teenage girl.

He nods. "So Lolli wants you to be the sexy version of Savannah."

"Basically. That's what frustrates me. No matter what, I was signed *because* of Savannah and Gwen. You know? I'm still proud of the record, I guess, but I hope I can make something better one day." I laugh helplessly. "Hopefully Lolli lets me."

"You will. Every time, you'll know more about yourself. You'll know more about the process." He bobs in the water, blinking up at me. "We wrote more on this upcoming album. I think I cowrote two, maybe three, songs. If I ever try to—" And he interrupts himself, starts to laugh. "Have I told you about the Clinton song I wanted to write?"

"No."

His chin skims the surface of the water. "I wanted to write this song about the Lewinsky scandal. It was calling out Bill Clinton a bit. I mean, I'm a Democrat, I just think Bill deserves a little healthy criticism." He ducks under again, then swims over, brushing his hand against my knees. "But I get why Axel didn't like it. It was a bad song. I had done coke that night in Stockholm, so I was up all night, and I thought it was brilliant and edgy at the time, but Axel looked at me like I was insane when I sang it for him."

"Axel?"

"Yeah. Our producer."

Something about this name is familiar. After a moment, I remember: Axel Holm. Gwen works with him, too. "What did he say?"

"He just said it wasn't an ETA song. Which is fair." He laughs again, louder this time. "He's very decisive. When he says no, it's no."

I splash him. "How did it go?"

"Oh, it was like . . ." He closes his eyes for a moment. "It went something like, *I'd give it all up for the girl in the blue dress.*"

"That is bad."

He smiles. "Thanks."

"I'm not sure if the songs I'm singing now would be any different from the songs I'd write. I mean, most of the time I am thinking about sex. Seriously. I really am."

He hesitates, then asks, "What do you think about?"

Heat strums through my body. He's plucked chords and I am the instrument in his hands. I wonder if I should jump in the water to stifle the feeling. "Things I can't have. That's the best part. The distance between two things. That's what I'd write about."

"What can't you have?"

I splash him again.

"Do you really think that?"

"What?"

"The best part isn't the real thing?"

"I haven't actually had good sex, Wes."

"I didn't know that."

"We haven't talked about it. I mean, I've done it once with this guy, a year ahead of me in school. I just wanted to get it over with. I don't know."

He shakes his head. "I promise my first time was bad, too. I didn't know what the fuck I was doing. I was worried this girl would judge me. You know? If I came too fast, or if I didn't know how to put the condom on right. I didn't really have a frame of reference either. I grew up in Texas. The only thing we were told about sex was to wait until we were married to have it."

"All *I* remember from sex ed is this video of a girl giving her boyfriend a blow job. Cut to black, of course. They didn't show anything. Anyway, she gets a cold sore, and it's big and ugly and red, not like any real cold sore I've ever seen. It looked like a punishment. Right after we saw that video, a girl at my school got pregnant. Anyway, this girl—not the girl in the video, the girl from school—told a few friends, then everyone found out. One day, she threw up in the pool during gym class. Every day we had to get into the pool and swim laps, but that day, we were all so happy because the pregnant girl puked, and class got canceled."

"What did she end up doing?"

"She got an abortion. But I remember thinking girls carry sex on their bodies. That was the lesson I learned."

He nods, and I get the sense he is really listening to me, so I continue, "What if the girl in the video enjoyed herself? Or, at least, what if she was thinking about sex each night before she went to bed? That's when I think about it the most. Right before bed. You know?" I'm communicating something to him desperately, weaving my feet through the water, grazing his chest. I wonder if what's between us has been clearly defined now, or if we can return to shapelessness.

"Always right before bed?"

"Usually. I think about it to fall asleep."

"Why don't you just watch porn?"

"Because there's no porn that's exactly the way I like it, exactly the way I imagine it." In truth: it is all too male. Sticky, salty, his alone. What I want is tension. When I imagine sex with Wes, we are usually talking at first. Just talking. We stare at each other, the frequency between us an earthquake monitor, ratcheting with every breath. Then I'm arched over his neck, biting his skin. His hands roaming up my thighs. His fingers inside me, so slow, and then faster. His mouth where his fingers were, and it feels different than it was with Nathan, because Wes knows what he is doing, has done it before. Eventually, my thoughts dissolve into sleep. The next night I imagine it all from the beginning again. I sit in the front row of this internal film for hours, my eyelids the screen.

Eventually we are kicked out of the pool by an employee who has come to clean it. We've left puddles all over the tiles. The elevator doors close on us, and we stand far apart as we're propelled up through the hotel. Wes has a towel loosely wrapped around himself. He's dripping water onto the floor; his hair is damp; he smells like chlorine.

When the door opens to my floor, he presses the topmost button to keep the elevator moving. He smiles at me sleepily. Steps forward, then stops. For a moment, he hesitates, waiting to see my reaction. All the former selves inside me stare up at him, wide-eyed and disbelieving.

He leans down. His lips are cold and wet from the pool. Our movement warms them up. He catches my bottom lip between his teeth and gently pulls, laughing when I moan. "You like that?"

I nod. I would let him untie me and untie me until something soft and hidden finally emerges, and now he knows.

He presses me against the doors with his hips. "What else do you like?"

"I'm not sure."

The elevator is back in the lobby, the doors opening to an empty hall, then closing. We push a button, and the elevator rises again.

When I encourage him, his hand slides along my underwear, rubbing back and forth at first, then pushing it aside so he can slip a finger into me. I bang my head against the buttons, hitting five floors at once.

He laughs and bites my earlobe. "Do you want another?"

I nod again. Yes. How did he know? I need more space filled, it's not enough, and when he pushes another finger in beside the first, I make a high-pitched whine I've only ever practiced alone, a noise hauled up from some depth I've never really explored.

"You're so wet," he says. "Fuck."

"I know, I know."

Suddenly, his fingers stop moving. "Is it for me?"

"Yes, all for you."

Even faster now. His face is scrunched up, and his eyes are closed. I can feel how hard he is beneath his sweats. He presses his lips to my neck. A red oval blooms there in the shape of his mouth, but I don't care about the hickey, even though it will have to be covered with concealer for over a week. I want this symbol, a reminder of where he touched me.

The next morning, mist rises thick and blue from the forest. The fleet of buses returns to the highway. It is the end of summer.

We know you loved "Sweat"—and you want to know what's underneath Amber Young's skin! The teen star filled out our test below.

1. When I have a crush on someone
I completely ignore them!

> **Name:** Amber Young
> **Birthday:** July 3, 1980
> **Star sign:** Cancer
> **Occupation:** Singer

2. My first kiss was
Awkward

3. If I were president
I would be a terrible president

4. I can't stand
Judgmental or bigoted people

5. My style icon is
Kate Moss

6. The biggest item on my bucket list is
Falling in love

7. My biggest insecurity is
My grades in school

8. Coolest person you've ever met
Gwen Morris. I LOVE HER! She's like my sister.

9. I knew I was famous when
My brother said his friends knew who I was!
Now he tolerates me . . .

10. Three things I'd like in a boyfriend:
Makes me laugh
Gives me the butterflies
Good kisser!

1999

Chula Vista, CA

I can't grasp the growing frenzy about Gwen and Wes because I'm shut away on tour. It's like Gwen said: I'm walking down a tunnel, and the world is happening around me. But from what I can tell, the fervor is like a little girl, stripping her Barbie dolls the way I used to, twisting their plastic faces together. At least, until the first-ever Teen Choice Awards, which I'm not invited to. I watch it on television from a hotel room, after a pathetic show at an outlet mall. Sonny had to corral shoppers out of stores to join the audience.

I sit cross-legged on my scratchy floral comforter, the reek of old piss lost somewhere in the beige carpet, too deep to ever be extracted, and find the right channel just as Savannah Sinclair is midbelt, standing in the center of a spotlight. She has no dancers with her—the performance is in the aerobics of her voice.

When Gwen and Wes step onstage together to present an award for Sexiest Love Scene, I finally see it for myself. I understand completely. Their shy, secret glances. How uncomfortable they seem together, which viewers will mistake as clumsily hidden lust. The little bit they perform at the podium.

"I wish *we* had a sexy scene together," says Wes, scratching his head.

"Oh, yeah? What would the scene be?"

"Hmm, I think we'd be standing just like this." He steps closer.

"And?" So does she.

"And I'd just—" He leans forward, cupping her cheek in his hand, and kisses her. It's chaste, innocent. A kiss you might have in middle school before tongues have been introduced. She pulls away first, flushing red.

"Um, I guess we should hand the award out, right?"

"Oh, um, right. Forgot we had to do that."

They become characters, not real people I know. And I have trouble distinguishing between these two things.

So the idea of Wes dissolves, like a mint on my tongue. He hasn't called, and it's been a week since the tour leg ended. When we said goodbye, he pulled me to his chest with one arm, then stepped aside so Ty could hug me, too. My body was screaming at him, and his was screaming at me, but neither of us said anything.

I'm handed a microphone, deposited in front of a cinder-block backdrop.

The reporter, a stiff and vaguely judgmental woman, says, "This is *L'Oréal Summer Music Mania*, the biggest show of the summer, and we're here with Amber Young. Who are you excited to see tonight?" She smiles so widely I know it is false.

Sonny stands beside the cameraman, frowning as I stumble over my words. I'm so honored to be here, I say. I can't believe I'm performing with Gwen Morris and Sol Sister and Chloe Woods, the whole lineup. I don't think anyone is here to see me, obviously, so I'll just get up there and do my best.

After, I watch Gwen open the show. She struts down metal stairs to the heat of the stage, joining her dancers for tight choreography, moving with the intensity and focus of a bullet. She wears a lavender leather set—a crop top and pants—and platform sneakers. I don't dare blink; I don't want to miss anything. It's the way I felt waiting for the senior's car to pull up in front of Lindsey's house: I can't look away, can't focus on anything else until it arrives.

Maria Colmenares is next. Then Check-M8, the rock band from Kansas, a sprawl of tattoos on ghostly skin, red hair flattened by backward caps. Sol Sister, the duo from Atlanta, who are number one on *TRL* this week with their song "Blinders." I've been singing it all week: *My blinders on / Can't look your way / No way, no way.* Chloe Woods, the R&B singer who won this year's Grammy for Album of the Year. Caleb Waterman, a guitarist from Cincinnati with an equine flop of brown hair. I'm last.

Before I go onstage, I find Gwen in the greenroom. She opens her arms for me, and I rest my forehead against her shoulder. There is new health in her cheeks. A Renaissance blush. She looks drunk for the very first time, as if she's just stolen rum from the family liquor cabinet. "This is a hot little number," she says, pointing to my studded bra and matching pants. "The boobies are saying hello tonight."

"They've had so many nights out recently."

She really laughs, which means hardly any sound comes out at all. Her fake laugh is loud and insistent, as if swearing it finds you funny. "Tammy," she calls over her shoulder. "Come meet Amber."

A woman, once a voice on the phone, now unfurls into a figure. Tammy is Black, petite, strikingly beautiful. She has wide-set eyes and a septum piercing. She tells me she grew up in Kissimmee, Florida, near Walt Disney World, and began dancing at three years old. Gwen says she couldn't take her eyes off her at the audition. There were hundreds of dancers trying out for the tour, and her eyes followed Tammy the entire time.

I can tell that Tammy scans people and immediately draws conclusions, the same way Gwen does. I desperately want her to like me, but I also know she'll sniff me out if I'm too obvious about it.

"What's this?" I ask, pointing to a tattoo of a vine running along Tammy's left arm, starting at her knuckles. She twists around to look at it.

"Oh, I got it when I was sixteen. I add a leaf to it every year to re-mind myself." Of what, she doesn't elaborate, but we've also just met. She points to the section she got this year, which includes a small budding flower.

"I want to get a tattoo now," Gwen says. "I almost did in North Carolina. Remember?"

Together, they share a memory I can't see.

Tammy laughs. "I'm glad I talked you out of that. Mike would have murdered you."

Light dances in Gwen's eyes. "I did get my nose pierced, though. See?" She leans forward to show me the new stud. "And this one." She points to her cubic zirconium belly-button ring, which looks just like mine.

"What tattoo would you have gotten?"

She shrugs. "Something meaningful. Anyways, what about you? What's going on with you?"

My face is hot next to hers in the mirror. I know I should tell her. Every second I don't, I just hate myself more: for all the misplaced longing, for the exhilarating hours I think about him rather than all the things I should. What will I risk for just one ferocious moment? What will I do to preserve the image she has of me? I should have told her long ago—and I know one of the many reasons I haven't. She thought he was lackluster from the beginning, and I was embarrassed to want someone she found so mediocre, so ordinary.

But there's no time—I'm called backstage. This is the biggest show I've ever done. Cameras are floating over the crowd; the performances and interstitial interviews will be broadcast to hundreds of thousands of people. I can't comprehend this number, and maybe it's best not to picture it. I hardly have time to coax my belief in myself. I can only close my eyes for a moment, then open them. There's nothing to do but sing.

Later, trash litters the beach. Plastic bags. Crumpled cans. In the dark, I think the shapes are nesting birds. The sand parts for us, supple and eager. Icy water laps at our ankles, turns our feet red. Gwen stares at Tammy sprinting into the surf until she notices me looking, and then, like a child whose hand has been slapped, she glances away. I draw vague lines between them in my mind.

Gwen lights a cigarette. Her face glows as she leans toward the lighter in her hands. With her pink hair and blue eyes, she looks like a fiery creature who leaped out from the flames.

She exhales. The cigarette darts through in the air. "So, this school principal from Texas went on the news, said my music is bad for young kids. Apparently, moms came into his office and complained about a teacher who played my song during class or something. The principal said I should be banned. That my music is evil."

"Stop, Gwen. Don't think about that. Everyone loves you," Tammy says. I get the sense that she is the hand on Gwen's back during spirals like these.

"What is love in this context? We have one word to encapsulate so much. They *admire* me. They *idolize* me. But love? Can you really love someone you don't know?"

Tammy drags sand with her heel. "Okay, well, we both love you." This laced with pride, and I feel it, too, because both of us do really know her.

Gwen takes another drag. "Maybe you shouldn't. Maybe the moms are right about me. I remembered something recently. When I was in middle school, my mom came into my room, and I had a whole song prepared about how much I hated her and what a terrible mother she was. I performed it for her and it made her cry. I don't remember why I did that, all I think about is my guilt, and I wonder if she sees me now and thinks, 'My daughter traumatized me with a song when she was in eighth grade.'"

"We've all done bad things, Gwen," says Tammy.

The cigarette plunged in the sand. "Growing up I was told to shine, to be special, and that doesn't always result in being the nicest kid. So

I don't think I was." She buries her face in her hands. "I thought I was better than everyone, but especially her."

"Gwen, it's okay. I had terrible fights with my mom. I've said some awful things to her."

"Your mom can be a cunt, though," Gwen says. "Sorry."

"Yeah, but still."

"But still," Gwen agrees, and we are silent for a while, listening to the waves break against the sand.

"I actually like my mom," Tammy says, and we all burst out laughing. "Sometimes she takes too much shit from other people, just because she wants to make them happy. She steps back so other people can fill the space. When it's just us two, we won't speak sometimes for ten, fifteen minutes. But I feel like that silence is saying something. We don't need to talk."

"Yeah, you know you're close with someone when you can be quiet with them," Gwen says. Wiping the sand from her palms onto her thigh, she takes both of our hands. "My best friends. Have I ever told you how grateful I am? I should tell you more often. You are the nicest, most beautiful, most talented, most wonderful people."

"I don't know about nice," I say.

Gwen smiles at me. "You are a nice person. I'm not. But I want to be."

Tammy lies back on a curtain of seaweed. She asks if there's anyone I've been into on tour. It is a casual question, meant to sew us together as friends, but I take a moment too long to respond. I dig my hands in the sand to meet the wetness beneath. Gwen rests her head on her shoulder and watches me hesitate.

I don't want to see betrayal or judgment unfold in her eyes. I want her to look at me this way forever. A lie is a small stitch one day, and the next, a tapestry of ugly knots. Later, I justify it to myself: she is the one lying to the whole world. Wes, too. But why is it that every day, I regret who I was the day before?

I tell them there's no one on tour. I add, "I actually haven't had sex in, like, two years."

"I packed my vibrator on the bus," Tammy says. "Maybe you should, too."

I wiggle the fingers on my right hand, and she laughs again.

Later, Gwen and I smoke a joint, just the two of us. Tammy has returned to the hotel, too tired to stay up any later, insisting that weed puts her right to sleep.

Gwen asks, "Are you going to Vegas for *Billboard*?"

"Nope." I take the joint from her and hold the smoke in my throat. Wasn't invited, I don't bother to add.

"Wes and I might walk the carpet together." She laughs. "You know, what he did wasn't even a big deal, but of course everyone was like, 'Damage control! We need a girlfriend for him!'"

And this shocks me—this buried knowledge, now excavated. "What do you mean? What did he do?" It's a struggle to keep my voice remote, disinterested.

"Nothing bad. He was dating an older woman during ETA's first tour. She was, like, over forty or something. They might still be together. Who knows."

"How did they meet?"

Gwen shrugs. I can tell she truly doesn't care. "I think she was his makeup artist. I forget the details. He told me ages ago."

The smell of salt hovers in the air as whitecaps crash on the sand. We look out. The water is stygian, and it is easy to imagine the depth of it—the monsters with lanterns hanging from their foreheads, illuminating deep ridges. I wonder if we are all so murky, if all our trenches are as dark and flammable as oil.

1999

New York

This age. It feels like walking barefoot on wood, every encounter a splinter that will remain embedded for years. They carry candy-colored spoils from the Limited and Rave and dELiA*s, wearing similar outfits stretched across different bodies. I look down at them, collected by my little stage in the mall, and think, We are the same. We are all mortified to be alive. We are still-adjusting worlds—tectonic plates shaking in place, sometimes submerging, pushing up, up, up, only to crumble on the surface.

Lolli sends its representatives to MTV to campaign for my new single "Work of Art," and eventually the video debuts on *TRL* in October. The shoot was inspired by the Demi Moore film *Ghost*: there's a potter's wheel, me spinning on top of it, male hands packing clay onto my skin until I am a sculpture, not a girl. The single moves up the charts, but not high enough. It doesn't surpass "Sweat." Won't ever surpass "Sweat." I am pushing a boulder up a hill, and I stumble back under the weight.

But in November, I hold my CD in my lap. The cover art is a close-up of my eye, my silhouette in the pupil. I take out the silver disc, stare at my reflection in it, smudge it up with my thumbs. If I do nothing else, create nothing else, at least I have this.

In Your Eyes peaks at nineteen on the US *Billboard* 200, which is slightly below label expectations after the explosive success of Savannah and Gwen. But all I know is the colors that move in my vision, the oily sheen of promotion. Even though critics and parents hate it, some girls buy it because they are just as lusty and horny and yearning as I am, dancing in front of their mirrors in their underwear, trying to release what moves inside them. The royalties—a little less than a dollar per record sold, after production costs—start to churn. This money feels like a sunrise beyond buildings: hazy, untouchable. Sonny handles the finances for me. He also accompanies me to all the press, herding me in and out of black Range Rovers. I perform on morning shows and late-night shows. I'm fitted for wardrobe by a stylist. My team decides I should differentiate myself from Gwen and Savannah, which means showing more skin. I hire a bodyguard named Dale, whose face is a bright window that can be shuttered by blinds at any moment.

My mom calls once. "If I fly out, will your label cover it?" she asks. They might, I tell her. But don't bother. It's mostly waiting around, smiling, answering the same questions over and over, crossing and uncrossing my legs on different seats. The real reasons I don't want her around: the miasma of her drugstore perfume, the liquor she stashes in her purse. Worse, the flattery or disdain leaking off her face, depending on the person she's addressing.

My dad doesn't call at all. This makes me feel very small, staring up at a towering, shadowy figure who won't acknowledge me, no matter how loudly I shriek. I didn't realize I had been expecting him to contact me until he doesn't.

On the phone with Gwen, I say, "I thought he would finally want to be in my life if he heard me, you know?"

"I know." She sighs. "Just pretend you're walking through that tunnel we talked about. Or maybe it's a hallway. Everyone else in the world is behind closed doors. Your dad. Whoever. Even if they're screaming and banging, even if they're dead silent, you don't have to open any of those doors. Don't pay attention to anyone else. You just keep walking."

I don't recognize the number, but I still pick up, expecting my brother, Greg, who said he would call from Arizona. It is not Greg.

"Hi," says Wes.

"How did you get my number?"

"Mike asked Sonny for it."

"Oh."

"What are you doing now?"

It is morning. Cold rain is tapping on the windows. I disentangle myself from the hotel sheets. "I'm in New York doing radio."

"Z100?"

"A few other stations, too," I say, switching the phone from one ear to the other.

"Did you stop home?"

"No, but I got dinner with my mom. She came into the city." I don't want to talk about my mom, how she cut into flank steak, the blood pressured out of the meat, then complained to the waitress that it was too well done. She swirled her glass of wine until they brought a new one out to her. Didn't reach for the bill because she assumed I would pay, and so I did. My new debit card slapped on the table, red and glossy, Amber Melissa Young stamped in silver. Sonny first handed it to me after I signed with Lolli, explained he would take a per diem amount from my advance and royalties and move the rest of the money into a checking account. My mom agreed and signed off—she didn't trust in my self-discipline.

"Where are you now?" I ask him.

"Stockholm." A pause. "Are you going to Vegas next week?"

"Funny. Gwen asked me that. I think I am now. I wasn't, but since the album is doing okay, Lolli got me invited at the last minute."

After a moment of hesitation: "Then we'll see each other."

"Yeah. I'll be the one no one knows, standing alone in the corner."

"No, you'll be the one everyone wants to be introduced to."

"Right." I pause, wondering if everything will remain unsaid between us. It has for months, but I can still feel his mouth on my throat.

"It's different without you here," he says.

"How is it different?"

"You know how."

I don't know. Maybe I do. I want him to tell me. "I saw you and Gwen on television."

"Oh." I hear his hesitation, as if a voice can fall in one moment the way a face can. "I mean, do you feel like it was wrong or something?"

What a complex question. They belong together in the eyes of the world, and so, in this way, it's completely natural. All is as it should be. "I think, maybe, I was being a bit thoughtless, you know, in the elevator."

He's quiet, which is unlike him. "Okay," he finally says.

"What I mean is I feel confused about it."

"You know I'm not really with Gwen, though."

"Yeah, I know that."

"I guess I don't really understand the problem." His breath is quick again. "Maybe in a way—well, at least to me, and I really can't explain it, but it really turns me on that no one else knows. Only us."

"No, I get that. The secrecy thing. It turns me on, too."

"Really? What else turns you on?"

I bite my lip. "Um, I think a lot of things. I have a weird one."

"Tell me."

"I think I would be into it if you flirted with other people in front of me. You know? If you made me a bit jealous, then chose me after."

"Hmm. Like, as foreplay?"

"Well, maybe it's just hot that so many people besides me find you talented and attractive. It's literally a universal fact."

"I feel the same about you. I bought your album, by the way. Well, I had Mike go and get it for me." He pauses, and I can hear him unzipping his backpack. "I was reading the booklet and saw that you thanked us. *To ETA, for welcoming me into your family and showing me the ropes.* That's nice. Nothing for me specifically?"

"I think of you all as one entity, actually. I'll be waiting for my thanks on your next album. *To Amber. For entertaining me during long stretches of boredom, breaking into hotel pools with me.* You can add the rest on your own." Through the crack in the bathroom door, I can see a slant of myself in the mirror: I'm smiling as I talk to him, surrounded by thin, gauzy sheets, a nest of room service.

Suddenly I'm afraid of myself. I have analyzed every interaction we've ever had, turning them over like coins, watching the light reflect off them in different ways. I take a breath to calm myself and wonder if, on the other side of the line, he has taken one, too.

"How has it been, though?" he asks.

"A critic called me nasty."

"That's fun."

"Very." I reach for a slice of grapefruit on my breakfast tray. "Another said something like, 'How can music be both prurient *and* banal?'"

"Big words."

"What do you think?"

"Do I think music can be prur—what? And what was the second thing?"

"No, do you think I should believe him?"

"Amber."

My name, which I've always hated, has never sounded so gorgeous.

"I say just keep moving forward. That's all you can do."

"That's pretty much what Gwen told me."

"Okay, good. Listen to her, though, not me."

An hour passes. Two. Dale knocks, reminding me to pack. I throw everything in my suitcase with one hand. The other is holding my cell phone up to my ear. Wes is telling me about growing up in East Texas. There was a pond where they used to swim during summers. Clogged with algae, brain parasites that travel up the nose, every childish wonder. When he heard stories about the biblical flood, he says he imagined the next one would start from this pond, pouring out in green ribbons into the suburban streets. He wants to take me there, but he hasn't been home in over a year, so maybe it's all dried up. "It's where I had my first kiss, standing on a log. I was home for the summer. We were taking a break from auditioning in Los Angeles, and my friend invited me to tag along to a party. Everyone was meeting in the woods by the pond. It was the only place to go, really. That, or a parking lot. And I remember I saw a couple hooking up against a tree, and there was this bonfire. A boy got knocked unconscious that night when he jumped into the pond and hit his head on a rock, but he was fine in the end. I don't know what I'm even saying. Only I want you to see this place. I keep picturing you there."

Then he asks about my childhood. For a moment, I imagine him in our little apartment, crouching low to avoid hitting his head. My room emptied, girlhood swept away, the pile of once-loved stuffed animals now collecting dust in a closet.

"Do you have trophies? From sports and stuff?"

"No," I say. "I wasn't good at anything but singing. Not school or athletics or anything. I had a lot of animal figurines everywhere. We had a lizard for a while, and he had a terrarium."

Does he want me to be exceptional in some way? Maybe he wants me to say I knew I was destined for this from the start, that I had my choice of pursuits that would lead me to whatever end. I could have been this or this or this. Whenever interviewers ask me what I would be if I weren't a singer, my mouth dries up. For some reason this question fills me with dread, so I make up something different every time.

"My mom has a wall of me," he says. "When you walk into our house, there's an entire hallway with photos from talent shows and my guest pass from *Star Search* laminated and framed, that sort of thing." He sighs. My hair flutters in the wind from the open window, but for a moment I think it is his breath traveling through the phone. "I'll never forget what she said about you that day."

"What did she say?"

"Something like, she's going to beat you, with a voice like that. Her voice is bigger than her whole body."

I close my eyes. "What are you doing right now?"

"I'm, uh, just hanging around. Alex is nowhere to be found, obviously, so we're waiting on him to start recording. I'm the only one here. Are you still in bed? In your hotel?"

"Yeah."

"Lazy," he says. His voice is deeper than expected when you first look at him, and now it rumbles through me.

"There are things to do when you're alone." I run my hand down my stomach, to the dark grove of hair.

"Hmm," he says. And then he pauses, as if he too is afraid. He must have heard the way my breath quickened. "Amber, are you touching yourself?"

"Yes," I say, and then I begin to.

On the other end, I hear the rustling of his hands. "Fuck. Are you really? Do you wish I was?"

"Yeah. So badly. But you know we can't." Even now, I'm thinking of Gwen.

"We can't," he repeats.

"Well, I think, in this hypothetical, you can. Imagine you can. What if you were? What would you do first?"

"In my mind, I was already putting my finger inside you. You were so wet, like you were in the elevator."

"Mmm. I think I'd want to go down on you after, though. Would you like it? If I did that?"

Our hands shuffling under fabric. Then, from his end, a door opening and closing. Voices. Softly, he says, "Shit. I have to go. Can I call you back?" And to someone else: "Nobody. I'm ready."

After he hangs up, I make myself come. It takes longer than usual. I stare at the ceiling, my limbs stretched toward every corner of the bed. Sonny and Dale are banging on the door. I call out for one more minute. I want to bask in this sunlit feeling, just for one more minute.

1999

Las Vegas, NV

Wes! Gwen! To the right, Wes! Gwen, Wes, over here, please! Can we get you over here? Wes! Gwen, right here! Their heads swivel in every direction. Gwen wears a blue bandanna tied around her back and flare jeans. Her pink hair waterfalls to her hips. She brushes it from her eyes as she moves for the cameras. At one point, she looks up at Wes and smiles. But Wes can't figure out where to put his hand. He removes it from her shoulder and places it on her waist, then decides to weave his fingers through hers. Back again to the shoulder. Back to the waist.

After I walk the carpet, she finds me with a drink in her hand. I smell the tang of alcohol on her breath. "Okay, wow," she says, running her hand along the carmine leather of my dress. "You look like a hot vampire. You could be in that *Dracula* movie with Winona Ryder."

The next day, the press will say my dress was distasteful, tarty, too tight around my breasts, too high on my thighs, like always.

"Where's your boyfriend?" I ask.

"Funny. He's gone backstage. They're performing first." She wrinkles her nose. "He stinks."

"What?"

"I mean he smells. He's wearing too much cologne." She points her finger down her throat, then laughs. A photographer flows toward us like a wave, the camera flashes, he falls away. Watching her, I think: it's time. I will tell her about the elevator with Wes, what we did on the phone. But then she says, "Is there a place we can go? I'm in a shitty mood. My mom is bringing my brother on the road, so I'll have to deal with that for over a month. I need a cig. Do you want a cig? Let's go—just for one second."

Her words are in such direct contrast with her smile that it disturbs me a little. I nod. We lean behind a potted majesty palm and light up.

"Which brother?" I ask.

"Isaiah," she says. She blows out smoke from the corner of her mouth, then fans it away with her hand. Her cigarette is tucked behind her back, so no one will notice it. "The little one. Thank god. I mean, Nate has his thing about guns. That's all he cares about. We keep hoping he will grow out of it, but I don't think he will."

"How old is Nate again?"

"Fourteen. My mom leaves him with his dad when she's on the road with me, and they're, like, the same person. They always go hunting together."

"Why can't your mom stay home?"

"I have no idea. Wish she would. Both my brothers hate me because they think all her attention is on me, and they're completely right. My stepfather hates me, too. He thinks I'm the reason she left him."

Gwen has glossed over lots of things about her childhood. About this man, her mother's second husband. The third is only eight years older than Gwen, a wannabe actor her mom met last year in Los Angeles and eloped with after a few months. From what Gwen's told me, it is a rotating home of fathers. I'm starting to think no unscathed kid has ever entered this industry. You have to have some emptiness, some cavity that needs filling.

The leaves of the palm suddenly bend, caressing our necks. One of Gwen's handlers has found us. He snatches the cigarette from her outstretched hand and crushes it beneath his boot. We are both led into the auditorium.

The sun leaks out of the desert. The air is suddenly cold. An after-party is hosted by a record executive at his second or third home. The most impressive feature is an infinity pool, built above a vertiginous drop, which a few drunken partygoers have already waded into. Beautiful couples are falling over each other. Drinks seem to emerge out of thin air. The night is hedonistic, wild as an ancient rite. Girls in sequined dresses could be the flash of nymphs in moonlight. Around the perimeter, the party folds and unfolds, spitting people out onto balconies and wraparound decks. Cocaine in bathrooms next to toothpaste. Joints and cigarettes mingling in ashtrays. I'm led into a room with an L-shaped couch filled with industry men. They offer me a bong, and when it's passed to me, I let the earthy smoke sit in my lungs until I'm calm. Because I know, I *know*, if I have to quantify love, I love her more, so I must finally tell her.

Down at the bar, I take a shot of vodka and chat to someone famous with a signature jaw, but the entire time I'm searching for pink hair in the crowd. Sonny weaves through the throng of bodies to join me. He grabs my arm and says he'd like to introduce me to someone, but I twist away. "I need to find Gwen. Have you seen her?" He shakes his head, then looks at me sadly, as if my priorities are all wrong.

As I stand in a bottlenecked crowd at the bottom of a staircase, I feel a warm hand on my waist. His lips on my ear: "Let's go somewhere."

I forget about my mission to find Gwen, gripped by want, and follow Wes up a different flight of stairs to the third floor. Here, the harder drugs are being done in locked bedrooms. I keep my head down as he tries multiple doors. A laundry room is empty. There's only a washer-dryer unit, piles of dirty clothes, a cat's litter box, the stink of bleach. In the dark, we assess each other. He is wearing a ridiculous outfit, typical of ETA: red paisley jeans and an oversize velvet jacket, and thankfully, I can only see the outline of it. I kneel on the ground, start to unbutton his jeans.

"You don't have to."

I look up at him, hoping he finds this angle sexy. "I really want to."

"Okay." He smiles as his head falls back. I guide his dick out of his boxers. He's already hard, curving up slightly, and I don't know how I'll fit him inside my mouth. I try to remember Rhiannon's blow job lesson from years ago, the banana between her lips. It is the same fear I feel whenever I am about to step on stage. I spit into my hand and rub his shaft up and down. Then I lick him from base to tip. Even though my knees are digging into the carpet and my jaw has begun to ache, I feel a sense of power having him wrapped up in me like this, his singular focus on me, the noises I alone can draw out of him. He's moaning my name; he's cursing and gasping. His body rocks back and forth. His hands are knotted in my hair and slowly he tightens his grip. When he comes, he tastes like salt. He watches me swallow, then leans down to kiss me.

"You know there's zinc in that. You got your vitamins."

I laugh. "My health is very important to me."

"You're so good at it. Do you like doing it?"

I say I do, because even if I don't necessarily like the physical, carnal act of it, I do like how satisfied he is. Then he steps forward, pinning me against the dryer, still warm from a recent load. His arms tense to hoist me up onto the machine. With me sitting on top of it, we are eye level. I pull him toward me, hooking my ankles around his waist. We press together like hot iron and cloth, and it feels like steam is released between us. He reaches beneath my dress, rubbing back and forth along the fabric of my thong. I whisper, "I want to. Please."

He nods and kisses me so passionately, so suddenly, I don't have time to close my eyes. I can see his fluttering eyelashes, the curve of his smile. He breaks off to search his wallet for a condom, to roll it on. He's between my legs and he's slid my thong aside, and I'm tense from years of anticipation, from how badly I want to exhale, and finally, at last, the space between us is closing and soon it will be nothing. Our breathing is so loud that we don't hear the footsteps. Behind us, the slit in the door suddenly widens, becomes a rectangle. A beautiful girl with pink hair stands in the light, and our eyes meet over Wes's shoulder.

1999

Las Vegas

The hall casts a spotlight between my legs. I pull down my dress and jump off the washing machine, standing beside the pile of dirty clothes.

"Wes, get the fuck out." Gwen opens the door for him and points out to the hall. He pulls his pants and jacket on. Won't even look at me as he closes the door. Then it's just me and Gwen in the dark.

I watch as she closes herself off, retreating into the bunker that is her body, and no matter how hard I dig, I won't be able to reach her.

Her eyes are the color of shrapnel as I explain myself. I tell her about *Star Search*, I tell her about the tour, I tell her she matters more to me than he does. She swirls the drink in her hands.

"So, you lied," she finally says. She's measured, still in control of every part of herself. I flail as she stiffens.

"You lie every day," I spit back.

"Can you just acknowledge you were wrong? This isn't about me; this is about you. Just look at yourself."

I deflate immediately, like she's stabbed me with a pin. "I'm sorry."

She asks why him of all people? What's so special about him?

I shake my head. I don't know. There is not a why, there is only a feeling. I wish I could pass it along to her, so she could see the shape and color of it for herself. I start to cry from shame, which makes her scoff. "You're such a liar. Like, it's actually crazy."

"I was going to tell you."

"When?"

"Soon."

"How long has it been happening?"

"Since the summer."

She laughs unnaturally, coldly. "You can fuck Wes. I couldn't care less. I genuinely don't care. What I care about is that you lied to me so much. So much. On the phone, on the beach, every single time we spoke. And I think you're selfish. I think you're a terrible friend. What if someone else had walked in here and found you?"

"You don't actually like him."

"Everyone thinks I do, though."

I hold my face in my hands. "I know."

"If this blew up, he wouldn't protect you. He doesn't care about you."

"How do you know that?"

"I just do."

I glance up at her. "Tell me."

"No."

I insist. She bites the inside of her cheek. "He's said stuff."

"What kind of stuff?"

"I don't know, Amber."

"You do know. Why would you bring it up to begin with?"

"Look, Wes cares about how he's perceived. He wants to be successful. We both feel—I don't know. You're not very driven, Amber. Not like us. You're just not. You have natural talent. Great. But what else?"

Anger whirlpools in my gut. Jagged rocks at the bottom, strong enough to grind down hulls. "I'm not interested in going back and forth about who works harder. I know how dedicated you are. I've always been proud of you. And I wish I was more like you. Okay? Like, I don't know why I act this way."

"Because you just want the approval of men. That's your entire career."

I laugh because this hurts so much, but I want to show her it doesn't. "Sorry I'm not repressed like the entire country wants me to be."

"But whatever they say goes, right? You say yes to whatever they want you to do. Yes to whatever outfit makes your video the most provocative. Yes, Sonny." She begins to mimic me, fluttering her eyelashes in an exaggerated way. "When have you ever pushed back on anything? Or, like, thought for yourself?"

"When have *you*?"

She gnaws on her fingernail. "All the time. I want this next album to be different. I'm going to handpick my own writers and producers. Mike can go fuck himself if he likes, but that's what I'm going to do."

"Yeah, right."

"At least I know what I'm doing."

I slide to the floor. All my anger is just barbed sadness. "You really don't think I know what I'm doing, too?" We stare at each other. Different insults are rising and falling in my mind, but I don't say any of them.

"I really don't," she admits.

I let that sink in. The truth. I remember when she taught me how to dance, and no matter how hard I practiced, there was something innate in her bones, something I could never replicate. I wonder if she's right, if I am selfish, if part of me just wanted to be with someone everyone thought was hers.

"I'm so sorry for lying to you." This in a small voice. "It was wrong. But Gwen, you never really talk to me, and I've never felt that I can really talk to you, either. Have you ever felt like this?"

"Some people like to keep their personal lives private. You go around talking about penis size and giving blow jobs and having orgasms, but I'm not like that. Doesn't mean there's anything wrong with me."

"Never said there was."

"You did."

"I didn't. I asked if you've ever felt like this. If you've ever loved anyone."

"No, I haven't. I've told you that. And if I loved someone, I would think it through first."

"You think through loving people."

"Yeah, I do."

"Well, that makes me really sad."

I slump against the washing machine, staring up at her, as if asking for absolution. There is an undercurrent beneath us both: I am over-worked, exhausted, just a kid. And I need you. I can't do this alone.

I glance back down at my feet. "I said there was nothing going on because I didn't want you to judge me. I'm always worried you're going to judge me."

Then I tell her how sorry I am over and over, as if I can give flimsy words more weight through repetition.

Staring at me, eerily calm, she says she forgives me.

"I won't do anything else with Wes, I swear to—"

She's turning toward the door. She's folded herself away completely. "I told you. I don't give a fuck. My team will break the story eventually. Our schedules were too hectic, blah, blah. Can you just lay low until everything settles?"

I'm starting to heave with tears. "But. Gwen. Please. I love you. You're my best friend. My only real friend."

"Well, I can't be your friend right now."

I sound like a little girl when I ask, "For forever?"

"I don't know." She opens the door, which offers a brief ray of light, then slams it shut.

Lying on the cold pile of laundry, I wipe my eyes on an anonymous satin bra. The breasts that would fill it are small and perky, the kind I've always prayed for.

I can hear two men talking in the hall. Both have greasy, unctuous voices; they keep oiling each other with compliments. One of the men says Savannah Sinclair and Alex Kowalczyk's recent engagement is the worst thing to ever happen for both their careers.

"How old is she?"

"Eighteen."

"Jesus."

"Can you imagine?"

1999

Las Vegas

When I was in sixth grade, I wrote an essay about ancient Greece. It was the only time I was ever praised for a school assignment. My teacher, Mr. Weaver, asked me to read it aloud in class. I stood on my chair and shook, trembling under the heat like batter starting to rise. As I flattened down the pages of my essay, my little voice bubbled with excitement.

Later, the rumors began: I showed my boobs to Mr. Weaver, maybe even let him touch them, and that's why he liked my paper. A push-up bra appeared in my locker with a note that said, "You should thank Mr. Weaver for all the support!"

I was called to the principal's office to explain myself, trailing shame down the hallway while the whole school watched. For some reason, I think of this moment in the laundry room.

Morning is a growing stain. I find Wes in a bedroom, sweat matting his hair, his pupils dilated from cocaine swept into his nose and rubbed along his gums. He pulls me through the bedroom and into a master bathroom with a golden claw-foot tub. I make sure to lock the door behind us. I'm not in the best state of mind to make decisions; I make them anyway.

I sit on the rim of the tub, and he stands between my legs. I ask him if what Gwen said was true. If he really doesn't think I'm driven, or that I won't succeed the way they have. And he hesitates for a long, suspended moment.

"I'll be honest," he says, running his hand through his hair. "I probably did say something like that. Years ago. But the point is that you're fucking talented. You're so talented."

He really does seem sorry. His eyes are very wide. And I want to believe people can change. I want to believe that, through my music, I can burst through all my faults, reach a higher plane. But the fight with Gwen has hurled me down into my own depths. "You were both right about me, I think."

"We weren't."

"No, I really do think you were." I pause for a moment. "Why did SMG want you to be with her?"

He shrugs.

"I heard there was another woman."

He blinks away surprise, then he says yes, there was. Reluctantly, he tells me about the makeup artist, Stacey Beau, who toured with ETA in the midnineties. In my head, she has curly black hair, heavy-lidded eyes. In the haze of touring, he hadn't even considered her, but he was eighteen and touring was lonely. She ran her hand along his thigh while applying powder to his face. He thought it was strange at first. Inappropriate. She was in her midthirties and married to someone back home. But the next day, she was slower with her brush, more deliberate. He found himself closing his eyes. When she leaned down to apply moisturizer to his cheeks, he kissed her. That was the first time. Later, they hid in the pockets between hallways and stages. She was eager to teach him; he was eager to be taught. While the young girls were chanting for him in arenas, she had him in forbidden darkness, and he liked how kind she was, how encouraging, how sometimes she'd make him laugh.

"Anyway," he says. "The whole team found out. She said she was going to publish something about me. Apparently. I don't think that's true. She wasn't like that."

"Have you talked to her since?"

He considers, then says, "She called a couple of months ago." I can't help but wonder how long they talked.

"That was your first time, though? With her?"

"Yeah." He scratches the inside of his wrist. "I'm just worried what you think of me now."

"You're always saying that. I don't think anything."

"Do you wish you didn't know?"

"I want to know everything."

Bleached strands frame his face. He's a little flushed. I've never paused to consider whether he's as insecure as I am. Maybe he doesn't want to be known so intimately. Maybe he's afraid of himself, too. He taps his fingers against his thigh, unable to keep still. Then he asks if Gwen is mad.

"Yeah, she's pissed."

"Okay." He exhales sharply. "What do you want to do?"

I rise up to kiss his chest.

"Amber," he says, eyes darkening.

I blink up at him innocently. "What?"

"What did Gwen say?"

"Um, she said to keep it quiet until your teams can figure it out. We can probably go public after that." Suddenly, I worry I've overstepped. "Unless you don't want to. Because you're my friend. You know? And if you don't want anything more, that's fine. I might have misread everything. I probably did."

He shakes his head. "Is the door locked?"

"Yeah. I checked."

And he leans down, takes my lip gently between his teeth, drags its slowly down toward my chin. I moan into his mouth. I unzip his pants and wrench them down to his knees. He steps out of them. Now that there's light, I notice he's wearing Batman boxers, the kind that come in packs.

"Don't laugh," he says, even though I am, but soon they are gathered around his ankles, forgotten. I put him inside my mouth and his eyes widen. He grips my shoulder tight, saying "Holy shit," over and over, but his dick is shrinking despite my effort. He insists this is because of the drugs he did tonight, apologizing even after I tell him it's okay.

"Just give me a second," he says. "Let me focus on you." He tells me to lie down on the bath mat, and once I do, he pulls my thong down my thighs, and then his mouth is between my legs. I ask for more, so he slides two fingers inside me, too. I arch, skull grinding into the cold tile. Suddenly he stops. He gently kisses my inner thigh, then he says he's hard again.

"Do you have another condom?" I ask.

"I think so." He pulls away and searches through the pockets of his discarded jeans, frantic, throwing old, crumpled receipts to the floor. With his other hand, he starts fingering me again and curses, asking how I'm still so wet. When he finally finds the condom, he tears the plastic wrapping and rolls it over himself, kissing me until I'm gasping, but I want more, I'm shameless, I'm begging.

He rubs himself back and forth across my clit. "You really want me?" he asks.

"Yes."

"How much?"

"So much."

He kisses up my body until we're parallel again, and his face is in the crook of my neck. Softly, he says, "Now?"

"Now. Please."

He finally pushes into me. My muscles are greedy hands clenched around him. As we move, I'm somehow compressed and vast at the exact same time. He asks if I want to turn over, and I say yes. He doesn't pull out, just maneuvers my body around his. We're both on our knees, cushioned by the bath mat, and he's gripping my hips so he can push deeper. The loose toothbrushes on the sink roll back and forth. A bottle of conditioner falls off the rim of the bathtub. When he slows his rhythm, my mouth loosens and drips with sounds of pleasure like a leaky faucet. I touch myself as he moves inside me, and this gets me close. We lose ourselves in this until I tell him I'm about to come, to keep going. His fingers dig into my waist, and he pulls me back harder and harder against him.

Lips against my spine, he says, "I think I can feel it."

"Don't stop, please don't stop, it's not over."

After, we're both left limp and wrung out, his body curled over mine. His heart is beating so fast, and his skin is hot. As I return to myself, I notice all his weight on top of me and make a noise so that he'll shift. He says sorry and sits up, running his hand through his hair. Our eyes meet. There's no need to say anything; we shared how it felt. I pull my dress back on and he zips it up for me, then he ties a knot in the condom and throws it in the trash. Before he opens the door, he says I should wait a few minutes before I follow him. He kisses my forehead, a stamp of warmth, then slips away.

After he's gone, I stare at myself in the mirror. I'm flushed, bursting out of my skin, and now I will have to live this way—I can't ever go back. Because now I know. I know sensation can condense and condense into one relentless peak.

SWEAT

Amber Young   Track 7 on *In Your Eyes*

Produced by
Andy Sacks

May 24, 1999

[Intro]
(Spoken) I don't know why this happens to me
How do I stop it?

[Verse 1]
Saw you from across the room
Don't know what to do
Never felt this kind of thing before
Now I'm melted on the floor

[Chorus]
Let's sweat, baby
Draw it out of me
Touch me there
Scratch my back
(Come on, baby) Make me swear

[Verse 2]
Don't be tentative, don't be shy
We both know what we're going to do
Never known what love was
Now we need our own room

[Chorus]
Let's sweat, baby
Draw it out of me
Touch me there
Scratch my back

(Come on, baby) Make me swear

[Bridge]
Don't you know what you're doing to me?
All the ways you touch my body
(Come on, baby) Make me swear

[Chorus]
Let's sweat, baby
Draw it out of me
Touch me there
Scratch my back
(Come on, baby) Make me swear

[Chorus]
Let's sweat, baby
Draw it out of me
Touch me there
Scratch my back
(Come on, baby) Make me swear

ABOUT

Genius Annotation   5 contributors
"Sweat" is the first single from Amber Young's debut album *In Your Eyes* (1999). It was released to radio a few days before the infamous music video of Young on a treadmill debuted on MTV's *Total Request Live*.

2000

Los Angeles

"I want Axel Holm."

Across from me, my A&R rep at Lolli, Pat Mackey, is frowning. He twists his wedding ring around his finger, which is what he does when he's frustrated. Pat is around forty, newly divorced but in denial about it, obsessive about his own musical taste. He prefers rock and punk to pop music, but now that all the labels have signed pop acts, Pat feels as if the earth has crumbled beneath him. He clings to Guns N' Roses and Mötley Crüe in private, *Rolling Stone* covers framed behind his desk. He has taught me more about music than anyone else, but his taste is firm: this is a good song, this is a very bad one. There is no nuance in his thinking.

Now he glances outside his window, to the sprawl of concrete, the green hills. "I think it's a long shot. It's not like I haven't considered it. But Axel is booked. Everyone wants to work with him. So, why you? That's what he'll be asking."

Sonny turns to me. "Honey, we might have to let this one go."

Pat nods, knitting his hands together. He says the album did pretty well, but Gwen's and Savannah's first-week sales were higher. He's printed out reviews. "It's as if she has studied her contemporaries and mashed them together into a cacophonous mess that unfortunately values provocation and lewdness over quality," says one that he's handed to me. The rest I don't read. The reviewer isn't wrong: I do feel as if I've grasped Savannah's and Gwen's limbs, sewed them onto my body, hoped the stitching wouldn't be visible.

As he waits for my response, Pat unscrews the cap of his water and drinks it all in one gulp, the plastic crunching beneath his hands. His assistant scurries over with a new bottle for him. I'm uncomfortable when I realize she's my age, or close to it.

"A headlining tour for this next album, maybe?" Sonny asks, licking his lips.

"Maybe," says Pat. "Depending. It's all Lyle's decision." He glances down at my hands, which are visibly shaking. Gwen's absent voice rings through the room: *What do you want?*

If Axel produces for me, the next album has a better chance of success: a headlining tour, a career with longevity instead of just one hit in "Sweat." This industry is ceaselessly churning out fresh talent, flipping them over, slapping on barcodes. I want to feel safe. I want to feel like I've solidified. Maybe this is an impossible goal—Gwen certainly doesn't feel comfortable, and her career is stratospheric.

I take a deep breath. "What will it take to get a meeting?"

Pat sighs. "Look, Axel *is* in town soon, which is a rarity. We can try to put you two together in a room, and see what happens?" His hands, fiddling with the pen before him, suddenly still. "You'll have to win him over."

Sonny and I exchange a look. I am on the cusp again.

Wes and I meet up at his new house in West Hollywood. Each time we are together, we make the most of it, because at any moment the tablecloth could be yanked away, revealing us crouched beneath.

There is hardly any furniture in Wes's house, and his pool is dry and full of leaves, the tiling laced with grime. When he's home, he doesn't bother unpacking his suitcase, just throws the contents on the floor in a pile. His refrigerator has only packs of Coors. His bed, which we're in now, has no comforter, just a top sheet.

I rest my chin on his chest and ask how Alex ended up proposing to Savannah.

"You've never heard this story? It's wild."

"Who would I have heard it from?"

He licks my cheek. "Don't be bad."

I rub his spit off with the back of my hand, then lean forward to lick his nose, but he holds me back. This is a game we play. When we've settled down again, he says, "Well, I think Savannah wanted to tell everyone she wasn't a virgin anymore. She was tired of the media's emphasis on it, and they've been having sex for a while now. Alex wasn't into the idea. He has this incredibly pure image of her, I think. He felt like he was protecting her from herself, and that annoyed her. Reasonably. I mean, I'm never on Alex's side. Anyway, they had this huge fight. We were in London at this point." He pauses there for a moment to kiss me. "Sorry, you looked so cute. Anyway, Alex wasn't focused at all during our show. He stops the entire thing and goes, 'I just can't stop thinking about my girlfriend. Do you think I should marry her?' And the entire crowd says yes. So he has a phone brought out, he calls her, and he proposes right there onstage, with her on speaker."

"She can't say no with the whole world listening."

"Well, yeah. Exactly. I think he knew that."

I run my hand down his cheek. "Hmm, what do you think of Savannah?"

"Oh, she's great. People think she's kind of passive because she's so nice, but she's not at all. She's super talented. She writes most of her own music, actually, which most people don't realize. I think her parents are in some band together. She's from a super musical family in Nashville."

"Why do you think she's with Alex, then?"

He's drawing patterns on my stomach now, and I close my eyes. "What do you mean?"

"They seem very different."

"I think she's the one in control, though. Their dynamic might surprise you."

Then his finger stills near my upper thigh, and he says he needs to tell me something.

"What?"

SMG is stalling, he says. They don't want him and Gwen to break up yet. Her album just dropped; ETA's is scheduled for next month. We'll have to be patient. Soon, he says. Eventually. More barren words. I turn over in bed and close my eyes. He kisses my shoulder until I turn back around. His thumb is nudging my lips apart. Our eyes are a key in a lock.

"I'm sorry," he says.

"It's okay. It's not your choice."

"I want you so badly."

He knows I love hearing this.

"More than anyone else?"

"Yes."

In response, I pull him toward me. "Have you been thinking about me when we're not together?"

"I always am. Seriously, I always, always am." He's kissing my neck, my breasts, my belly-button ring, slowly stirring my body, and it feels like each of my nerves is straining toward his mouth, waiting for its turn to be woken up.

"Fuck, that feels good."

He looks up at me from between my legs and laughs. His breath steams my thigh. "Yeah? What else?"

"I don't know. How do I know what to say? Like, where did it all come from? All this stuff we say during sex? Maybe you should call me a few names, just so I can see what I like."

"Which ones?"

"Whatever comes to mind."

He laughs again. "Okay. But I want you quiet for now. See if you can be quiet."

I smile, my head falling back.

When we start having sex, the rhythm sounds like a song I've heard, or maybe sex is just what a drum sounds like, what the underlying beat of so many songs sounds like, and this is why it's so familiar.

Axel Holm doesn't want to work with me. This is obvious from the start. Pat's assistant deposits us in a conference room, where he is already swiveling around in an office chair. He is younger than I expected—still in his twenties—which surprises me, since he's already so accomplished. He has full lips, a square jaw, and a cleft chin. An angular, sharp face that encourages shadow. Dark-blond hair curls behind his ears.

For a while, no one speaks. Then Axel coughs, and slowly the vertebrae of his back extend until he is standing at full height, looking down at us all.

"Hello, Pat." His accent is slight, barely noticeable.

"Maestro," says Pat. "Good to see you again. This is Amber."

Axel studies me, frowning. "I heard your first album," he says simply. No hello.

"And?"

He shrugs. "You have a nice voice."

Axel checks the time on his watch, clearly disengaged. Pat glances at me, which feels like he's pushing me forward.

I take a step. "Do you want to talk here or somewhere else?"

Axel frowns.

"I just thought, maybe we could take a walk and get to know each other, if you'd like. It's beautiful out."

At first, I think I've made a mistake. He spends all day in the studio, maybe he dislikes the outdoors, the sunshine. But he shrugs and says okay, so I find myself in a car on the way to the Venice Boardwalk, which he says he would like to see on this trip. We each look out our own window, our bodies pointed away from each other, until we arrive. Sand has blown into the parking lot. We slam the doors shut and walk in silence, passing sunbathers lying on beach chairs in the grass and tourists flocking to kitschy ephemera. We follow them into a stall selling T-shirts, flags fluttering above in the slight breeze, thumbing tags and running our hands along the different fabrics. He inspects a white shirt, then neatly folds it up again.

Outside again, Axel is quiet as he observes the mayhem. A skater skids around us on the path. A man is jamming on the bongos, surrounded by a circle of dancing women, who rotate around him and flail their arms.

He nods along to the beat, then turns to me. "So how old are you?"

"Almost twenty."

"You look older."

"How old are you?"

"Twenty-six."

"You actually look younger," I say. "I heard your studio is in Oslo now, but wasn't it in Stockholm before? Why did you move?"

"My mother lives in Stockholm, but my father is from Oslo. I wanted to spend more time with him. I can do my work from there well enough." He uses his hand as a sun visor. "So why do you want to make music?"

"Oh. Well, I don't know." I stop to think for a moment, intending to continue my thought, but he breaks through the pause.

"You do not know," he repeats stiffly.

I turn toward him in the grass, my toe kicking up a disk of dirt. "No, I *do* know. I just have never said it out loud. No one has ever asked me that before. I guess it's just assumed."

"What is assumed?"

"That I like making music. That I want to keep doing it."

He crosses his arms. "If we are going to work together, potentially, we have to be honest with each other. There has to be a—" He pauses, searching for the right word. "Symbiosis. I want to get to know you."

Our feet push and pull on the hot sand as we walk onto the beach. We find a spot to sit beneath the shadow of a lifeguard chair. I pick up a fistful of sand and filter it through my fist, taking my time before I respond.

"Singing is the only thing I'm good at."

"So you came to it by default."

I shake my head. "It was the only thing that made me feel like, you know, that feeling. That feeling when you're in love with someone. Heat in your stomach. I can't explain. Maybe that's the point. You can't put music into words. It's, like, feeling in motion."

He looks out toward the water. "Okay. When did you feel like that for the first time?"

I tell him about my Christmas talent show, and he nods. "What did you like to listen to?"

"Whatever was around. I wasn't picky. Mostly pop, I guess. My dad left some of his records behind, so I sometimes listened to those. I felt like I got to know him through those albums a bit. Others I bought myself. I listened to so much alone in my room. Mariah. Janet. Madonna, of course. Um, Joni Mitchell. Whitney Houston." I tell him how, when I was young, I used to stand in front of my mirror and lip-synch to women with big voices, a power they knew exactly how to wield. And I hoped I might find that power in myself, too.

"I like shoegazey stuff, too," I add. He doesn't respond. "You know? Dream pop. Mazzy Star."

He grimaces slightly. "Too slow."

I shake my head. "That's not true. Have you ever heard 'Fade into You'?"

"I'm sure I have."

"That song feels like this big ball of sadness and longing just rolling around inside you. I love it. I'm not making that kind of music, obviously. But when I'm feeling moody, I like to listen to it."

He scratches his chin. "Maybe I'll try again."

"What made you want to make music?"

He blinks, surprised. "Me? Oh, I think—I think for me, it was—" He trails off, deep in thought.

"See? It's not such an easy question."

"I have an answer. I just need a moment." He pushes sand into a mound with his hands. "For me, it was probably to escape." He doesn't elaborate on what he was escaping from. Then he turns to study me again. "You're not what I expected."

I still under his gaze. "What do you mean?"

"You're not how Gwen described you."

"How did she describe me?"

He shrugs. "Natural talent you don't cultivate. A lack of drive."

This would be a blunt thing to say to someone's face if I hadn't already heard it before, from Gwen. It hurts less the second time. "I know succeeding in this industry isn't just about natural talent. It's brutal, and talented people fail all the time. You need more than ability. Are the most successful songs always the best-written ones? The most well-sung ones? Probably not."

He takes a cigarette from his pocket and lights it, cupping his hands to nurture the flame. Smoke blows into my eyes. "So what *do* you need?"

"Really, really good people around you. Smart people. People who make you want to be better, who push you. And a good song doesn't hurt."

His mouth cracks slightly. "Well, I think a good song is about feeling. It transcends communication. If you can play it anywhere in the world and people get lost in it, if they say, 'I can't get this out of my head' or 'I just *have* to sing along to this,' no matter what language they speak? That's success to me."

"So your goal is to irritate people."

He laughs and takes another drag. "Maybe. But I think a good song is like an affair. It lingers long after it's over. You can't forget it, especially when you try to. It's the lover who stays in your head. Who drives you mad. Didn't 'Bubblegum' drive you a bit mad?"

I admit it did. "That's what I want. I want to make music that's played in twenty, fifty years. Music like that first love you can't get over."

I feel his eyes on me, a slow sweep of interest, then their abrupt absence, as if he's a scholar turning the pages of a book. He seems like the kind of person who thinks deeply before he speaks, who will write it down beforehand if it's important enough.

"That's a beautiful thought," he finally says. He stands and wipes away the sand from his jeans. "Let's walk back to the car now, okay? We will be sick of each other soon enough."

I must look confused because he laughs.

"After many hours in the studio. I have some songs I think will work very nicely for you. I'll send some demos over to Pat, so you can get a feel before you come to Oslo. Okay?"

The cold sand, protected by the lifeguard chair, turns hot again once we're hit by the sun. We collect the shoes we've abandoned by the grass, and I smile up at him. "Okay."

Back to myself in the mirror: a girl, six years old, her fist a microphone, lip-synching to iconic voices. I was too young to perceive myself through the world yet, so I gave myself everything I lacked. I was not yet reframed, because I was the frame. I was not in their eyes, because I was the eye.

In Lolli's downtown office, I excitedly pull my phone to my ear. Just as it starts to ring, I remember Gwen won't pick up. She's gone, but she's also everywhere: *What If?* is her new dreamscape of an album, produced in part by Axel. It has three irresistible hits that are all getting plenty of radio play. One song in particular, "After-School Project," is constantly being cycled through, and when she played it for me months ago, I said it should be the first single off the album. I loved the hook—*You're my after-school project / Spending all my time on you*— and the detached tone of her voice. When it hit number one, I wasn't surprised.

Her friendship was my skeleton—it held me up. It moved my limbs and gave me strength. I wonder if she's sagging with loss, too.

The next time I see her, we're both wearing mermaid tails and seashell bras, filming a commercial for Poppy's Patties. The concept is this: a pirate drops his cheeseburger into the ocean, we find it, and it's so delicious we swim to the surface to ask for another. The pirate has us compete over the burger, each of us singing a few bars, and he hands it over to the most beautiful voice. In the commercial, and in real life, Savannah Sinclair gets the meal.

In the makeup trailer, Gwen avoids my gaze, tilting her chin so someone can apply powder to her forehead. Her entourage—publicist, assistant, two bodyguards—settles on the steps of the trailer and leaves the door swinging open to the parking lot.

She asks for a cigarette. I bum one from the production assistant, too.

"Jesus Christ," she says. "This tail is so constricting. Don't you think?"

Her tone isn't inviting. She just wants to say something, and I'm the only one there to say it to.

Savannah Sinclair is led to her chair, waving hello to us as a stylist fits the mermaid tail around her waist and legs. They'll drive us to set on golf carts, since we can't walk in them.

She closes her eyes, and her makeup artist bends over her, rubbing more swaths of eyeshadow across her lids. All her features are fighting for space, the result a harsh beauty of straight, symmetrical lines. Goodness wafts from her. She's said, "Hi, hello, how are you?" to every crew member, and I can tell it's not false. She's full to the brim with kindness and likes to pour it into other people, which in turn refills her.

Eyes still closed, she asks, "How are y'all?"

Gwen laughs, the cigarette between her teeth. She removes it. "Oh, fine. Congratulations, by the way."

"*Thank you.*" Savannah opens her eyes and smiles up at her makeup artist. "Zane said we were insane."

Zane pecks her on the forehead. "You are fucking insane."

"I was telling Zane, like, if I could have a baby and not have to go on another world tour for a year, I would have one this second. No joke." She smiles, twisting her blond hair into a knot. "What about you and Wes?"

Gwen coughs, fans away smoke.

"Like, will y'all get engaged, do you think?" Savannah presses. It is obvious she cares deeply about other people's lives. Most people ask questions out of politeness, but she genuinely wants to know.

Gwen's shock travels through her, through me, through Savannah. "Um," she says. "No idea."

Savannah's eyes widen. "With Alex it was immediate. I was like, 'That man. Him. I want to eat him.'" When she speaks, her Southern accent gains strength in the middle of her sentences, then dissolves.

"But are we talking about attraction, or love?"

"I think attraction."

"Well, I don't know if you need that immediately. Haven't you ever wanted someone unexpected?" Gwen asks.

"Never," I say, attempting to join their conversation.

Savannah nods at me. Zane tells her to look up, so he can apply mascara. "Blink, babe," he says. She thrusts her eyelids down as he strokes upward.

I continue, "I think if you don't want someone when you first see them, you never will."

"Yeah, totally," Savannah agrees. "You have to have that feeling. Like, boom. Hello, I want to carry your child." She laughs girlishly. This tear in the fabric reveals the layer of child beneath. Sometimes I forget she is two years younger than I am, barely old enough to get married.

The trailer door opens. Strangers filter in, then Chloe Woods, wearing a casual T-shirt and sweats, a designer purse swinging on her arm. Her lips are lacquered in gloss and her box braids are dyed a cool gray. Her presence shifts something subtly, like an ear suddenly weighed down by a diamond. The rest of us stop talking.

Chloe knows Gwen the best out of all of us, so they catch up as Chloe's makeup is applied, passing Gwen's cigarette back and forth.

On my way out the door, hopping in the tail and holding a production assistant's arm, I tap Chloe on the shoulder. "I really wanted to say, I love your music so much. I'm really, and I know honored sounds weird, but I'm honored to be working with you."

The only reason I'm here is because Maria Colmenares dropped out due to a scheduling conflict, and they needed a fourth mermaid. The paycheck was big, and I probably shouldn't have it. Compared to them, I am no one. An afterthought of a pop star. She must know this. But Chloe realizes I'm intimidated by her and soothes me because of it.

"Stop, you're too sweet." She touches my arm.

I can feel myself redden. She politely asks how long I'm in town.

"Only for tonight. When do you think we'll wrap?"

"At this rate? No idea. Four a.m., maybe later?"

Gwen coolly glances over at us. Her look says I'm a suck-up. And she knows my eyes are trying to thaw her, so she immediately turns away.

2000

New York

My mother was a greedy woman: she wanted a different life for herself. This is the most dangerous, incendiary thing to want. I know because I've wanted it, too.

Seventeen and broke, she hitchhiked from West Virginia to New York City. It was the seventies; the city was dirty but also furious and alive. She started working part-time as a waitress, spending nights looking for men; she couldn't conceive of a way to raise herself up without one. She had no degree, no useful talents, only her looks. And she thought making art was a religion practiced by fools, not a respectable pursuit. Eventually, she found a nice accountant who was unexceptional in every way other than his stability, which was the trait she valued above all else. But he surprised her by knocking her up at eighteen, again at twenty-two, and leaving her for another woman at twenty-three. She decanted her new life into an empty glass, let it breathe, swallowed it. Then poured again.

New York is sweltering. No use wearing clothes. In the hotel room, Wes and I draw the shades, but the sun still proclaims itself through the slits. We have sex in the bed first, then I wrap my legs around his waist and he picks me up, pushing me hard against the wall. I kiss his shoulder, the scatter of freckles there. The silver cross bounces up and down on his chest.

After, the sun still beckons, so we head out to the balcony. I'm wearing his creased basketball jersey and ratty boxers, my oily hair twisted into a loose bun. Wes is shirtless, leaning against the railing. A sunburn on his back is peeling, the skin drooping like dead flowers. We are in various poses of ease. We don't think we can be photographed from such a height. We don't know that a man has taken the stairs up fifty flights in the opposite building and pressed his camera against the glass.

We slip the balcony door closed and toss our clothes in a pile again. It is the last time we'll see each other before he travels to Southeast Asia and I go back on the road, this time with Sol Sister, the R&B duo who hit it big with their song "Blinders." In a hot bath, I lie between his legs and lean my head against his chest. He sculpts beards onto my face with bubble bath. We order a pizza and I eat two slices. Back to bed. He tackles me and blows a raspberry on my belly. Our damp towels lie discarded on the floor. The television is left on mute. A moment is ours, and then it is taken.

WHY SEXY SELLS

Amber Young begs for controversy with her over-the-top, skimpy looks. Why we think she knows *exactly* what she's doing.

Exclusive photos! AMBER'S AFFAIR: SEDUCING
WES KINGSTON IN NYC!

AMBER AND WES'S BETRAYAL:
The heartbreaking moment Gwen Morris found out

Gwen Morris and Wes Kingston BREAK UP!

INSIDE AMBER'S GRIP ON WES:
His bandmates are worried!

GWEN VS. AMBER

• What Gwen really thinks

• They can't even be in the same room together!

• Turning to Savannah behind the scenes

VERSE 2

2000

✦

2000

Los Angeles

It happens at once, a flood of humiliation. I'm a late-night punch line. I'm a tabloid tossed over chicken cutlets and eggs in a shopping cart. A crude angle of my body. A frame on a balcony with someone I love.

I hide out at Sonny's house. The huddle of paparazzi grows outside the gates. I'm expecting a call from Lyle and Pat: Lolli is dropping me, they'll say. No second album, no sessions with Axel Holm in the fall. That day in Venice, after Axel said he wanted to work with me, I watched the sun shiver over the ocean and thought I'd finally arrived.

But Sonny says Lolli is very happy. In fact, I've reinforced my own image. This is who I am, who I've always been. Being called a slut and a whore won't impact my career. Haven't I been called these things already? Notoriety is preferable to obscurity, hon. This is America's favorite kind of foreplay.

On my bed, the mattress springs clench under his weight. He continues, "In the meantime, you can't stop working. You have six days to learn choreography, Amber."

"You also won't get your money if I sit in bed."

I turn away from him and start to cry.

Because I have no self-control, no discipline, I seek out ETA chatrooms on Sonny's computer. I know what the tabloids are saying, but I want something uglier, something with even sharper teeth.

> *Ladytune4: Wes never even liked her, but she came onto him so hard that eventually he gave in. I don't think he would ever betray Gwen like that. Amber wanted to be famous, and her album wasn't doing that well, so she knew she had to use Wes to get ahead and maybe she thought if she slept with him he'd do a song with her or something.*
>
> *Hotdg78 has entered the room.*
>
> *Cdd4: Amber is so ugly I threw up in my mouth when I saw the pictures*
>
> *Cam4ever23: Using Wes is really gross she knew she had a dead-end career and Wes was way more famous than her. I wish she would just go back to wherever she came from, wherever the fuck that is. No one cares about you!!!!*
>
> *GaryN: My cousin went to high school with her in New Jersey and says she was always a huge slut*
>
> *Cdd4: Just die Amber thanks* ☺
>
> *Soccrlover912 left the room*
>
> *Hotdg78: She looks like a slug and a beaver mated.*
>
> *FLgirl9 has entered the room*
>
> *FLgirl9: hi*
>
> *Sexyboyzluvr: no I think she looks like a dog, a fat dog.*
>
> *Hotdg78: amber ruined everything* ☹☹

For days, I am sick. Nausea is the only feeling that lasts. I fill the bathtub and sit there, knees against chest, until I'm purple and pruned and shivering. I turn the lights off in every room. I wonder, what percentage of people in the world have to think you are bad to make it definitively true? Does immorality travel like blood through water, slowly reddening the liquid until it is forever stained? Can the water ever be clear again?

I turn inward until I'm convinced it would be better to die like this internet person wants. Or, not to die—to disappear into a void and then reappear as someone new. Isn't this also a form of death? My promise to Gwen to lie low, to be careful, was made by an idea of myself. How many of these do I have? Hundreds. They are stacked inside my head, these paper girls, all patient, selfless, capable of restraint.

"Five, six, five, six, seven, we're holding here on seven, and eight. And one, two, three, four, five, six, hold seven, and eight. Can we pick up the speed, Amber? And one, two, three, four—"

"Can I have a second?" Waves of nausea curl and break inside of me. The world is foul.

"Fine," says Alicia, my choreographer. She's got cropped black hair and sleeves of tattoos on both arms, muscles that look like sand dunes. "Gloria, Tiff, can we rework the chorus section again, while Amber's gone?"

I sprint to the bathroom and heave, but my stomach offers only yellow acid. I try calling Wes. No answer again. So I slump against the cold tile by the toilet, and in my head, Sonny's voice is cruel. Oh, honey, he says. You thought you would be remembered for your derivative music? You thought you would be taken seriously the way Gwen and Savannah are? Oh, little fool. Didn't you know? This is all there is for you.

I dial Gwen's number. She doesn't pick up. I dial again and again. The fourth time, sounds pulse in the background. She doesn't say anything, but I can hear her slow, calm breathing.

"Gwen," I cry. "Please. I know you're there. Please just listen. I'm so sorry."

No response.

"You told me to look at myself, and I am. I see everything. I know why I did what I did. I need all this proof I deserve love. I need so much proof from so many people, just to believe it's real. Maybe I'm this hoarder of people to love me. I'd do anything. It was so wrong to lie to you. To put Wes before you. He's not even calling me back." I pause to collect myself, blinking away tears. "I'm so sorry. I need you. I need you always. I wouldn't even have this career if it weren't for you. You pushed me when I was afraid, and I had no idea why you would do that. But now I understand, I think. It's because you know you're so talented, there's room for you and for anyone else. That's rare confidence, confidence I don't have, and I should have thanked you. And now I'm so alone, Gwen. I'm so alone. And I need you. I can't do this without you."

The harsh bathroom light feels accusatory. What has my friendship ever done for her? All I did was take.

I press my forehead against the wall. My voice is wavy from crying. "Please. I don't know what you've read or what you've seen. Just, please, if you ever want to talk, you can call me, and I'll pick up. I miss you so much. I'm all alone. There's no one here for me."

"Amber, stop."

I'm so relieved I close my eyes and start shaking. In the dark I'd been stretching my hand out but there was nothing. Now I've touched a door. "I'm so sorry."

"I know you are."

"Do you think you could come over?"

"I'm at the studio right now," she says. "I need a few hours, okay? You know how I need to keep working when I'm stressed. Just give me a few hours. Everything will be okay."

When she knocks on Sonny's guest room door, we both melt down. What is there to say at first, other than I wasn't whole without you?

She folds beside me on the bed, placing her chin on my shoulder. "I know I can be so cold," she says softly. "I shouldn't have cut you out of my life like that. But I was so angry, I had to punish you. Maybe there's something wrong with me, if I acted that way."

"There isn't anything wrong with you. I'm sorry if I made you feel like there was."

She shakes her head. "No, I'm sorry. If I made you feel less than me, I want you to know you're not. In a lot of ways, I think you're stronger than I am. Just don't lie. Whatever it is, I'd rather know."

"Okay. Do you hate me?"

"I could never. You're my best friend."

Hearing this makes me cry even harder. For a few moments she's quiet, combing my hair with her fingers. "You aren't what they're saying you are."

"No, I am, actually. And we could have been way more careful."

"Some random guy followed you to the opposite building. There's no way you could have known. The press thinks they have a right to us. If we complain about it, they say we asked for it."

"I just feel so young," I say. "I feel so stupid."

"We are young. We are stupid."

"I know. So what they're saying about me is true."

"Amber, if you were in college and hooked up with some guy, if it was Wes or whoever, it wouldn't fucking matter. It just wouldn't matter, okay?"

"What about you? What are you going to do?"

"Me? I mean, my publicist says the press is really one-sided right now." Her hand returns to my hair. "You know I can't say anything right? I wish I could."

"Yeah, I know. I get it."

A tear travels slowly down my chin, falling onto her hand. I turn around to face her. "I need something else. I hate to ask you. I haven't told anyone, you're the only person."

"What is it?" She scans my face. "You're scaring me."

"I need a test."

"Like, a pregnancy test?"

When I nod, panic flits through her eyes. Then a glazed expression settles; she has tightened all the emotion inside herself. Somehow she has the ability to tell her emotions where to go and when to surface. "Are you late?"

I say yes. A few weeks. And I've had strange peachy stains in my underwear. Finally, I've said what my body knows to be true, what it's been forcing me to acknowledge.

"What does Wes think?"

I shake my head. "Haven't talked to him."

"What? Why?"

"He won't answer his phone."

She scoffs. "Look, it really could be nothing. I'll ask Tammy to buy the test and bring it over here. Okay? We'll check, just in case."

"Thank you." I close my eyes, sinking into her warmth, her composure, and think this is what a mother is. She is a mother to me, and sometimes I am to her. "I love you."

"I love you, too."

In the bathroom, the drip of water taps against plaster. Gwen's arms are folded across her chest. We are tightly packed, our bodies pushed up against the door. Tammy shows us a cut on her leg from hopping Sonny's fence.

"There are so many cameras out there," she says.

Gwen inspects the scrape. "You okay?"

Tammy waves her off, saying she's fine, then she pulls an inoffensive pink box out from her purse.

I pee on the little stick, then set it down on the sink.

"Don't think about it," Gwen insists. "Let's just wait. No point in being anxious twice."

"Have you ever taken one before?" Tammy asks me.

I nod. "Once, in high school, but I was being neurotic. We actually used a condom, but I was nervous anyway."

"The only one I've ever taken was when I was pregnant," Tammy says. "The second line was fainter than I thought it would be. It was like, 'Hi, I'm barely here, inside of you. Surprise!'" She squeezes my hand. "And by the way, I don't regret anything. I couldn't afford a baby. Couldn't dance on tour with a kid."

"How old were you?"

"I was sixteen, I think. Sixteen or seventeen. Just starting out."

I blink at her wordlessly, unsure what to say. This feels like an intimacy I don't deserve. Before I can speak, she calmly indicates the stick. "Should be time now."

I ask Gwen to look for me. She reaches, slowly, so slowly. The world tips over. She sees the result, absorbs it, then sets it down in front of me. "We should take a few more, just to be sure," she says. So we do. I don't process the movement of my limbs, I just pee on the sticks, and when they are all lined up, I sit on the lid of the toilet with my head in my hands. A baby coalesces in my mind. A baby like fruit, soft and plump. Then it cleaves apart, only slivers of an idea.

Tammy asks if Maura, Gwen's assistant, can make an appointment. Gwen shakes her head. "That might make it look like the appointment is for me. Amber, you need to tell Sonny. There's no way Lolli hasn't handled something like this before."

"Lolli is going to drop me," I say through my hands. She tactfully ignores this.

"Do you have cash on you?"

I raise my head. "Cash? No. Why?"

Our lives are handled by others; we don't ever have much cash on hand. We are ferried from city to city, recording studio to radio station. In this way, and in many other ways, we are like children at their parent's knees, pulling at fabric, asking for change. Sonny handles all my business interests—the negotiation of contracts, the endorsement deals, my cuts from royalties and mechanical rights. I only have the debit card he gave me. Though I can buy whatever I want, technically, he sees all my statements.

"For the abortion," Gwen clarifies.

And I realize I don't know the true cost of things.

"I didn't know I had to pay," I admit.

"Of course, you have to pay. This is America." She crosses her arms. "After you tell Sonny, you need to call Wes. He should know before you make any decisions."

I shake my head. "I've already decided."

Even so, I try Wes again. This time, it goes through, but it's not his voice on the other end. It's Axel Holm's. Higher than Wes's, more polished. "Hello?" he says. "Wes can't talk right now. He's in the vocal booth."

"I thought he was in Asia."

He's clearly annoyed at the interruption. "The boys must rerecord here first, or else the album will be turned in late. We are very busy."

"Can you tell him I called?"

He pauses on the other end. "I will." Then, to someone next to him: "Yusuf, can I hear that again?" To me: "Goodbye, Amber. Talk soon."

Sonny ends up driving me to a Planned Parenthood in Reno in between tour stops. Gloria wanted to come, too—I told her where I was going in hushed tones on the tour bus—but Sonny said no. It has been a week since I took the test. As the van whips along the freeway, the land flat and sterile, I feel like we are driving against creation itself. Billboards ask if I'm going to hell, whether I want to find God. And every second the baby is growing larger inside me.

We've signed up for the earliest appointment at the clinic in the hope that it'll be relatively empty, and it is. Just in case, I wear one of Wes's baseball caps and a pair of Sonny's reading glasses that blur my vision. As he signs us in, no one seems to recognize me, and I sink into the plush seat, wondering if the receptionist thinks Sonny's the father or my father.

I don't look at the sonogram during my ultrasound, just my hands clasped in front of me. A kind nurse sticks an IV in my arm, puts me under, and when I wake up, I'm in a waiting room, and the baby is gone.

Back in the van, I clutch pads for the spotting and ibuprofen for the pain in my lap. Sonny taps his fingers against the steering wheel. "You've become like a daughter to me, hon. Your mom trusted me to take care of you. I'm just glad you told me."

I stare out the window and force a smile.

"You okay to perform tonight?" His voice doesn't tilt up at the end, like it should with a question.

I tell him I'll be fine.

He doesn't say anything else as the pad in my underwear fills with blood and cramps wrap their hands around my uterus and pull. The nurse told me I could return to normal activities after, and this is a normal day: pulling the microphone closer to my lips, looking out into the roar and the light and the faceless heads. The crowd has no idea; my job is to make sure they have no idea.

A few days later, Wes returns my call in the middle of the night. When I pick up, we sit in silence together, my breaths responding to his.

"I'm so sorry," he finally says. "It's been busy here."

"Do you know what's going on?"

"I've heard."

I stumble over my words. "Two girls. Cool. Good for you. I'm the one who broke you two up. Everyone hates me. Everyone wishes I was dead. Some of your fans are saying I should just roll over and die."

"They don't know us," he says. "They thought Gwen and I were dating for, like, an entire year. It doesn't matter. It will all go away." He sounds like he's trying to convince himself, too, though.

I say at least we can be together for real. Silence on the other end.

"SMG doesn't like the idea of us right now. Maybe when things settle down."

"Maybe," I repeat, my voice hollow.

"What do you want me to do? Honestly, what can I do? Because I feel like I'm in an impossible situation right now. They're telling me one thing, they're over here saying it doesn't look good for me to be with you. I'm sorry, but that's really what they're saying. And then I feel like a piece of shit for listening to them. I don't know what to do."

"Listen to them. It's okay. It's done."

His voice breaks a little. I can't tell if it's our connection or not. "Please don't say it that way, Amber. I love you."

"Why?" I really do want to know.

On the other end, he sighs. This is when it starts to sour, when the plush skin begins to bruise. This night. When he tells me why he loves me and the answer doesn't please me and we fight about the reasons you should love someone, as if such things can be counted on one hand. When I tell him about the abortion and he's silent on the other end for a long time. This is the night I cease to be an outline of a person, and he's forced to color inside me for the first time.

He starts crying. A guttural, strange sound I've never heard before. He says he can't believe he didn't answer the phone. And as I listen to him, I'm thinking, we're finally here, inside of each other, aren't we?

2000

New York

The stage is cold, the way sand at night is cold: all the warmth has seeped out, but the memory of it is still there. Gloria, Tiff, Jay, Max, and Tony, my dancers, are huddled together backstage. I fold into their circle of arms. "Tonight, we are grateful to get this chance, to perform for a living, to entertain all these people night after night," says Jay. "To be here with Amber."

"Amen," I say.

After each performance, there's a high, then a comedown. Life becomes a twitchy seismograph.

The Sol Sister tour pulls into cities crusted with fading industry. Minneapolis. Des Moines. Kansas City. These cities rise from flat plains, like brooches pinned to the country's chest. America blurring into cornfields, rusted railway cars, graffitied warehouses. Strips you could pick up and deposit anywhere else.

Vanessa and Simone Adams are kind to me backstage. We sometimes watch television in the greenroom together with our dancers, our plates balanced on our knees, spilling over with food from catering. I always take the same amount of food Simone and Vanessa do, whether it's a handful of chips or a sandwich, so I won't stand out. I pick at charred animal skin, soggy salads, and whipped frosting, and force myself to swallow.

There are hard truths I swallow, too. Three years into my career, I'm still an opener, not a headliner. Younger girls are more successful than I am. I've been abridged to just my body.

Sometimes I want to reanimate my own life, but conversely, I also want to return to my mom's womb, to grow fingers and toes all over again. To float in amniotic fluid and warmth. From the safety of this sac, I could decide when to finally emerge again.

In my seat, I pick at an errant thread. I'm wearing a sepia cutout crop top, lace-up jeans. My exposed belly is taut and flat as a pond. Onstage, Gwen is dressed as a nymph, draped in moss and sylvan light, singing the hook of "After-School Project." I almost don't recognize her, this woman onstage made of lunges and hair flicks, the movements of her body rippling out through the auditorium as wider circles of awe.

A few silvery Moonman statuettes are awarded. Then ETA debuts a new single. As soon as they start to sing, a camera trails down the aisle and presses on me for a reaction. I soften my face and try to focus on the performance, pretending I can't distinguish Wes's voice from the others during their harmonies. But it's easy to follow, because it travels right to me. Listen, it says. Don't you dare forget me.

Later that night, a little drunk from an after-party, I arrive at his hotel.

One of ETA's bodyguards swipes his key card and swings the door open. The shower is on and the bathroom mirror is covered in steam. I leave my clothes in a pile on the floor and step inside. Wes doesn't say anything at first, just pulls me closer. His dark chest hair is flattened and splayed in every direction. I cry for a long time, his lips on my forehead, and my tears mix in with the water, so it is all indistinguishable.

He starts rubbing body wash onto my back. While he does this, I draw our initials on the glass door, like a teenage girl in her journal. A heart surrounding them. Finally, a question mark.

On another pane of glass, he answers with his own question mark. Underlines this twice.

I draw a sad face. He writes, "Not right now." His handwriting is like a little boy's. I've never seen it before. He sets down the bodywash and both of his hands find my hips. His chin, the crown of my head. I like when we are touching in multiple places at once.

"When?"

"I don't know," he says. "We can still see each other like this, though, if you want." I look back over my shoulder at him, and I'm also looking beyond him. What he's not saying is far more important than what he is. I know him. I know how he thinks, and it is this: I don't think your career can recover from this. I'm ashamed of you. I'm embarrassed by you. If they're calling you a whore, and I'm with you, what does that say about me?

But I still wonder if he can shock me back from a flatline. I need to feel something, or maybe I just need to be wanted. My mouth hovers an inch away from his, another question. He answers. I'm backed against the shower door, and our bodies throw it open. We close it again. My body erases all the markings we've made on the glass, creates new ones.

Sonny tells me we are heading to Oslo on schedule, despite everything in the press. He was right—Lolli hopes my notoriety will translate to cash. They are desperate for their Savannah, their Gwen, so they will throw artists at the wall and see what doesn't break. I've heard Lyle recently signed a new teenager, Lauren Li, a bright-eyed, pretty fifteen-year-old from San Francisco.

For weeks, this is all I've wanted, the only thread I could find to tug on: another chance. A redemption. To be edited and snipped, all the bad parts cut away.

During the car ride from the Oslo airport, I lean against the cold window. Sonny snores against his. Pat is in the middle of us, squeezing a bottle of hand sanitizer and rubbing it into his palms. He tells me to try to get some sleep, or else I'll be jet-lagged.

But as soon as we reach our hotel, I stare at the ceiling for hours, my mind spiraling down dark shafts, the night outside my window smooth, endless tarmac.

2000

Oslo, Norway

We enter a nondescript building in Old Town. Three floors down, there's a cozy soundproofed control room. Inside, a hand-knotted rug, a keyboard, a boxy computer, a mixing board, and a sleek leather couch. Behind a glass wall, a vocal booth. Axel is hunched over his computer. Two more producers, Yusuf Hassan and Oskar Aasland, are beside him. They are a little older than Axel is, maybe by ten years or so, and both have scraggly facial hair, forks next to their eyes when they smile. Yusuf is plucking the strings of a guitar. He is quiet but welcoming, all warmth. Oskar is a little moodier. He's thumbing knobs on the mixing board. When he makes a joke and I don't pick up on the sarcasm, he mumbles something under his breath.

Axel ignores our round of introductions, focused only on his screen. After a moment, he looks back at me expectantly, eyebrows raised. "Won't you warm up?"

I nod. And so we begin.

Axel is shaking his head. "No falsetto. I need a little more power behind it. Use your head voice. Try again."

I push my stomach out and sing the note.

"Great. Again."

I scan the lyrics. "Can we change this, though?"

He enters the booth and leans down. "Change to what?"

"I think we should do, *You're the disciple, I'm the heaven.*" The original line is *Being your disciple feels like heaven*, and I like my idea better. There is a current moving between us, which is: Who will give in? Axel doesn't want to make many changes; he already has a vague idea of how I should sound. Most producers do. So throughout this first session, any input I make feels like picking at skin. Each time, he flinches as if a scab has been ripped away too early, drawing fresh blood.

"Sing it for me?"

I do, and he frowns, which means it sounds just as good. I smile to myself when he returns to the control room.

"Axel," I say, pulling my headphones around my neck. Our eyes meet through the glass.

"Yes," he says patiently.

"What about, *Our sex is my church?*"

"Where?"

"I don't know. It's just a lyric."

He makes a face. "Maybe we can use it later."

Even though we won't, it's an initial burst of creation. A sprout in dry, crumbling soil.

During a break from the booth, I watch as Axel, Yusuf, and Oskar create a rough mix in Logic. To me, the software looks like rows of scribbled signatures, although I've been told each row is a different track. Here is where my voice will be immortalized: in a dark, wood-paneled room, the trash overflowing with crushed Red Bull cans, smoke flowing from the cigarettes dangling in their hands.

I watch Axel's fingers dart across the keyboard, studying each minute change he makes. After each playback, the song improves. Eventually Axel breaks his concentration, glancing back over his shoulder, where I've been hovering behind his chair. "Don't you want to see better?"

"Oh, sure. Sorry."

"Why are you sorry?" Yusuf pulls over a chair so I can sit beside them.

The screen is reflected in Axel's eyes. He bites his tongue, his lips. His hands glide back and forth until early morning, when he stabs the space bar with his thumb for a final time, and we all listen to the play-back together. My voice explodes into the control room, floating on their kicks and snares like a boat on choppy, energetic water. Axel and Yusuf glance at each other; Oskar's eyes widen; morning light stretches over Oslo.

We all sit down for dinner together. The restaurant is aromatic and musky, pulsing with the ebb and flow of those who leave and those who enter.

"So, Axel, are you a vampire?" I ask, breaking the silence.

Across the table, he looks up. He had been staring at his silverware, deep in thought. "Huh?"

"I asked if you're a vampire. Do you ever sleep?"

He shrugs. "I work best at night."

"And during the day."

He fights against a laugh but loses. It opens his face up. "You've found me out."

I take a sip of beer. "I knew it."

"Back home she couldn't have that yet," Pat says, pointing to my drink.

"What are you going to do about it, Pat?"

"This is better, isn't it?" asks Oskar. "This way, you can learn to drink responsibly."

"I do like the taste of it, and how it makes me feel. I just don't want to get carried away."

"Get carried away if you want," says Sonny. "I won't tell."

I shake my head. "I think I have an addictive personality."

Sonny laughs. "You don't even know what that means."

I know exactly what it means. It is my mother and her stained teeth. Her lies. "Yes, I do, Sonny. My mom is an alcoholic."

The table of men stare at me, blinking. Maybe I've revealed too much.

"My father is the same, actually," says Axel casually. He takes a sip of water, the only drink he's ordered. "When I was young, I used to visit him in Lillehammer. That's, ah . . ." He draws a vague shape in the air, pointing toward the ceiling. "North of here. A few hours north. When they hosted the Olympics in '94, we went together. I was still a student then. He came to pick me up at the train and he didn't recognize me. I waved to him, and he just stared at me blankly." He laughs to himself. "He was fucked already, you see. He doesn't remember the Games at all. I asked him about it the other day. It's strange to me how I can remember an event so vividly, while he has nothing at all. It is like I shared this memory with someone who was already dead. Is that like your mom as well?"

Listening to his story, it feels like we've been punctured in the same exact spot.

"Yeah, my mom would stash her bottles away, and my brother and I would find them. It was always surprising, coming across one. It would explain the behavior from three or four nights before. We'd go, oh, there it is. This bottle was when she got home and screamed at us to go fuck ourselves." I sip on my own drink. "She had all these hiding places. In her dresser, under piles of clothing. In the dishwasher. Under the bathroom sink with the toilet paper."

"I had no idea," says Pat, and he really does seem concerned for a moment. Cheeks ruddy from his own alcohol, his face lying slack. He turns to Sonny. "Did you ever tell me that?"

"Donna is a piece of work," says Sonny, throwing me a look. "She hardly checks in on her own kid."

"I guess the alternative is a nightmare, too," Pat says. "Some parents are way too involved with their kids' careers, in my opinion. Savannah

Sinclair's mother manages her. I hear there have been problems. She's mishandled finances, donated a lot, maybe millions, to this one pastor."

"That must be a fun Thanksgiving table," says Sonny with a laugh. Axel is watching this back-and-forth silently, tapping his finger against his chin.

I take another sip of beer. White bubbles float to the top and settle on the surface. I watch Pat through the amber glass. I tighten up in his presence; he is the one steering my entire career, the one who will report back to Lyle Michaels and tell him whether I'm still worth Lolli's investment or if I'm already spoiled goods.

On the way back to the studio, he explains why we are in Oslo, not Stockholm. "Axel's father is dying, you know," he says. "He refused to move out of Oslo once he got sick, so Axel is taking on fewer projects to take care of him. The fact that he's chosen to work with you, well, it says something. It really says something."

Back in my hotel room, Wes is calling, which is a rarity, but I don't jump to my phone. I just watch it ring. Last year, loving him felt like a forgotten word, always on the tip of my tongue, never pushed forth. Now we've both grasped it, but it has several definitions when we thought it had only one. At the very last moment, I pick up.

"Hello?"

"Hey. Are you on break?"

"We just had dinner. But I have to be back at the studio in an hour. We'll probably work all night."

"Ah, yes. Axel. Is he being hard on you?"

"A bit." But this isn't the full truth—Axel is exacting and honest. When he challenges me, I know I will be better for it. He is critical but never cruel.

"He tends to do that."

"At least I'm not thinking about what happened." I close my eyes. Because when the baby is larger than a toddler in my mind, when its cheeks have grown sallow and the rosiness has leaked away, I remember my fear. The terror of holding the test in my hands, and the whole world looking down alongside me to see those two lines. I think of Argus, the hundred-eyed giant. There are so many eyes on my body, and I can't move without them all narrowing in judgment.

"That's really good," he says softly. A moment passes.

"What are you thinking about now?" I ask.

"Now? Just you."

I run my fingers over my breasts. Cup the weight in my palms. "Anything in particular?"

"Well, I was imagining you surprising me. You, in my bed when I get home."

"Just waiting there?"

"Exactly," he says. I feel turned over in his hands.

"Am I naked?"

"Uh-huh. I think you are, yeah."

"Nice."

He laughs. "So, you're naked, and you're waiting for me. You're such a good girl."

"Wes. That voice."

"What voice?"

"It just makes me laugh. Sorry."

"What do you mean?"

"No, I don't know. I'm sorry."

"Okay," he says, but his voice is clipped.

I lie back onto my pillow, closing my eyes. I speak into the darkness behind my lids. "For some reason, I couldn't get into it that time."

"Okay. I mean, we don't have to do anything. We can just talk."

"Yeah, okay."

I apologize for calling him so much last night. The press coverage leaks back into my head whenever I step out of the studio, so I had called him again and again, called Gwen, called my mom, called Greg, called every one of my dancers, but only silence answered in the end.

He asks what was going on.

"Nothing. I think I just needed to hear your voice."

"We had a show last night. And we had an annoying interview. This random reporter asked us all, 'Screw, marry, kill: you, Savannah, Gwen.' I said something like, 'I'd marry all of them. They're all great girls.' Something like that."

"You didn't want to screw me?"

"Well, I did, but I felt like that's what he expected me to say."

"No, I get it. Very respectful."

I continue, "I think he probably wanted you to kill me, though. Marry Savannah, screw Gwen, kill me. That's the national consensus."

He must agree, because he's quiet for a long time.

The lights are dim in the studio. I'm lying on the leather couch, watching Axel's golden head nodding along to the playback.

"I want to leave a space for a harmony here, something like—" And he demonstrates for me, his voice scratching against his throat. He flushes. "Well, you try."

I sit up on the couch to sing for him.

"More control." He draws a straight line in the air. This time, he nods when I sing. He says to do it just like that from now on.

The praise rises through my body, settles somewhere in my chest.

"The texture of your voice has a velvety, smooth element to it, like honey, but it can also sound like you chain-smoke. That rasp is what I want in the bridge."

"Well, I do chain-smoke. So do you."

He rolls his eyes.

"Axel?"

"Yes?"

"Is the stick up your ass uncomfortable?"

"Very," he says, leaning back in his chair. It rolls a few inches, hits the wall. I return to the booth. The entire time I'm singing, I feel his eyes. He isn't concerned with the way I look—it's meaningless to him.

He cares only about the capabilities of my body as an instrument. I am sure he can see the organs inside of me, the pumping, churning machinery. My diaphragm expanding and contracting. The breath ejected from my lungs. By taking me seriously, he has stoked me with fuel.

As he compresses my vocal, he hums to himself. He is always humming to himself. I swing around in an empty rolling chair. Every so often, he glances back at me, amused.

"Your voice isn't so bad, you know," I say. "If you just hum, it's not so bad."

He smiles. "Very funny."

"Do you ever sing for other people?"

"No, never."

"You've never been in a band or anything?"

"Absolutely not."

"So you don't mind that no one ever hears you, or knows who you are? You're like the Wizard of Oz."

He doesn't turn away from the monitor as he says, "I've never seen that movie."

"Well, the whole point is that he's an anonymous man behind a curtain."

"I prefer it this way. This way, I can create, and my face is unknown. For most people, especially in your country, the art and being the face of the art is interchangeable."

"What's wrong with that?"

"There's nothing wrong. I just prefer it this way. It's not very important to me if people know I wrote a song. The fact that I did write it, and it's out in the world, is enough for me."

"That's kind of brave."

He snorts at that. "Brave? No. Not brave. We are all a small part of something larger than ourselves. This is a good way to think. You and me, we are working toward a common goal." He forms a bridge with his fingers. "You, the artist. Me, the producer. My individual aspirations, people knowing my name? No, that does not matter very much to me. As long as the work gets done, I'm okay."

"Do you hate that it matters so much to me?"

"You are American," he says simply.

I tell him I'm embarrassed.

"Of being American?"

"Of wanting to be famous." All because I was desperate to mold some powerful semblance of self, which could be wielded like a scepter whenever I was hurt or scared or insecure.

"Wanting to be known is normal," he says. "We all want to be known by other people. We all want to connect."

"I used to think I sang to escape my family. But that's not right. I really wanted them to pay attention to me. One time I ran away from home, and the entire day went by. No one cared. I showed up for dinner and my mom had a microwave meal on the table. She was, like, 'Oh, you're late. Clear your plate when you're done.'"

I slip back. It is so easy. And I am there, I am in the apartment again. There is the sconce that looks like an upside-down breast. There, the little Virgin Mary statue, a garage sale purchase. Mom and Greg are fighting. When I turn the stereo up, feet stomp down the hall. A fist slams into my door. Shut the fuck up, Amber, they say. Shut up. But their arrival just makes me sing louder.

"This is what I mean," Axel says. "You wanted to connect with her. You wanted her to notice you. That's your drive, and it's nothing to be embarrassed about. It's human. You are a human being, Amber."

I'm staring down at my hands. "But I'm not. Haven't you read about me?"

He shifts in his chair. "No, I haven't."

"Don't you know what the press is saying?"

He says he's heard a few things. Wes and I were photographed together in a hotel room, weren't we? When I nod, he asks why we don't tell everyone the truth. I'm not surprised he already knows Gwen and

Wes were never a real couple; he's spent a significant amount of time with both of them.

I say it doesn't matter. This scandal is delicious, and our real lives don't have that kind of flavor. It's like choosing between a mass-produced candy bar and a microwaved vegetable.

"Gwen doesn't want anyone to know," I add. "Neither does Wes. Everyone thinks they were madly in love. It's easier to blame me. It was all my fault, anyway." Then I tell him the public's idea of me is incorrect. That's obvious. What's less obvious is that my own idea of myself is also incorrect. I'm wrong about myself all the time. I think I'm good, then I make bad choices. Each day, I make a new mistake to bury tomorrow.

He runs his hand along his nose, back and forth along the bridge. "Have you read the poet Mary Oliver? An American poet."

"No."

He nods. "Okay. I will bring something for you tonight."

At dinner, he slips me the poem under the table. The title is "Wild Geese." Beneath this, he's written "For Amber." He's clearly torn the page out from a book because it's speckled with his coffee stains. He's underlined certain lines in pen. Drawn squiggles to coax out the last of its failing ink. In the bathroom, I flatten the paper against the sink and water blooms across the bottom corner. I dry it off with my sweater as best I can, but I've given something else to the poem, some new damage.

I read it under flickering lights. I read it again and again, searching for new understanding each time, and when I've dried my tears, I face myself in the mirror, running my tongue over a pale canker sore on my gum. Here I am. Between me and this reflection, there are years of tension. Maybe I've been aimless. Maybe I've been afraid. But I don't want to be that way anymore; I want to know what I'm capable of.

Streetlights reveal the contours of the cobblestones below. It is cold, and very late.

Axel walks ahead of us, and I jog to catch up. "Thank you for the poem," I say.

"Listen." He hums a melody. "Do you like it?"

As he stretches the melody out, we recognize its potential at the same time. His eyes are suddenly wild, frantic. His strides lengthen. "Keep up. But don't distract me, please. If I don't repeat it to myself, I'll forget it."

I'm silent the rest of the way. We all follow him up to his apartment. His place looks bare and untouched at first. A tabby cat slinks around his ankles. He scrapes wet food into her bowl with a fork, still humming, then leads us to his bedroom. Here, his life pours out. Sweaters and instruments and books. A tipped-over mug on his comforter. Unopened boxes of pasta stacked in a tower. "You live like this?" Pat asks. Yusuf settles against the wall, arms crossed, and says something to Axel in Swedish or Norwegian. I can't distinguish between the two languages, and Axel has told me they are very similar.

"Where is it?" asks Axel, throwing aside a pair of sneakers and a blanket. "Ah." He holds up a tape recorder. His cat settles at my feet, and when I lean down to rub her head, she arches in pleasure.

Axel hums, his foot tapping against the floorboards. He already has the chorus and a partial verse.

"Is that going to be our hit song?" Sonny asks.

"Yes, most likely," says Yusuf, cross-legged on the floor.

Axel turns to me, brow raised. "What do you think?"

Together, we listen to the playback.

"We need more layers in the second verse. It's too sparse, a letdown."

He nods, twisting in his chair. When I enter the booth to record, time passes, and I don't notice its weight. Then I am lying on his soft rug, smacking a pen against the lyric sheet we've printed, Post-it notes scattered around my legs. "Do you like, *Won't show you what's inside my room*? Or, no, actually, *The room is mine, won't show you what's inside*. That's way better." I cross the first one out.

"You answered for me."

I fiddle with a knot on the rug. "Axel?"

He makes a gentle noise, so I know he's listening.

"How do you come up with this stuff?" It seems miraculous to me—"Bubblegum" while riding his bike, this new melody walking home from the bar.

He shrugs. "Not sure. I'm always listening, I guess. Listening to silences, wondering what could fill them. How do you?"

"What?"

"Where do your ideas come from?"

"Which ones?"

"You had one just now."

"Axel, you don't have to be polite."

He clicks his pen. "Polite how? You have many things inside you to say."

What a thing to hear, after a lifetime not hearing it at all. If he's right, if there was a well inside me once, when did it run dry, rust over? When did I decide the water was all polluted? He turns back to his computer, shakes his mouse. Staring at the screen, he asks, "What is your mother doing now? She doesn't travel with you." This last part an observation, not a question.

"She's at home."

"Is she very proud of you?"

"No, I don't think so. She felt I should do something more responsible, something I couldn't fail at. She always wanted me to go to college."

He bites his tongue, which he does when he's concentrating. "It's funny. My father said something like this to me."

"I hope he knows he's wrong now."

He scratches his head, smiling. "Maybe."

"I don't think she saw anything in me. My mom, I mean. I think she knew that to succeed in this industry, as an actress, a singer, whatever, you have to have something extraordinary. Eyes have to be drawn to you, instead of all these other people next to you, for whatever reason. She didn't think I had it, so she tried to discourage me."

This makes him frown. "Come here. Listen."

He pulls a chair over for me and hits the space bar.

"Is this the second verse?"

"Yes."

It is so much fuller now, a buildup that sweeps us right into the next chorus. We exchange a look. He raises his hand, I high-five it, and the gesture feels juvenile, but in a nice way.

What's the time? Given the pearly light, it must be morning. This time of day makes me understand what he's said about listening to silences. They hum with potential, waiting for some impact. And sometimes, when your instinct is right, you don't need to fill them at all. They can stretch on and on. Every time he's quiet, I know something wonderful must be churning inside his head. If only I could be seen in such a way, too: as a mind brimming, about to spill over.

My memory is heavy or light, depending on the thickness of the paper. Sometimes ink can't leak through time. Sometimes everything is transparent, as if held up to sunlight. During these two weeks in Oslo, I remember: Axel's hair hanging in front of his eyes, his fingers brushing it away. Yusuf's tentative laugh, and Oskar's booming one. Being afraid, at first, to suggest an idea, then the joy of approval. The joy, the joy. Hours passing without glancing at the clock. Circling the room with Axel, throwing ideas back and forth as if they are corporeal. Pinwheels of inspiration twisting from his brain to mine. Axel asking for my opinion and listening when I offer it. Burning with a new kind of desire—creation, something that begins in the mind and ends in the body. Forgetting to call Wes because all the space in my head is taken up by this album, and there's no other room. Waiting for the muses. Working all night even when they don't arrive. Axel's eyes fixed on mine in the vocal booth, the same gray as early mornings here. Again, he says. Try again. You can do better, Amber, I just know it.

And the night before my flight back to America, Axel says we're going to a club so we can test out the rough mixes.

"This is where we find out the truth," he insists. "This is the real world."

Inside, there are dancers on platforms. Chartreuse lights and artificial smoke create a dark, seamy swamp. Darude's "Sandstorm" is playing, but then it melts into a song I don't recognize. When I tell him I like whatever it is, Axel says, "It is 'Heut' Ist Mein Tag' by Blümchen."

"Do you know every song ever made?"

He snorts. "Of course not."

Axel goes off to hand the mixes to the DJ, a friend of his. The rest of us sit at a corner table, sweeping crumpled napkins and crumbs off the surface. When he returns, he slides into a chair between me and Yusuf. He tells me he was raised in clubs like this in Stockholm. As a teenager, he would ride on the handlebars of a friend's bike through the city—toward the music, into which he could disappear. He felt its power as something vaguely religious. Something to be experienced in congregation, with other people.

"Everyone here," he says, indicating the crowd, "will stay until closing, until they are forced to return home to their beds. Then they will come back the next night, and the next. Tell me that's not worship."

One of my songs begins to play, and the dance floor shimmers like light on fish scales. A couple grinds against each other, moving like it is their last night on earth, surrendering to forces greater than themselves. Total abandon. A basic, primal instinct: lose yourself, and you will be found again through release.

Axel is watching the couple, too. "Look," he says. "This is how your music feels, how it makes a crowd move."

It is too much. I have to be inside of it. "Come on." I reach for his hand.

"What are you doing?" he asks. But he doesn't drop my hand, just looks down at it, confused.

"We're dancing."

Yusuf points at Axel's panicked expression, laughing with Oskar.

"Why are you just sitting here?" I ask.

"I need to watch!"

"Well, *I'm* not watching anymore." I release Axel's hand, but his sweat remains on my palm until it dries up. The crowd parts for me. The beat pushes my hips one way, then another. My hands float above my head. I am molten; parts of me break off and flow away. In this moment, my voice gushing from the speakers, my body transcending its barriers, I just think: I'm alive, I had forgotten and now I remember, I'm so grateful.

Outside in the cold, I hug my coat tight against my chest, jumping up and down, then light a cigarette. I know it is bad for me, but I always want the wrong things, the things that heat my blood.

Pat comes outside to join me, threading his hands through his jacket. "I sent the rough mixes over to Lyle and the other execs," he says. "They were nervous, and I wanted to assure them the sessions were going well. They like it. I think they'll want it all on the record."

They like it. Slowly, this sinks in.

He continues, "I hope we can get the first single and video out in the winter. We can't know for sure, but I think we've done it. I think we have hits here. And you know what? Everything that happened back home with Wes and Gwen . . . Look, I think people will be interested in you. It's low-hanging fruit."

I consider this. "Do you know that myth?"

"What myth?"

"I don't remember the king's name. But his eternal punishment is to stand in a pool of water he can't drink, beneath a tree with all kinds of fruit he can't eat. They are dangling just out of reach."

"Are you the dead guy or the fruit in this scenario?" Pat asks.

"The dead guy," I say, but later I change my mind. I am the fruit.

PLEASE DON'T DISTURB

Amber Young   Track 1 on *Amber Young*

Produced by
Axel Holm & Yusuf Hassan

April 3, 2001

[Intro]
See that sign on my door?
Won't let you disturb me anymore
No!

[Verse 1]
I heard you talking about me
You think I asked for it (Oh!)
Won't wait and see before judging (No!)
How can I clear up the misconceptions?
You've got too many damn questions

[Chorus]
See that sign on my door?
Please don't disturb me anymore
It's closed now, the room is mine
Won't show you what's inside

[Verse 2]
Get out of my ear
You're calling me this one that one (Oh!)
Won't wait and see before judging (No!)
How can I clear up the misconceptions?
You've got too many damn questions

[Chorus]
See that sign on my door?
Please don't disturb me anymore

It's closed now, the room is mine
Won't show you what's inside

[Bridge]
I've got to be honest . . .
Something's going down in this room
But what's it to you?

[Chorus]
See that sign on my door?
Won't let you disturb me anymore
It's closed now, the room is mine
Won't show you what's inside

ABOUT

Genius Annotation   **3 contributors**

"Please Don't Disturb" is the opening track and second single from Amber
Young's eponymous album *Amber Young* (2001). Fans have speculated it
is about what was going on in the press at the time surrounding Young and
ETA's Wes Kingston, which Young has subsequently confirmed.

2000

Los Angeles

I am a cyborg. I have crimson contacts in my eyes and I'm wearing a metallic bodysuit. During a short break in filming, I'm escorted off the soundstage and to my trailer in the parking lot. Wes is waiting inside. When I wrench the door open, he perks up, yawning. His hair is pointing in every direction.

"How many hours have you been gone?" he asks.

"I'm not sure. Maybe five or six."

"I'm sorry, I'll come watch."

"It's okay."

He tugs me into his lap. "I want to watch."

"We'll wrap in a few hours anyway." He can probably sense the annoyance I'm trying to tuck away. I lean forward to show him my contact lenses up close.

"Creepy." He kisses my neck. "Is this the song you wrote with Axel?"

"Not this one."

Lolli has decided "One More Chance" will be the first single off the new album. I fought for "Please Don't Disturb," the song I co-wrote, but Lyle says "One More Chance" is the sure hit, so in a conference room full of men, I was overruled. I'm afraid Lyle will say I'm difficult now. That his opinion will disperse through the industry. He's always calling women difficult or demanding—just euphemisms for bitch.

"Well, Axel said something about you on the phone. The other day, you know, when Ty and I called him to go over ideas."

This shocks and excites me at once. "What did he say?"

"You know Axel. He never says much. But we talked about how talented you are, how everyone underestimates you. Even me." He tugs on my hips. "Can we undo this suit?"

"No, it took forever to get into it. And I feel gross. It's so tight."

"Okay, well, you're not gross. You know you're not."

"I'm just saying it's uncomfortable."

He sighs. "Sometimes I feel like you only say you're ugly so that I'll say you aren't."

This is sometimes true, but not right now. I stare at him, and I'm not sure what we are to each other. I want to know. I want him to finally draw a circle around me and say, mine.

"Have you talked to Mike about us walking the AMA carpet together, by the way?"

For a few moments, he doesn't answer. He sighs, but he's really saying, *I can't believe it, this again?* "You know we have to wait."

"What are you worried about? That everyone will think you moved on from Gwen too fast? That everyone will think *you're* the slut?" This makes me laugh.

He looks out the trailer window to the lot. "No. I just know SMG won't like it."

"What are they going to do?"

"I don't know. They can do whatever the fuck they want. That's why I'm being cautious. You're asking me to piss off my label, my manager, my mom—"

Softly, almost too soft for him to hear, I say, "I just thought maybe I was worth it."

"You think a relationship is giving up everything for each other, but I don't know if that's love."

"I don't think that." What I think is ETA has to remain preteen friendly, and I'm a reminder that he's a man having sex. These two ideas are so incongruous—I can see why his label is concerned. His private life must bolster his public one. He prefers relationships in corners, in dim lighting, because of it.

"Okay."

"Okay."

"Amber."

"I said okay."

"You don't sound okay." He's very still. There's a knock on the door and we both turn toward it. Another knock, then Sonny's hand waving in the doorframe, gold rings winking in the sun.

"Coming!" I shout, pushing off Wes's lap. He's still holding my waist. Suddenly, I see his thumbs, just there, and maybe my entire life is beneath them.

"Can we not do this?"

"Do what?" I remove his hands, then pull on the trailer door more roughly than I intended. It slams behind me, shaking before it settles.

"Careful," Sonny says, inclining his chin toward the window. The fleshy wattle of his neck shakes.

"Of what?"

"The kid."

"He's not a kid."

"Oh, really? Honey, from my vantage point, he's a little shit, and I've always thought so."

"I'll keep that in mind."

"Yeah, I bet." Sonny escorts me back to the set, where my dancers are already shooting, most of them men a foot taller than me. We've rehearsed for over a week; the choreography is deep, well-traveled grooves for our bodies to follow. Our director also did "Sweat," but the budget for this video is astronomical: this time, we have green screens and special effects.

A makeup artist touches up my foundation as the director points to my mark. His face is crooked, permanently suggestive.

I incline my chin toward the green screen. "Is that where the giant city is going to be?"

"Yes, right there."

"I want it to look futuristic, like *Blade Runner*."

"It will. You're the sexy, evil cyborg invading the metropolis. Capturing all the men who tried to control you. It'll be fabulous. We're going to do the wide shot first, okay?"

Wes emerges from my trailer and watches me from behind the director's chair, picking at a turkey sandwich and a bag of chips. Taking a fistful, licking the yellow dust off his fingers. We exchange glances between takes. I remember how, when we first had sex, I was desperate to join myself with him. The lining between our bodies was too thick—I wanted it rubble. First love is ravenous in this way. It's starved. It's consuming the idea of someone else until your teeth snap against an unexpected bone.

For most of his childhood, Wes lived alone with his mother and two small Chihuahuas named Pearl and Garnet. After his parents separated, his mother moved through men. He doesn't remember most of them. Only one face is clear: the man who introduced his mother to the megachurch with a cross visible from the highway, to the preacher with the voice like God. This cycle of men made Wes think love was continuous loss. He saw his mother broken down on the couch, crying in her room, unable to sleep or eat or do much of anything, and he didn't understand why she kept putting herself through it. He blamed her for trying again and again to give him a father, when he was more than capable. When he helped pay the medical bills, when he won *Star Search*, when he was discovered through the walls of that dingy apartment in Los Angeles, he felt as if he had emerged from his childhood as his own father and mother and brother and sister; he had been all things to himself at once. So the fear is not just that he will lose everything with one misstep. The fear is that maybe he does need other people.

RADIO TRANSCRIPT
January 2001

Interviewer: We asked passersby what they thought of a few of your outfits.

Amber Young: Okay.

Interviewer: Here's the response to one of them. You wore this to the *Billboard* Music Awards. This sheer dress. And a passerby said: "Was she born in that?"

AY: Ha. That's funny.

Interviewer: Does that bother you?

AY: No. I mean, I have no control over what they think. All I can do is wear things that make me feel good. I felt good in that dress. The stylist I work with—actually, her name is Brenda, thank you, Brenda—we picked it out together and I love it. That's a special dress for me. It's the first time I was invited.

Interviewer: Yeah, but what if kids hear you on the radio and want to copy what you're doing? Are you wearing that to get attention?

AY: Not for attention, no.

Interviewer: Okay. There have been a lot of rumors about you and Wes. Is Gwen's song "Touch and Go" about the whole situation?

AY: Well, that song was recorded before, actually, so I don't get why everyone thinks that. We're all good friends. Gwen and I are really close.

Interviewer: So no drama?

AY: None.

PRE-CHORUS
2001

2001

Los Angeles

Celebrities float across the carpet in front of the Shrine Auditorium. When we cross paths, Savannah wobbles over on her heels and hugs me. Two crystalline bodyguards trail behind her. By now, she is mononymous. Just Savannah. I wonder if she's lonely with only this one name, if she feels constricted by it.

A journalist thrusts her microphone into my face and asks who I'm wearing. Together, we glance down at the faux snakeskin bandeau top and matching pants, which flare out by my ankles. I'm shaky as I try to engage with her. Hunger swirls in my stomach; I've neglected to eat much for two days. And the voices arrive all at once, from every direction. *Look here, Amber, over here! Amber, this way! Amber, are you excited to be performing at the AMAs? Amber, to the right, please. Amber, smile for us. This way. Turn this way. Have you seen Gwen yet? Amber, are you excited for your performance tonight? Amber, smile! Over here! Look here. To your left.*

I feel the warmth of a hand on my waist. An anchor. Beside me, Gwen smiles. She waves calmly to the photographers. "I think I'm dying," she whispers to me. "For real this time. I've had a headache for an entire week."

"Can you step over there, Gwen?" Her publicist points to an interviewer on the carpet.

She squeezes my hand, then releases it. The photographers short-circuit over this.

In the auditorium, an elegant chandelier hangs from the ceiling. Gwen is a pastel head on the other side of the room. Too far away. But Wes is seated with the rest of ETA in the row behind me. I try to get his attention. He's speaking to someone else, deeply entrenched in conversation, but his eyes keep flicking over to me.

Eventually he pushes through his row and meets me in the aisle. I close my eyes for a moment, then ask if he will come to the restroom.

"Now?" he asks quietly.

"Please."

He says okay. He'll follow a few minutes after me. Through the auditorium, down the hall, to the empty bathroom with its deceitful mirror. I close the stall behind me and sink to the floor. Eventually he squeezes inside and takes my hand. I tell him I'm going to throw up.

"You'll be fine," he says firmly.

"I'm telling you I can't do it."

"You've been here before."

"But I've never sung."

"Gwen will be in the audience. She wants to see you."

"Look. I can't do it. I've done the rehearsals and my body knows what to do, but I can hear what they'll all say. Especially if I screw up. Anything I am, anything I do, they will find something to hate." I lean my head against the stall. "Do you ever get like this?"

"We all get like this. You have to push through it. I've told you before."

"I can't sit out there right now. I'm shaking." I hold out my hand to show him. "I just need a minute. I'm sorry, I'm sorry, I'm sorry." How many times do I repeat this? Enough for him to unlatch the door. I wonder if he followed me only because he thought I wanted to have sex.

I reach for him. "Wait. Stay. Please."

"I really have to go, Amber. Just head backstage. Warm up. Listen to some music, that'll help." He takes my face in his hands and kisses me. The warmth of his mouth lingers for a few seconds, then it's gone. Two women enter the bathroom. I watch them through the slit in the stall. They fix their makeup, then start to gossip. I can't hear anything other than a fragment of a sentence: "—dressed like a prostitute." The other laughs, the door slamming. I count to five hundred with my head between my knees, and then I find Dale waiting for me in the hall. He stands in the shadow of any door I close.

Backstage, Sonny is frantic, claiming I gave him half a heart attack by disappearing. I warm up in a chair while my makeup is retouched. I pace around using my vocal steamer. Then I burrow my hands into my purse, searching frantically, tossing out junk. I find the piece of paper I've been looking for at the bottom, rolled into a tight ball. "For Amber," it says. I trace the swirls Axel made with my thumb.

"Here we go," says Sonny, rubbing my shoulders. A producer hands me my earpiece, then guides me to the wings. The host is announcing me. I step into the light on cue.

I don't remember much of this performance—only Wes's retreating footsteps and the slam of the door. I don't sing for myself; I only want Wes to watch. His eyes are hooks in my body. They fasten, pull me under. And in the din of my performance there is a hush in my chest. It tells me I shouldn't have shown my true self to him, because now he has turned away.

The next morning, we're in a hot car, our skin stuck to clingy leather seats. We weave through the hills and park at an overlook. The sun melts the ice in my coffee, forming a top layer of milky water, and all the flavor has seeped out by the time I take a sip.

Slowly, he says, "Everything feels different now."

I tell him I know. It does. I lie against his chest. Close my eyes and listen to his pulse. Light, quick. It never falters. He's absentmindedly combing my hair.

"Maybe we're too similar. We want the same thing at the same time. Or maybe we bring out the worst in each other. That's what it feels like. Everything is heightened. I feel everything more because of you, and that includes every bad feeling."

"All the bad feelings are because of outside circumstances. Everything is heightened because it's all out there." I point out the window. "You're making a decision because of what everyone else thinks about me, not what you think. Or maybe it's the same thing."

His hands are on my back, drawing circles. I twirl in his arms, like a dolphin through a hoop. "What did you think would happen?" I ask.

"I don't know. I just wanted to be with you," he says simply.

"You could change your mind."

He leans against the headrest. Hits his head against it a few times. I brush his hair back.

"I've made up my mind."

"When did you decide?"

"Last night."

"Not before then?"

He shakes his head. Some organ twists in my chest. There are so many truths: he might love me a little; it is not enough; there is no changing his mind; he is not all evil or all good; he is a person who has made a choice. But there are knots to untangle. I've thought so little of myself, and his need for secrecy reflected this, so I let it drag on and on because it confirmed what I always suspected.

"Do you love me?" I ask.

"Yeah, I do."

It sounds like an echo, though.

"But I can't—I can't pretend like who I'm with doesn't matter," he continues. "That's awful, I know. But we talked about this years ago. We said we cared. We said we cared who people saw us with."

"I didn't think I'd ever be the person you were ashamed of. I know you think I'm a slutty piece of trash, but I performed at the AMAs last night. Or were you not watching?"

He sighs. "That's not how I see you at all. When I first saw you, I thought you were—I don't know."

"You saw Gwen."

He shakes his head. "Gwen wasn't there. You were backstage, getting your makeup done for *Star Search*. Your mom was with you."

"Oh."

The sun has lowered itself over the hills to rest. We are deflated, blinking slowly at each other. There's no other direction to turn, so we just keep tunneling down into the past, both of us crying, both of us making embarrassing, miserable sounds.

"I think about your abortion sometimes." He wipes his face with his T-shirt. "I know I fucked up, not being there. Will you always blame me for that?"

"Maybe," I concede. "I don't know. I did hate when you told me how upset your mom was about it. Why did you even say anything to her? Like, how did that help? That made me not like your mom, if I'm being honest. I guess I can tell you that now."

"She doesn't like you either."

"That's fine."

We sit in silence for a moment.

"Why doesn't she like me? She hasn't even met me."

He sighs, running his hand along the steering wheel. "She mentioned something she read about you. You were talking about a photo shoot, and you said it isn't your problem how people react to you. It rubbed her the wrong way. She said you were begging for attention, then complaining about it."

"Well, I have a lot of shame and guilt, okay? She can rest easy."

"We all do. I have to deal with my own shit, too."

I look over at him in disbelief. I feel as if Gwen, her blunt force, has animated my body. "When I signed with Lolli, they asked me if I was a virgin. When I said no, I thought they were going to freak out. But they were so happy about it. 'Great!' they said. It's fine, though. I haven't done anything wrong. I know that."

"I felt guilty, too, when the photos of us came out."

I rest my feet on the dash. "Really? I didn't feel guilty at all. I was happy to be with you. Happy everyone finally knew. I only felt guilty once it was, like, imposed on me by the entire world. I started to believe I really was the other woman, that I had destroyed a real relationship."

He looks down at his hands. "I feel like everything was better before we actually got together. When it was just an idea. You know?"

"Maybe," I say. But he is right, it was. "Do you think we should go back?"

This could mean anything. Back to the jellyfish tank. Back to the hotel pool, its water clear and still before we disturbed it.

"One more minute," he says. "Let's stay for one more minute."

We watch the last burst of sun. Eventually, he turns the key in the ignition. Now night is spread around us, as if a campfire has been smothered. Our car curves downhill, the heap of city beneath. And I remember driving down this road years ago, during my first summer in Los Angeles, when all my lust flowed in his direction, like tributaries into one lake.

2001

Los Angeles

For a while, each day is full of little agonies. But time erodes our relationship, taking more and more away. When weeks have gone by, and I haven't cried for a day or two, I think it's over and done, maybe I'm strong, maybe I've healed, but then an ETA song plays on the radio, and I'm in bed sobbing. The intervals stretch wider. They stretch so wide that a week without crying becomes a month, until I'm hurled backward again.

Soon it is spring. In Los Angeles, there is a tentative breeze, fickle clouds. Gwen has a rare day off, and I've just finished an interview with KIIS-FM. The publicity spin for the new album, *Amber Young*, is about to begin. There will be a release party in New York. Performances on *Rosie O'Donnell, Live with Regis and Kelly, TRL, Top of the Pops*. I carry my anticipation around with me; my nerves keep me up at night. I take hot baths and hold my breath for as long as I'm able, and when I emerge, I tell myself the universe has shifted subtly, and in this world my album will succeed.

But for now, respite. Gwen and I spend a few hours lounging on floaties in her pool. She has a trucker hat pulled over her eyes. Leaves drift through the water. Sometimes she floats over and picks them out one by one, throwing them back onto her lawn. Her rescue dog waddles over to sniff them.

"I had a dream last night," she says. "Tammy was on tour with you for some reason. You said the world was ending and I had to jump on a plane or else I would never see either of you again. The plane went down over the ocean. People say you can't die in your dreams, but I always do. I die and die and die." Softly, she adds, "You know. It's been hard. With Tammy."

Our floaties bump against each other. "What do you mean?"

"Mike threatened me. Made me fire her. She joined the Sol Sister tour a few months back. Right after you left for Oslo, actually. You almost overlapped."

"What do you mean he threatened you?"

She shrugs, but this is a mask of a gesture. Gwen encases herself in enamel. She was taught to deny herself, to harden. I can see how difficult this is for her, but also that she's desperate to unclench her fists. "He said we were too close."

"I'm sorry."

"It's okay."

"It's not. You always say that. You can tell me."

"It'll change how you see me."

"Nothing will change."

"How do you know?"

"Because I know, Gwen."

She flips onto her stomach, trailing her fingers through the water. The rim of her hat skims the surface. She tells me Tammy was lying in her bed, then pauses here, glancing over at me. What does she expect to see? Shock? Fear? I meet her gaze, squeeze her hand, an encouragement so she can continue. I've noticed the tugs between her and Tammy, the small adjustments they make to be near each other. I notice everything she does. And so I know she doesn't want an effusive reaction from me. Just the squeeze and our eyes locking: I see you, all of you.

"Okay," I say. "Okay. Go on."

She sucks in a breath, then continues her story. They are in bed. Gwen is tracing the tattoos across Tammy's back, marveling at how they shift whenever she moves. Tammy says she loves her, very softly, and Gwen hears it. She stiffens. While I grasp for love, Gwen crosses her arms over her chest—we have always been this way.

Gwen rests her palm on the surface of the pool. "I couldn't say it back, so I just lay there as she cried. I just fucking lay there. And I do love her, that's the thing. But I couldn't say it, because to tell her would be to release it into the world. You're the first person I've told besides myself."

"Maybe she knows."

She shakes her head. "Amber, I *fired* her. And I keep thinking about what would have happened if I had let her in. If I had told Mike to fuck off. I think I'm so strong but then I hurt people. Seems more like weakness to me."

"Have you tried calling?"

"What would I say? I do love you but I'm one of the most famous people in the world, and if I get into any relationship, let alone this one, people are going to talk, and be invasive, and I don't want to put you through it? Selfishly, I don't want to put myself through it?"

"Yeah, you could say that."

She sighs and something inside her breaks. A dislodging, a rush of tears that she quickly wipes away. "There's no point. Anyway, I've been seeing other people."

"Have you?"

"There's someone in my tour crew, yeah. And someone in LA, whenever I'm here." She smiles. "Ladies know what they're doing."

"Oh my god. Tell me more."

"Absolutely not." Then she laughs, but this tumbles into a sob. "Look at us. We're a goddamn mess."

She drops off her floatie, wading around and collecting leaves, twirling their stems between her fingers. "You know what I think? I think we should go out. You're sad, I'm sad, and we might be less sad. I have a handle in my liquor cabinet."

"Excellent idea, Gwendolyn."

We pour vodka into any container she has, which isn't much, since she's never home. She drinks from a Tupperware tub; I use a toothbrush holder. Gwen writes a ditty as we take shots. "You go 'I'm so sad,' then I go 'I'm so sad,' we cheers, and together we say, 'We're so fucking sad.' Then throw it back. Okay?"

"I'm so sad!"

"I'm so sad!"

"We're so fucking sad!" The alcohol slices down our throats. We both grimace and chase it with pulpy orange juice.

"Did I just come up with a hit? Get Axel on the phone. Let's get Axel on the phone!"

"Gwen, *no*, don't." But she's already pulled away, her Nokia pressed to her ear. "Don't worry. He's no fun." She smiles like she's a kid, which she never really was. "Axel, you won't believe who I'm with. Amber is here and we came up with your next num— Oh, shit, it's his voice mail. Dammit. Should we sing it for him anyway?"

I take this opportunity to snatch the phone out of her hands.

Later, in the car, we've mellowed out. She's leaning against the window, her hand slapping the wind outside. "It's really amazing," she says sleepily.

"What is?"

"That we're friends. An entire industry wants us to hate each other. Maybe we have, a little bit. But we also really love each other."

I take her hand and squeeze it. Outside the club, cameras almost impale our windshield. Gwen grimaces at the flashes of light, the sounds battering against us, while her bodyguard carves a pathway through it. She's started to fear these men. Not only because they follow her everywhere, to pump gas, to get her nails done, but also because every day they inch closer, emboldened. Her bodyguard pushes us through a side door, through a deserted hallway, into chaos. She streaks to the dance floor like a comet, and where she lands, there's a crater wide enough for us to dance. Double takes. Triple takes. The entire crowd glancing over their shoulders. Her name reverberates through the bodies. A man calls out to her. He's pale, wearing a wifebeater and baggy jeans. She doesn't just roll her eyes, she cuts him down with them, as if he's a tree she's felled.

A new beat drops, a remix of Gwen's song "R U Serious?"; the DJ has clearly spotted her. And so we shed ourselves, becoming girls in their early twenties. Girls able to get gorgeously drunk, to press against a night that might shatter. We're radiating with a rare, particular excitement: for once, we don't care about the impressions we leave behind. Maybe the pictures taken outside the club will be in a tabloid tomorrow, but we anticipate this coverage constantly, steeling ourselves against it. We'll spend many more years doing this. Tonight, we'll move so rapidly, any photograph would turn out blurry. We'll become lens flares.

Gwen tires out first. She slumps into a booth, tugging on my hand so I'll follow. Both our drinks shudder over their rims. "Whoops." She wipes up tequila from the table with her sleeve. "Mike wants me to do a movie. Did I tell you that?"

"What do you want to do?"

"Anything but a movie. It freaks me out. I already feel like a character playing another character. Too many layers. Anyway, the script is shitty. It's about this girl who dreams of starring on Broadway and moves to New York." She snorts into her drink. "I'd tell this girl to stay home."

"Go to college."

"Don't say yes to the first manager who wants to take you on."

"Don't hook up with the guy you're on tour with."

We collapse with laughter. The club is familiar, suddenly. The laughter shocks me back. Over two years ago, I was here with ETA, spilling like a drink in Wes's hands; every time he moved, I would tilt in his direction.

"I've been here before."

"With who?"

"Wes."

"Oh." She frowns. "What was it about him, really?"

"I don't know. Maybe I just wanted him to love me."

"I think he does."

"I doubt that."

"I just want to understand, like, *why* do certain people work together? Tammy and I are super similar, and she saw me and all my
anxiety, and was like, okay, I get you. Mom and my stepdad—the first
one, not this new one—are also very similar, but they clashed, stoked
each other, and it was terrible."

"Maybe different people need different things."

"Yeah, maybe. So, what do you think you need? What do you think
you could give to someone else?"

"I thought you were drunk."

She smiles pleasantly. "I'm very philosophical when I'm drunk."

Just then a familiar face appears, hovering in the dark. He has a col-
lection of features like a replayed infomercial. Nicky Land, the actor.
He extends a hand and we both shake it in turn. His face and arms are
more orange than his palms, which are very pale. His eyes remind me
of northeastern beaches in the winter.

"Big fan," he says.

"Of me or her?" Gwen asks.

"Both of you."

"Aw, shucks," I say. "Gwen, do you think we should let him sit
with us?"

"Might as well." When his back is turned, she mouths, "You should
fuck him." Scoots over so he can sit beside her. Rubs the dark leather.

"I'll get us another round first," he says, catching the bartender's
eye. "Vodka? Tequila?"

We say either is fine. To him, I mouth, "Water," pointing at Gwen.

Once he's gone, she turns to me, lowering her voice. "Who is he again? I've seen him before."

"Nicky Land. He's in that movie franchise about the explorer. You know? The explorer with the map of the world tattooed on his body. He looks at it for directions and he's like, 'We go north!'"

"You're kidding."

"You haven't seen that movie?"

"Um, no."

When Nicky returns, he's carrying three shots. His hands are covered in tattoos, thick stacks of rings. "Here we go," he says, setting the glasses down in the middle of the table. "That one's for you, Gwen."

She sips it and makes a face. "But this is water."

"I heard somewhere that you two despise each other," Nicky says.

"You believe tabloids? You should know better," I say.

"That's true," he concedes.

"What about you?" Gwen asks. "Tell us about you."

He shrugs and twists a ring on his index finger. But I can tell he's being humble; he really likes to fill space with himself. He uses heavy pauses, goes on wide tangents. His humble beginnings: born on a cattle farm in Queensland, he eventually landed a role on an Australian soap opera when he was fifteen. Reluctantly, he turns the conversation back to us, asking if we both really dated Wes Kingston from that boy band. His daughter is in love with him, he says.

Gwen nods. "We did. Both of us."

"Lucky guy."

It is easy, shallow attraction; I can wade inside it and still see my feet. He asks for my number as we're about to leave, and I write it down on his palm, which is rough and callused, experience ground into his skin. Wes's were baby-smooth.

I tell him I'm actually flying to New York in the morning.

"Ah," he says. "I'm in New York often."

"Then I have to go to Europe."

"Ah," he says again. "I'm in Europe often."

Our eyes meet, and we smile.

I perform "One Last Chance" on *TRL*. Afterward, I pace around my dressing room. The international number is written on a slip of paper by Pat, who has atrocious handwriting; I can't tell if the slashes are sevens or ones. I almost give up. But Gwen would ask. Wes would ask, too. So I gather my courage. The phone rings and rings and rings. I redial, substituting the sevens for ones this time.

"Hello?"

My stomach flips. "Axel?"

"Amber," he says. He sounds genuinely surprised to hear from me. "Congratulations. I've heard the song is doing well. You've worked hard."

"A compliment?"

"I'm capable of compliments. Enjoy your night. I hope you're celebrating."

"Wait. Can you be honest with me about something?"

"Of course."

"Do you think 'Please Don't Disturb' is the better song? I wanted it for the first single, but maybe my instinct is wrong. Lyle said it wasn't a hit, that I was kidding myself."

"You are not wrong. You never trust yourself." He pauses. "I do think it's the better song, yes. And I wrote both, so you know I'm telling the truth. I'm choosing my favorite child, but yes, I do like one child a little bit more."

"I feel like it must be the worst song on the album, if I helped you write it."

He laughs. "Amber, do you see yourself, truly? You have a record deal. You have producers like me. You have a whole team behind you. Most people do not have things like this."

"I think Lolli should release it as the second single. I think I should debut it tonight."

"Well, you're the boss."

"The boss? I like the sound of that."

"Good." Then, in his blunt way, he adds: "I'm going now."

We say goodbye. I tell Sonny I want to change the setlist for *SNL*. I watch his eyes, how they flit away from me and back. He shrugs, says if I feel strongly. I tell him I do. I feel strongly.

I am in love again: with this new album, *Amber Young*, and the way it makes me feel to sing it. The simplicity of the cover, which is a plain black-and-white photograph of my face. The spin of the globe, a rapid, shifting schedule, just like Savannah's and Gwen's. The entire summer I'm breathless, collapsed against my knees. Number fourteen on the US *Billboard* 200. Top 40 radio plays. It never bothers me that I don't have Gwen's or Savannah's level of success, because for once I am enough; the world doesn't hate me as much as I thought it did. And when "Please Don't Disturb" is released as the album's second single in April, it peaks at number seven on the *Billboard* Hot 100 and tops the charts in several European countries. Now my royalty cut comes from writing, too, not only from being the artist. My song. Mine. It is the fly circling around every ear, driving the country mad.

Lolli plans my first headlining tour to support the album. When Lyle calls me into his corner office to tell me the good news, I say, "I told you about 'Please Don't Disturb,' Lyle."

He laughs. He's too accustomed to excess, doesn't remember hunger. "We all get lucky sometimes, don't we?"

A girl steps forward. She's twelve, maybe thirteen. She hands me a poster of myself, torn from some magazine. There are four strips of tape on the back; it was hanging somewhere, maybe on her bedroom wall. The rest of the queue pushes forward behind her.

"What's your name?"

"Zoe."

I sign it. *To Zoe*. A heart. *X Amber*. I hand it back to her. "Thanks for coming. I love your bandanna. So cute."

Another girl. Eleven, maybe twelve. She has my new CD. A mouth full of braces.

"What's your name?" She hands me the CD, and our hands accidentally skid against each other. She flinches, then looks down at her palm in awe.

"Daniela."

"Hi, Daniela. Great to meet you." I sign *To Daniela*. A heart. *Big hugs. Amber*. "I hope you like the album. Do you have a favorite song?"

She hugs it to her chest. "I like 'Please Don't Disturb.'" Her eyes light up, excited. "Because when I listen to it in my room, my brother knows he's not allowed."

"That's my favorite, too. My brother also wasn't allowed in my room when I was growing up."

A boy, accompanied by his mother. Ten, maybe eleven. He's trembling like a far-off star. I push up in my chair to meet his eyes. "Hi, what's your name?"

Muscly men with beards and leather jackets. Clumps of fizzing teenagers. A grandfather with his little granddaughter. A man who wants me to sign his ass, before Dale steps in. Girls about to erupt into women, growing into their features, out of adolescent insecurities. Girls brimming with subterranean desire they cannot name but can already feel.

2001

Paris, France

Early morning, my phone rings in discordance with the birds. It's Axel, asking if I'm in New York. I tell him I'm not, then, sensing something strange in his tone, I ask what's wrong.

"Turn on your news."

I search for the remote in the couch cushions. Severe light streams through the curtains. A reporter is speaking in rapid French, and I can't understand a word he is saying. The coverage is of smoke billowing from the Twin Towers.

"What is it? What happened? Was there a fire?"

He tells me all he knows, which is not much.

"Do you want to stay on the phone?"

"I should make other calls. Do you know if Wes is in New York?"

"I don't," I say. "I haven't spoken to Wes in months."

"I had no idea."

"That's okay." On the television, firefighters drag a hose the size of a large snake through smoking rubble.

"Well, I should go," he says after a few moments. "I have to go now."

We hang up. I'm numb facing the television, watching for hours with Dale and Sonny. A before and after is drawn, right in front of our eyes.

I don't want to fly when my tour begins. No one wants to fly.

I am twelve again. First time on a plane. My life a steady churn of firsts: period, kiss in a closet, this flight. When did I use up all my beginnings? The route is Newark to Orlando, paid for by the *Star Search* producers. My mom chews Nicorette gum and flips through a magazine. I press my small hands against the window. It never occurs to me to be afraid. Of her, maybe, but not the plane cutting through the sky. It was made for this; we are safe in its aluminum belly. Every movement it makes is resolute, on course. The plane is taking me somewhere, and in this new place, I might be different.

Subject: Ideas
From: amberforeveryoung23@yahoo.com
Date: 12/1/01 11:45 PM
To: aholm@aol.com

Hi Axel,

Pat gave me your email address. I hope it's OK that I'm writing you. I have
a few ideas and Pat said it would be fine to run them by you. Let me know.
Amber

Subject: Re: Ideas
From: aholm@aol.com
Date: 12/2/01 9:13 AM
To: amberforeveryoung23@gmail.com

What are they?
A

Subject: Re: Ideas
From: amberforeveryoung23@yahoo.com
Date: 12/5/01 3:09 PM
To: aholm@aol.com

Hi Axel,

It's a random melody I can't stop thinking about. It's driving me a bit mad,
as you like to say. Maybe I can call and sing it to you sometime?

For the hook, I'm thinking:
You're just pulling up weeds
You're seeing things half-empty
You have too many needs
Amber

Subject: Re: Ideas
From: aholm@aol.com

Date: 12/6/01 10:56 AM
To: amberforeveryoung23@yahoo.com

Sounds good. Excited to hear it.
A

RADIO TRANSCRIPT
September 2000

Interviewer: Okay, okay, so this is what we're playing. We're playing screw, marry, kill with ETA. Okay. Let's do your albums. *Lightning in a Bottle, Brotherhood, Comeback.*

Alex Kowalczyk: Screw *Lightning in a Bottle*, kill *Brotherhood*, marry *Comeback.*

Cam Barone: Yeah, I agree with that.

Interviewer: Okay, let's do Amber Young, Gwen Morris, Savannah Sinclair.

[laughter]

AK: You're going to get us in so much trouble.

Interviewer: It's all in good fun. It's a game, boys.

AK: I'll answer. Marry Savannah.

Ty Jefferson: This is just becoming an opportunity for him to brag.

Interviewer: Okay, Wes, you go.

Wes Kingston: Nah, I can't answer that.

TJ: Yeah, we're not answering this one.

Gabe Barone: I'm going to say marry them all.

CB: Yeah, marry them all.

Interviewer: Wes, I really want to hear your answer.

WK: It's just a hypothetical, right?

Interviewer: Sure.

WK: Okay, I'd probably marry Gwen. I'd screw Amber.

[laughter]

Interviewer: This is good, this is good! Why screw Amber?

WK: She's real hot, obviously. But now I'd have to kill Savannah, which I don't want to do. Okay, I mean, look, I'll marry them all, too. They're all great girls.

TJ: Can we get the next one?

CHORUS (REPRISE)

2002

2002

London, UK

Elevator doors open to a rococo lobby. Dale steps out first. He guides me to the table they've set up in the banquet room, where journalists are seated in rows of folding chairs. Once I've settled in my seat, Sonny claps his hands, stepping behind the podium. "Let's get started. Right here. Front row."

A man stands. "Hi, Amber. Just wondering what's different about this album compared to your first. Thanks."

"I think this album is me coming into my own, redefining myself. It's very personal to me. I worked with so many wonderful producers, a lot of great, brilliant people, and I think it's really bold. Thank you."

Sonny points. Another man rises. The other hands fall, but don't lose their tension, since they are about to shoot up again. "Thanks, Amber. My question is whether you plan to do anything fun here in London?"

I exchange a glance with Sonny. "That's up to him," I say, and point to the podium. The men all laugh politely.

"Thanks," I add, and the journalist nods.

Another stands. This guy clears his throat before speaking. "I do hate to ask, Amber, but to get it out of the way, are you dating anyone?"

I reach for the water bottle on the table, break the seal, take a cooling sip. "No, I'm not right now. There's really no time for me to date anyone. Thanks."

This same man continues, "What would you say to people who think the Wes Kingston and Gwen Morris scandal was the only reason for your success with this album?"

"Um, well, I think I'd say that if you're only listening to me because of who I've slept with, then I don't really understand that. I do get the curiosity, of course. It's natural. But I think it's a difficult claim to make overall. That it's the *only* reason? I mean, I think it could have easily gone the other way—it could have ended my career. But now I'll have lovely questions like this for the rest of my life, you know? Thank you so much."

"You next, please," says Sonny. "Yep, there. Fourth row."

Another swig of water. I wait expectantly. "On a similar note, what do you say to people who are taken aback by your look?"

I lean forward, squinting. "Sorry, my look? I don't know what you mean by that."

"Your sexuality," he says plainly. "A lot of young girls around the world are fans of yours. I'm just asking if you believe you're setting a good example for them."

These types of questions are really just their own opinions.

"I'm setting the only possible example I can, which is being myself, or trying to be. I can't worry about how that's perceived. If I worried about the example I set for every girl on the planet, with all these different value systems, I'd lose my mind. Thanks."

On and on. A photo shoot in the lobby, then, finally, we head to the venue. I lie on the floor of my dressing room with Gloria. My eyes slip shut. Costumes are wheeled inside and someone pops their head in. "We're ready for you in five, Amber," they say.

I turn on my side. The floor is cold against my cheek. What relief, to have five minutes of rest. Gloria softly asks if I've heard from the actor.

"Nicky? Yeah. He's coming tonight. Bringing his daughter."

"His daughter?" Her round face lengthens in shock.

"Yeah. Have you ever been with someone who has a kid?"

"No, never."

"I thought I'd feel weird about it. Or maybe I'm pressuring myself to be? But I find all his life experience attractive. I don't know." I roll over again, opening my eyes. Sonny's voice booms from the hallway. Time to get up.

After sound check, Nicky Land and his daughter are led down the hall by my security. There's a knock on my dressing room door. Dale shoots me a knowing look before stepping outside.

The girl is so small. She shakes with eagerness, and I remember this exact sensation, when it felt like I was a balloon drifting through a sharp world. Tonight, her very first concert.

"I've heard about you," I say. "You're Camila, right?" She nods shyly. I can't tell if she is six or ten, and so I decide to adjust how I treat her depending on her reaction, but her eyes betray a surprising intelligence. Nicky told me her mother is the actress Lila Rodriguez, and I can see the resemblance: the long eyelashes, the warm brown eyes. The mother so clear in the daughter.

She is curious about the products my makeup artist left behind. She picks up tubes of lipstick, twisting them so she can inspect the color, humming her approval. Then she points to a gold leotard hanging on a rack. "Why do you wear stuff like that?"

Nicky chokes on a laugh.

I walk over to it. "This is one of my costumes. You'll see. I have seven costume changes in this show."

Nicky takes her shoulder. She stares up at me, blinking fast, almost puzzled. She must be thinking: This is her? This is Amber Young? I wonder if I'm a disappointment.

Nicky searches in his backpack, pulls out my new CD, and hands it to me. "She wanted you to sign this," he says. "Didn't you?"

I take it from him. There are scratches on the plastic; perhaps it has been well loved. I sign my name on the insert and write her a longer note than I usually would. I draw two hearts. "Here. Sorry if my hand-writing is bad."

She reads my note. "It is kind of bad."

Nicky squeezes her shoulder.

I turn to him. "Don't you want me to sign something for you, too?"

His eyebrows fly up. I pull his hand toward me. Slowly draw the loops of my signature over his palm. "Just want to be fair."

After the show, I invite him up to my room. Camila is with a sitter. We place an ashtray between us and recline on my hotel balcony. I still have a performance high, even hours later. I wonder if the show was impressive to him: the arcs of fire, the long cones of light crisscrossing the stage.

"You were amazing," he insists. "You really were. You have such presence."

I look out, to the city. "I think I become someone else. But I fucked up a few times. There's so much I could improve, you know?"

"I couldn't tell at all. And Camila loved it. She was dancing like this." He mimics her hands in the air. "I think she was a bit nervous in the dressing room. She can be shy."

"She must be used to this sort of thing though, right?"

"Her mother keeps her very secluded. I think it's more with me that she sees—" He makes a gesture. All of this, he means to say.

"I remember being her age."

"Yesterday, wasn't it?"

"That's sick. Shut up. I'm twenty-two." I hate the whine in my voice as I insist on it.

"I was twenty-two when I had Camila, you know."

"I didn't."

He stretches out his arm, the tattoos yawning on his skin, reluctant to tell me anything more. "So what do you remember from being her age, then?"

"Everything just felt so full of possibility."

He laughs. "And now, at the ripe age of twenty-two, you're terribly jaded?"

"No," I say, stamping out my cigarette. "I just know how things work out. I'm not delusional anymore. Back then, I thought I would be famous, and it would be magical. I would be happy. Now I understand that this is a job. This life. It has drawbacks like everything else. It's not a destination you arrive at. It's lonely, it's tedious, it's a lot of fucking work. I love it, and I'm so grateful, but it's still a job."

"How long are you on tour for?"

"Nine months."

"Jesus Christ," he says. "And then?"

I shrug. "I'll record a new album."

"Did you go to school?"

"Yeah, but I didn't finish. I wasn't any good at school. At least, that's what I was told throughout. What about you?"

"Me neither. I was always skipping class. I thought I was above it."

"I actually tried really hard. I was good at following directions. If there was an assignment, I turned it in on time, but it was always average stuff. Never anything special."

"You're special. Come on. I remember I first saw you on stage at the Teen Choice Awards. It was a year ago, maybe. You were presenting with some other singer. Someone from that boy band."

"Ty. From ETA."

"Yes, him. And you were wearing this black dress. I was nominated so I was sitting up close. I remember seeing your profile." He runs his pointer finger along my jaw. "You were just . . ." And his finger slips into my mouth.

His other thumb circles my knuckle. I shift into his lap, then take the finger from between my lips, inspecting it. "What's this tattoo?" I ask, pointing to an inked date.

"Camila's birthday," he says.

I lean down and kiss it.

"What about this one?" A triangle on his wrist.

"That's the Trinity."

"Are you religious?"

"Not at all."

"Me neither." And then our mouths meet. He picks me up, carries me past the sliding door, and tosses me onto the bed. His shirt lands beside me. His entire chest is covered in tattoos, and there is a scar on his arm I don't ask about. He takes a while to get hard, so I use my hands, then my mouth, faster, faster, and then he's above me, his hands are nudging my knees apart, and he's swinging between my legs, teasing me, asking if I want him, and I do, so badly that I'm whining into his ear to see his reaction, but more importantly my own. Every encounter is new understanding. I am shading in my desires. *What do you want?*

"Can I go on top?" I ask, and he flips us over, pressing his face between my breasts.

His hands grip my waist, pressing me down harder, lifting me back up. I tell him I want him even closer. He likes this idea, too, and I'm flipped again, this time onto my side. His broad body cupped around mine, finding exactly the right angle. I bite down on a pillow to muffle myself.

"Too hard?" he asks.

"No, no, keep going."

He does. The bed shakes with obvious effort. He asks if he can come, his face and skin burning hot. I tell him he can, but only on my stomach. He pulls out, and after, he wipes me down with his T-shirt. Then, his mouth is between my legs, and I'm guiding his tongue, and when he makes me come, I am a tree shaking in a storm, roots ripped clean out.

The press discovers the relationship. We are on a few covers, our photoshopped faces pressed together like a strange chimera. They say I'm pregnant with his baby. I'm pregnant with twins.

Why can't it just be sex? Why can't it just be the growth I experience whenever we are together—of pleasure, yes, but also a deeper knowledge of myself?

Whenever he is lying beside me, silent and still, I know he is thinking about Lila Rodriguez. He turns over in bed, revealing the tattoo on his back: *Lila*. I wonder if anyone will ever tattoo my name onto their flesh. Should I aspire to this? It's like Wes said: I think love should be catastrophic; an impact, blasting debris up into my life. When I was younger, I thought if someone gave up a part of themselves for you— space on their skin, their family—it was true devotion. But I only believed this because my dad left us for a woman he met at the YMCA, and I had to find some meaning in this loss. Sometimes I picture the scene. How he glanced over: there, emerging from the pool, his ruin. She must have looked delicious. I imagine small lemon breasts, the water dripping from her hips. Maybe it was an easy decision. Maybe, in that moment, he knew he would give up everything just to fuck her. Or maybe it took weeks, months. Maybe he looked down at me sleeping in my crib and was torn apart.

"How did it end? With Lila?" I ask Nicky one morning. The sheets are damp with our sweat.

"Our nanny." He throws a pillow over his eyes to block out the light.

"Camila's nanny? I think I did see something about that. I didn't know that was you."

He nods, the pillow shaking above him. When he emerges, he tosses it to the side. "It was a mistake. Many mistakes." He tells me they were living in Spain. Lila was away for two months on a shoot in Toronto. He continues, "Her name was Sofia. She was around your age. Anyway, one night, we were alone in the house. Camila was sleeping. She had left some books or dolls on the ground, that sort of thing, so I went downstairs to clean up. Sofia was awake, eating cereal. We spoke about this and that. She listened to me. It's sad that's all it required—her listening to me. I was drinking a lot, and I was so tired. Lila and I were raising Camila in between filming, and I think we both hadn't had time for ourselves in many years. So, I spent the night with Sofia. I thought it wouldn't happen again. I felt terrible. But, of course, it happened again. It happened a lot."

I ask how Lila found out.

"Sofia was pregnant. It was hard to conceal."

"She had the baby?"

He nods.

"How old is it?"

"He's two years old. I'm surprised you didn't know."

"I didn't want to read about you. Well, I did, but only briefly. I wanted you to tell me about yourself. I hoped you'd do the same for me."

"Sometimes I worry about Camila," he says quietly. What he means: How can he raise a daughter in such a world?

"When I was a kid, no one told me I could be anything I wanted. I'm glad you tell her that, even if it's not true."

"What did you want to be?"

"What I am now. I just imagined it differently."

"Different how?"

"I imagined I would be happy."

He runs his hands along my body. "I wish I could help with that. If only you knew all the things I want to do to you."

"Tell me."

And he does. I close my eyes and listen. Such good things.

Here he is, lying naked in bed, breathing softly. His weight crushing me. His smell crushing me. Not in a bad way, just in a human way. I maneuver out of his arms to pee. Down the hall, his daughter is sleeping.

All is dark. I run his tap and wash my hands. In the mirror, I look very young. He treats me like I am very young, too. He asked me plenty of questions about myself early on, but not so much anymore. Now he mostly talks at me or answers questions I ask him. Maybe he's reached some border, the rim of what he wants to learn about me. Are there people out there we'd want to endlessly discover, someone we can sink down into and never find a floor?

There is so much food in his refrigerator; he always has it stocked for Camila. I open drawers packed with raw meats, fine cheeses, loose vegetables. Nothing packaged—so what will I snack on? I find whole-grain cereal in a drawer. I guiltily take the box over to his couch, always thinking of Sonny, what it will look like in photographs if I eat too much, what it will look like in photographs if I eat too little.

Nicky's floor-to-ceiling windows reveal the spread of London below. I watch the city breathe with light. I've been here many times, but never stepped inside it, never gotten lost. I've been driven in a connect-the-dot way for years. Nicky says I should see the restored Shake-speare's Globe, but I don't know if I'll have the time. It is a dark mound in the distance, sitting somewhere along the banks of the Thames.

I feel very calm about not loving him. It proves something vital to me: I can be with someone, find pleasure in it, and remain myself. I throw individual cereals in the air, catching them on my tongue.

After a while, I turn on the lights in his office, half of which has been converted into a makeshift gym. I'm on his treadmill, my legs churning over the belt, when Gwen calls. I put her on speaker in the cup holder. "You didn't hear it from me," she's saying, "but Alex is going solo. He was recording at Electric Lady, too. I ran into him."

I pause the machine, then twist my limbs around in the mirror to inspect their shape. "I wonder what Wes thinks about that."

On the other end, Gwen reacts to the tug of a brush through her hair. A hiss of pain. "He's comfortable," she says. "He's always been too comfortable. He's the best singer, and then he fails to differentiate himself. He wants everything handed to him."

"No, that's not it. He wants to prove he doesn't need anyone's help. He cares too much about everyone else's opinion of him. It's all he thinks about."

"All he thinks about is himself."

"Well, maybe we're saying something similar. Maybe caring about the opinions of others that much makes you self-absorbed, in a way. But if that's true, we're also pretty self-absorbed."

"I never said we weren't. We make art. We're not, like, helping people."

"You are helping people. Stop thinking like that. So many people look up to you, love you, would do anything for you. When girls are crying in their rooms, they start listening to your album, jumping up and down on their beds, and they finally feel like they might be okay. That's you. That's what you can do. Okay?"

"Okay. Thanks for saying that."

"Have you ever thought about Cloud9? I've been thinking about it recently, for some reason."

"I literally thought about it the other day. Rhiannon, Claudia, the whole thing. I was so scared. I don't know if I ever told you how scared I was. I thought if I didn't leave, I would never become somebody. *That's* what I was terrified of." She laughs. "Isn't that so sad?"

"I only left because you did. I thought I should be grateful to even be in the group. I felt guilty for wanting more."

Gwen is quiet for a moment. "I mean, they were always telling us how many girls wanted our spots. That's how they get you. That line. They can treat you like shit because there's a replacement right behind you. Someone willing to accept the same treatment you're complaining about and be thrilled about it for a while."

"That's what Rhiannon said when you left. Everyone can be replaced."

"Yeah, well, if I hear Mike say Lauren Li one more time, I swear to God. Or your name. He won't shut up about you." She pauses. "Maybe we should have just made our own group. The two of us, together. Then we would have had each other this whole time, instead of being alone."

"We have had each other this whole time."

She sighs.

"Where are you now?" I ask.

This is one of the questions we throw back and forth. Where are you now? Where are you going next?

"New York."

"Are you really okay?" I have seen the coverage—the untouched, crude photos of her clubbing, wearing heavy eyeliner. Photos of her smoking from a bong on a rocky beach, which she had to respond to with a carefully worded statement. But I'm aware of how distorted, how slanted, this may be.

She takes a long time to respond. "I'm trying to be."

"Who's with you? Mike? Do you have anyone you can talk to?"

"My mom is here."

"Okay. That's good. When we're both back in LA we'll live together, and we'll take care of each other."

"I'm not living at your apartment."

"I meant at your house, obviously."

"When will you be back?"

"Soon. After Oslo. I'll tell Axel you say hi."

"Okay," she says. She doesn't match my excitement about recording albums. She feels trapped in the vocal booth. Onstage, in a rehearsal studio, she can move, and she's not confronted by herself.

"Have you spoken to Tammy?"

"Nope."

"I thought you were going to call her."

"Changed my mind. It'll go straight to voice mail. I know it will. How's the old man?"

"He's not old."

"He's, what, forty?"

"He's, like, thirty. And he's sleeping. But you're changing the subject. Don't do that."

"I'm not," she insists.

"What if she does want to see you? Let's picture it together. You meet up at some hotel. Grab a few drinks. You make your way to a room. You tell her how you really feel. She says, 'Yes, Gwen, I've loved you since I first started dancing for you.' Because that's the truth. You have the best night. You have super hot sex. You're so happy you can't even breathe. You're in love and it's all very beautiful. How does that sound?"

"Or," she says, whispering now, "I call her. It goes to voice mail. She screens my call because she thinks I'm a bitch, which I am. She's found someone else, someone she met on the Sol Sister tour, maybe another dancer with an amazing body, and they're having hot sex instead. She sees me in the tabloids, and she knows she dodged a bullet."

"Maybe you could text her first."

"No."

"What if we write her an email?"

"No, Amber."

"What if I draft it for you?"

"No. I've got to go now. Love you."

A *Rolling Stone* reporter is meeting me at the Luxembourg Gardens. Paris is cloudy today. Sluggish. My car pulls up to a park bench where the reporter waits with his notebook and a brown accordion folder.

He extends his hand. Says, "Nice to meet you, Amber," but I can feel the heaviness of his distaste. It is not nice to meet me. He must miss the early nineties, when the magazine covered Nirvana and Sinéad O'Connor. Now he's assigned to write about Gwen, Savannah, ETA, and me: the Teenage Dreams. To him, we are the fizz in soda, the sugar and chemicals that make junk food so addictive. Not a mirror of the culture, his culture, that created us in the first place.

He's wondering: Why this girl? If you remove the wrappings of her life, she is nothing extraordinary. Pretty enough, some say. Pretty in an unsubtle way. She's in your face. She's all at once. She is, as she will insist in every interview, just an ordinary girl. But America has a way of making its own gods. It revels in it. It lights the bonfire and watches the flames lick the sacrifice. The so-called ordinary girl becomes a walking advertisement for albums and collectible tour merchandise, for tabloids and perfumes. She's immortal and, simultaneously, tragically mortal.

"Shall we stroll around a bit?" the reporter asks, pointing into the park.

I say sure. We walk through titian foliage, past a fountain with a pool covered in a sheet of fallen leaves, abandoned chairs that must be fought over in summertime. One of his first questions is whether I consider myself a sex symbol. This makes me pause. Do I? I don't know. I'm aware that's how I'm perceived, how Lolli intends me to be perceived. But this feels like handing my sexuality over to everyone else.

He sees me wrestling internally, jots down a note. I eventually tell him no, which makes him frown. Then we discuss my album, which is the best part of the interview. I am promoting something—myself, but mostly this album—and must convince this man there is something of interest beneath a greasy surface. But the question about Wes is inevitable. I wait, and it arrives. His tone is familiar, a casual lean, as if we're friends. "I wouldn't be doing my job if I didn't ask. What really happened with Wes Kingston and Gwen Morris?"

I'm careful with my words. I've learned how they can be wielded against me. I say, "I've known them both for forever. I met Gwen back when we were in Cloud9 together, and she's one of my best friends. Wes is a friend. We're all cool. That's it. It's made out to be more than it really is." I pause. "I'm sure you wanted a different answer. Something sexier."

"No," the journalist says. "I wasn't expecting an answer at all."

Sometimes I wish I could swallow my own voice. "All I'll say is this. We're all so young. We're so, so young."

Weeks later, at an awards show after-party, I hear ETA before I see them. Their laughter is a memory of a different time. In the years since we toured together, they haven't changed much. Their stubble is still neatly trimmed, their hair still sticky with gel. But something hungry was scratching inside them before, growing fur and muscle, and now this animal has been drugged.

What differences do they see in me? Maybe my success is visible. My hair is longer, dyed back to my childhood auburn. I have a team rotating around me in elliptical orbit: my makeup artist, my stylist, an assistant named Brianna, my publicist Cara, Dale, Sonny. A whole system of moons. I have a new endorsement deal with Poppy's Patties, which Sonny says will consist of an upcoming Super Bowl commercial and a few print ads. A house I bought for my mom in New Jersey with that money. A tour with my name on it. A public persona, a specific version of myself that radiates beyond the bounds of my body. And maybe they can see the good sex on me, too. I don't mean the skin I'm displaying—good sex is far subtler. It screws a light bulb tight in your core.

A tap on my shoulder. It's Ty, grinning widely. He pulls me toward him. He really is someone to cup in your hands and bring close to your chest.

"God, how long has it been?"

He scratches his head. "I have no idea."

"What's going on with you?"

He shrugs, a little sadly. "Been busy."

"How's Gabe?"

His smile jumps back onto his face. "He's good. He's around here somewhere. Very ticklish tonight."

Just past his shoulder, Wes is pulling light to himself. Every eye is on him. Ty follows my gaze across the room.

"Does he know I'm here?"

Ty nods.

"Should I say hi?"

"I wouldn't. Let him come to you."

"Okay, you're probably right."

And almost as if he's responding to the thoughts flowing in his direction, Wes glances our way. He raises a hand. I raise mine. My body still remembers him; I wonder if it will always be this way between us. Then he turns away, ducking to respond to someone's question, and even though we haven't said a word, I feel as if we've spoken. On me, he probably sees sex, success, the world tour, the bestselling album, everything he didn't believe I would have without him. I'm satisfied by this, but I'm also a little destroyed, because now I know the truth: no matter what I do, who I become, there will always be lack in his eyes.

He reaches for someone behind him, then tugs her into his circle. A woman. She is tall, pale, about his height. She tilts her head, watching him speak to someone else, absorbing their conversation but not participating in it herself. She stands there, waiting. She opens and closes her mouth.

"Who is that?"

Ty hesitates. "Shannon."

He tells me she was in the music video for "My Paradise," the lead single from their fourth album. The boys walk through the Garden of Eden wearing tunics of ivy. Shannon plays the beautiful serpent-woman. Scales spray-painted onto her skin flare in the sunlight. She holds a ripe apple aloft to tempt Wes, and, together, they bite down, taste the soft flesh. Even though he knows she is bad, he wants her anyway. Then she slithers away into the undergrowth, exposing her fangs, and it all ends in corruption.

Now he's taken her hand in front of all these people. He can't stop touching her: his fingertips graze her elbow, her hip. I turn away, because it feels like seeing a place you once lived in decorated differently, with furnishings and rooms that didn't exist when you were there, everything that was once habitual now unfamiliar.

During the *Rolling Stone* cover photo shoot, I finally grasp it: I am inside of my life. This is not a costume I am trying on, this is the skin.

The set is cold. Either the studio we're shooting in has faulty heat, or they've turned it low. Stylists drape me in velvet and silk the color of my name. Highlight my cheekbones, my breasts, the bridge of my nose. Spread tanning lotion and bronzer all over my body. Honey dripping from my lips and fingers, flower petals scattered over the ground like in a honeymoon suite.

I look back over my shoulder at the camera. The world was once blurry, but it isn't anymore. The lens is slowly focusing—then, suddenly, there you are.

ONE MORE CHANCE

Amber Young   Track 7 on *Amber Young*

Produced by
Axel Holm

February 20, 2001

[Verse 1]
Quit calling at night
And start praying
Getting back with me
Might take divine intervention

[Pre-chorus]
Do you know what I need?
Do you know how to please me?

[Chorus]
You got one more chance, baby
Don't take it for granted
If you want to be my man
It's a little complicated
I got demands, I got plans
You need to understand
You get one more chance

[Verse 2]
Come on, make it right
And start changing
It's not that hard
And I have patience

[Chorus]
You got one more chance, baby
Don't take it for granted

If you want to be my man
It's a little complicated
I got demands, I got plans
You need to understand
You get one more chance

[Bridge]
How are you going to impress me?
Show me what you'll do
I don't need nothing fancy
I just want you

[Chorus]
You got one more chance, baby
Don't take it for granted
If you want to be my man
It's a little complicated
I got demands, I got plans
You need to understand
You get one more chance

ABOUT

Genius Annotation   1 contributor

"One More Chance" is the lead single from Amber Young's eponymous second album, *Amber Young*.

WE'RE ALL CAUGHT IN AMBER

Moms hate her, boys love her, and the rest of us love to hate her

ROLLING STONE, 2002

Amber Young licks her lips before she speaks. Now they are wet as sap. Her auburn hair is the color of redwoods, her eyes mahogany brown. She speaks so softly I have to lean in closer to hear her properly. This is what she wants, right? When she looks up at me through thick lashes, I can't help but wonder if the rumors are true. Did these eyes blink and, like a Trojan horse, cause the great city to come crashing down? The city, in this case, being the relationship between Gwen Morris and Wes Kingston?

"I know people think the music is provocative. Especially compared with what Savannah and Gwen are doing. I get that," she says. Her doe eyes are wide. "But I think there's nothing wrong with being confident in myself and my body. I'm not a virgin. I'll say that outright. I'm sorry if that shocks people." She laughs. I think to myself: Who is Amber Young, this girl who so easily declares herself to the world?

Before all that, she's walking at a leisurely pace through Luxembourg Gardens. A bodyguard trails behind her, never allowing her to leave his sight. Young is fresh from an interview and far quieter, more introspective, than expected. As stated, she speaks very softly. It's almost a come-on. And that's not all: she's wearing a corset top and a short skirt, a full slice of belly and bounteous cleavage on display.

"Wearing this makes me feel good," she says. "I don't understand the preoccupation with it. It's, like, I want to express myself through my clothing. If I was in college, I would feel comfortable wearing this."

When asked if she considers herself a sex symbol, she says no.

"That's a lot of responsibility," she explains. "I don't want to be responsible for anyone but myself."

Young was born in Montclair, New Jersey, in 1980, to a stay-at-home mother and an absent father who left the family shortly after she was born. He now lives in Columbus with his second wife and two young sons. Donna Young raised Amber—and elder brother, Greg—as a single parent. To give her daughter something to do while she was at work as a receptionist, Donna signed her up for the school talent show, which is where Amber first caught the eye of an agent.

Amber always wanted to be a singer, and her mother knew right away that her daughter was a star. "It was obvious," Donna Young says. "I did what I could to get her to auditions." Amber's talent intrigued an A&R representative at Siren, who saw her tape and an opportunity to bolster the lineup of their new girl group, Cloud9. "She just had a knockout voice," says Simon Riordan, the Siren rep who discovered her. "I couldn't believe she wasn't trained. I said, okay, let's train her, let's get her in this group. She'll do big things."

Another early member of Cloud9 was Gwen Morris, who left the group to begin her own solo career. After watching Morris's star rise and thinking she was capable of something similar, Young auditioned for reps at Lolli and signed a new contract shortly thereafter. It is reported that the two don't get along well and can't even be in the same room together without a cat fight. What's the problem? Maybe Amber's highly publicized affair with Gwen's boyfriend Wes Kingston. As for the Kingston-shaped elephant in the room, Amber won't say much. "He's a friend," she demurs. But what is that knowing look in her eye? Difficult to say. I ask about the photos of them on the balcony of a hotel room, which sent shock waves through the press. Nothing. She shrugs nonchalantly.

"Look, we're all so young."

Press her further and she gets a little defensive.

"A lot of people say that scandal put me on the map. It's hurtful. I thought my career was over, actually. It could have been over."

But didn't interest in the scandal help her record sales? Doesn't her bad girl image, boosted by the affair, help her record sales, too? "I just hope people can see me as separate from him and all that," she says. "Maybe there is an element that helped me, which was never having an innocent, girl-next-door image like Gwen or Savannah. There's no good girl to shatter because she never existed. I've always been flawed and that's okay." She shrugs again. Her attention shifts to her first headlining tour, promoting her sophomore album, *Amber Young*. Her debut, *In Your Eyes* (1999) was in the teen pop vein that had already been well mined by contemporaries Savannah Sinclair and Gwen Morris, and *Amber Young* has been better received by critics and listeners. But Sinclair can riff, and Morris can dance. What does Amber have to offer?

She picks her nails unhappily. "Of course, I want to be liked," she says. "Everyone does. That's a normal human emotion. But all I can do is put the music out there and hope people listen to it. I'm making music for girls like me, and hopefully they feel inspired or less lonely because of it. I'm making music because I love how it makes me feel. I'm not trying to say it's revelatory."

Patrick Mackey of Lolli Records says they are expecting more from Amber's third album. "Amber knows who she is, which we think will appeal to a lot of young girls who want to have confidence in themselves. At that age, girls are starting to explore and experiment. They need a role model."

What about all the mothers who say Amber's outfits are skimpy, her makeup too heavy, her sexuality oozing and blatantly obvious? She is, frankly, their worst nightmare. When I ask about the parents who are afraid of her influence over their daughters, Amber doesn't appear too concerned. She says, "Teenagers are going to learn about sex one way or another. It's a shame we have little to no sex education in America, so kids are going to the internet—or finding other outlets—for information that should be taught responsibly in a classroom. It is a parent or teacher's job to have that conversation, not mine. I'm a singer."

She tells me that she isn't religious, doesn't drink or do drugs, but she has had experience with boys. She isn't ashamed of that. "Young girls are going to explore their sexuality. It's a given. I'm not doing anything wrong."

In other words, Amber skips right to the chorus, no verses necessary.

After the tour promoting *Amber Young*, Young says she is looking forward to returning to Norway to record her next album with producer and cowriter Axel Holm. She loves the solitude of the country, with its gorgeous vistas and a population largely indifferent to her fame.

"No one knows who I am there. No one cares," she says. "I don't know what's going on. I'm in total isolation when I'm working on a new album. I love it. It's refreshing. It's a pool on a hot summer day. Then, after a while, you miss the heat again."

BRIDGE

2003

2003

Oslo

Winter is melting down the street. The sun is gentle on my face. Soft light bounces off buildings, blooms in windows. This brief time in Oslo has been stillness in my world of movement, even though we're working on a song or two each day—it is almost miraculous how quickly this album is taking shape. I kick a small block of ice back to the studio door. Dale's footsteps are heavy behind me; sometimes, I try to forget he contractually follows me everywhere. He's a stalker I pay to protect me from real stalkers. When we reach the stairs, he carefully watches my descent.

Axel waves when I enter the studio but doesn't turn away from his computer. Since I last saw him, he's grown stubble. It is the color of sand just after the tide has pulled out.

He clicks his mouse aggressively. "How was your stroll?"

"Cold."

"That's because you have no clothes on."

I gesture to my sweater, my bucket hat. "I have clothes on."

"Here," he says, handing me his thick winter coat, full of goose feathers. "This is better."

I slide into a rolling chair. "I don't need it now."

"For next time."

"Fine."

When he spins in his chair, he over-rotates, his foot brushing mine accidentally. Then he hits the space bar, and we listen to the playback together. He frowns and cracks his knuckles, one by one down his right hand, a habit of his. I point to the screen. "I think we need even more texture. Let's double this."

"Yes, good idea."

I return to the booth, pull on my headphones.

His voice in my ear: "Ready?"

"Uh-huh." I close my eyes. "*In the dark of the night / There's no—* Shit. Can I do that again? That was way off. *In the dark of the night / There's no dream / There's no light / Only shame.*"

Through the glass, he gives me a thumbs-up.

"*In the dark of the night / There's no dream / There's no light / Only shame.*"

"That was nice. Just do the 'shame' again. Like this. Bring more emotion into it. *Shame.*"

"*Shame.*"

"Again."

"*Shame.* One more?"

"Just once more, yeah."

"*Shame.*"

He shakes his mouse. "Yeah, that's really nice."

I glance down at the sheet on my music stand. "When did you write this melody again?"

"Sometime last year."

"It doesn't sound like me."

"Why does it not sound like you?"

"It's a little angsty. I don't know. It's more like—it sounds like there's almost a dream pop influence here. Just a little bit."

"You told me you liked that."

"You don't, though."

"Maybe I listened again and changed my mind."

I shake my head. "It just surprises me."

He leans back in his chair. Taps his pencil against his chin. "But why?"

"I don't know. The song is so sad. There's so much longing."

He shrugs. "It's not from my perspective."

"Whose perspective is it from?"

"Someone who is sad."

"So insightful, thank you."

He laughs as I dig through my purse. Then I throw a crumpled piece of paper on his keyboard. One of many scribbled, infant ideas that found their way onto napkins and scraps during my tour, and eventually into emails to him:

You're just pulling up weeds
You're seeing things half-empty
You have too many needs

When he's finished, he looks up at me and runs his fingers over the paper to flatten it. "Yes, I remember this one. Who is this about?"

"I don't know. Maybe it's my mom talking to me. Though everyone will assume it's about Wes, I'm sure. Maybe it is about Wes. Whichever way you want to interpret it. I don't care."

"Is this what he said to you?"

"Now you know why I've sworn off love forever."

"What about your actor?"

I shrug. "That wasn't serious."

Axel rubs his chin. "Do you have more?"

I reach into the bag where I've collected all my scraps, passing a handful over to him. We are both silent as he reads my words and I eagerly hand him more, like a child whose finger paintings are getting put up on the fridge.

"This one really is quite good," he says, holding up the original sticky note. "Let's try this for the second verse." Something inside me wobbles with joy. I return to the vocal booth, and our eyes meet through the glass. We have done this so many times before; we can decipher each other's gestures and tones, and, sometimes, when he's speaking with Yusuf or Oskar in another language, I can understand the essence of what he is saying from his expression alone.

Time compresses in here; I never know where we are in the day. I glance at the clock. Just past midnight. I should have known—Axel comes alive at this time of night; when peals of laughter resound off cold cobblestones, when the sporadic groans of car engines disappear around the bend. As soon as I begin singing the new verse, his eyes narrow. "You and I both know you can control it better," he says. "I want it smooth."

I tear the headphones off my head, raising an eyebrow. "Smooth, huh?"

"What?"

"Sorry. I'm just tired and being weird."

He shakes his head and sighs. "Can you begin again, please?"

My Nokia's messages screen has a little graphic: a note in a bottle, an orange starfish. I press select, text messages, create message.

Let me know u r ok?

Gwen calls back instead: she hates text messaging; says she has no time for it. "Honey," she says, mocking Sonny. "You don't need to check up on me, dear. I'm rehearsing for the halftime show."

"I know. I'm sorry, and I'm becoming your mother."

"Don't say that. She's so much worse. She's terrified I'm out snorting my body weight in mystery substances, even when I'm right in front of her. I think she believes I can clone myself, truly."

What's it like to have a mom leaning over you? "Okay. I'll let you go."

"You'll watch? Skip the football part, of course."

"Of course."

We hang up, still laughing. Axel is hosting dinner in his apartment. It is warm, well lit. Sonny is here again for this trip, and as a result the conversation is lively. When I return to the table, he's telling a story about a famous actor, Tony Wexler. I pull back my chair.

"It's true," he's saying. "I've been with as many actors as Amber has."

Everyone laughs but Axel. He's wearing a maroon turtleneck the same color as my wine.

Yusuf asks, "Who is Tony?"

"He's a movie star. Very dreamy," I say. "Sonny always brags about a love affair they had in the eighties. They were neighbors in New York."

"No, we weren't *neighbors*. I met him because he was the lead in a show I was casting."

Sonny takes another sip of wine. Pointing to Yusuf, he asks, "What's the craziest thing that ever happened to you?"

Yusuf squirms under our collective gaze. He is almost as attention averse as Axel is. "Following Axel around at this club in Stockholm. I went every single night, and eventually I put a demo in his pocket. It felt like a long shot." He grins. "But the next night he comes up to me and says, 'Was this yours?' He had my tape. When I said yes, he asked if we could write together."

"And I'm so glad I did," Axel says, raising his water in his direction. "What about you, Amber?"

I swirl my drink. "This is more surreal than crazy. But on tour, I looked out into the audience. There was a girl on her father's shoulders. She was holding up a sign. It said something very simple: *I love you, Amber*. I never expected to see anything like that. For a long time, the general consensus was that I was terrible. You know, because of the Wes and Gwen thing. Even before all that. I came up after Savannah and Gwen, so everyone said I had no originality."

"There's no such thing as pure originality," Axel says, frowning.

"Nothing comes from nothing. All we can do is try to create with the same ingredients we all have."

After dinner, I excuse myself to use the bathroom. I notice Axel all around me: a hairbrush left on the side of the sink, threaded with golden strands. A stack of music zines above the toilet. A single earring left abandoned on a shelf, the brass rubbed down to silver in spots. No other remnant of whoever it belonged to. Curious, I open the door to his bedroom. Even though the floor has been swept, there is a stray sock. Everything else has been piled onto his bed. Heavy wool sweaters, checkered boxers, old paperbacks, a cat scratcher. I sink deeper and deeper into him, running my hands along the fabrics, the papers, the life. His record player is still spinning, the speakers turned down low. A Billie Holiday album sleeve lies on the floor beside it.

"What are you doing?" Axel leans against the doorframe.

I startle, embarrassed. "Looking at your records."

"You can turn it up," he says, nodding to the player. "I was listening to something before you all arrived."

I lift the tonearm so it catches on the first groove. Twist the dial. Music seeps into the air around us. "I'm a Fool to Want You."

He takes a step forward into the room, I back up against the bed.

"This was fun," I say. "You're a good cook. I can't cook at all, you know. I have most of my meals in hotels, and I can't do anything myself—" I cut myself off. Suddenly unsure. Why did I come here?

"It's strange." He smiles to himself and gets down on his knees before his records. His fingers delicately coax them from their sleeves, holding them by their edges. "I have artists coming and going so often. I don't usually host dinners."

"So, you're saying I'm special."

"I don't choose favorites, Amber. You know this."

"You do, you're just too nice to tell me who it is." He responds with a small smile, which must mean I'm right. "Who else do you work with, again?"

"Gwen, of course. We're good friends. I don't believe I'm doing anything for her next album, though. Change in direction."

"She loves R&B. I think she wants to experiment with her sound. Try new things."

He nods. "Pop has stolen much from R&B, you know. Well, pop borrows from everything, really. It's the scavenger of music. We must be honest about that." He pauses for a moment. "Who else? Hmm. ETA, obviously. I just did a song for Alex's solo record. Chloe Woods. Lauren Li. Carly Ramona. She's very talented." He names artists as I lie back on his bed, in between all his things, staring up at the curling paint on his ceiling. He continues shuffling through his records. He holds one up, but I can't see what it is.

"Oh, this is good. I want to play this one for you," he says. He stops the spin of Billie Holiday, humming a melody, always filling silences. I sing a few absent-minded lyrics on top of it.

He stills. "What was that?"

"Huh?"

"Do that again."

He hums his little melody and I continue to ad-lib. His eyes are wide. "Don't stop."

He searches for something in a drawer, then holds his old tape recorder up to my lips, watching intently as I sing, as the recorder tucks the sound into itself.

"Damn, that's pretty good. Don't you think?"

I tell him it is. He asks how early I can get to the studio.

I smile. "Do we have to sleep?"

He runs his hands through his hair. "Yes, we should sleep. You should, at least. But we'll get up first thing, and we'll start the session with this." He hums the melody again. "That's nice. I love it."

His face looks like all the clouds have parted. We are both electrified, giddy. I can't believe he lives his life this way: walking along, then tripping on an edge of brilliance.

"We should go, shouldn't we? Back to everyone else?"

"We probably should," he agrees. He opens the door for me, watches me pass, then turns the record back on, Billie Holiday's voice trickling into the hallway.

"—Amber about Wes," Sonny is saying from the kitchen.

As we turn the corner, everyone looks at their laps.

"What about Wes?" I ask, pulling back my chair.

Sonny opens and closes his mouth. Oskar's eyes are wide. Yusuf pushes food around his plate.

"What about him, Sonny?"

Sonny digs into his scalp, like a dog with a flea. Eventually his hand falls. "He got married to his girlfriend in Vegas, honey. That's what I read. But it might be a load of shit. It might not be true."

I reach for a knife. A swipe through supple butter. I spread it across a slice of bread. It's been so long since I've had bread and after a moment of enjoying the pillowy feel of it on my tongue, I swallow. "What a dumbass."

Sonny laughs, but he grabs the slice from my plate, taking a bite so I can't have the rest. "See?" he says, the food spinning inside his mouth. "She doesn't care. What did I tell you all?"

After the plates are cleared, I smoke a cigarette on the curb. When I feel warmth radiating from another body, I turn to find Axel beside me. His tabby cat races around a trash can, a dead mouse dangling from its jaws. The limp body falls. The cat scoops it up again.

"I'm glad you're wearing my coat."

When he says this, I huddle deeper into it.

"Are you upset?" he continues. "I thought you must be. Wes talked about you often, so I know he cared for you."

"That's nice of you to say. I really am fine, though. I'm not surprised. It's okay, really. We weren't right for each other in so many ways."

"Why is that?"

"I was going through a hard time. I was really—I don't know what was going on with me. But that's when you know if a relationship is right or not. If it can withstand turbulence. So, it's fine. Shitty, but fine." He's silent, so I explain further. "He was embarrassed by me."

"Embarrassed?"

"Maybe embarrassed isn't the exact word. I don't know if you, like, know this or not, but back in America I'm not considered very family friendly. Once the press started covering me a certain way, he couldn't really get over it."

He takes the cigarette from my mouth, which makes me smile. He flicks ash from it and sparks spill onto the street. His brow is furrowed. "That's the most ridiculous thing I've ever heard."

"It's okay. Now the space he took up is full of all this stuff, all these ideas I'm excited about."

"That's good. You're learning about yourself."

"Yeah, I am." I turn to face him. "What about you?"

He looks uncomfortable. He always is when he's asked about himself. "I'll tell you some other time."

I'm aching to press further. Who are you? Who are the people you have loved? Who has loved you? A familiar warmth has settled in my stomach. My first impulse is to let it expand, my second is to smother it. All I know is I can be quiet with him. Everything is quiet. The air is pointy with cold, and the sky is a deep blue, and I realize night cannot be pure darkness because it's always growing lighter in increments, as morning inches closer. The city is still. Beside me, he shifts, and maybe he's damming himself up, too.

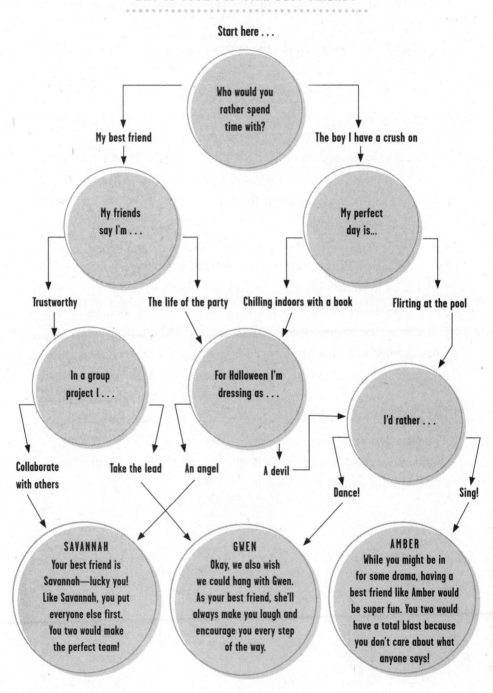

2003

Oslo

In the windows of Oslo, families are gathered around tables. A mother leans close to kiss her child's forehead in bed. A group of teenagers pass a bottle around. A couple is having sex, each thrust and exhalation fogging up their window. Night sounds. Humanity. Each time I am here, I remember life can be soft.

Axel unlocks the door to his control room. The overhead lights flicker on. The computer stirs when he touches it.

I point to the keyboard wedged in the corner of the room. "Play me something."

"Okay. But only if you sing."

I sit down beside him, forcing him to scoot over. Our thighs brush against each other. Our knees. "How about 'The One I Want'?"

He snorts.

"You wrote it, didn't you?"

"Fine." He holds his fingers over the keys. Slowly, he begins to play. I know every word, all of Wes's parts. It has been stuck in my head— our collective heads—for years.

When I saw you again
I tried to forget
But your image was stamped on me
An imprint

It's been years, babe
I still feel regret
I can't move on
Time without you is wasted

It's obvious to me
Should be obvious to you
You're the one I want
What more can I do?
Girl, I'll plead
I'll be your fool

It's obvious to me
Should be obvious to you
You're the one I want
What more can I do?
Girl, I'll plead
I'll be your fool

Make me your jester
Make me your king
I'll do anything

It's obvious to me
Should be obvious to you
You're the one I want
What more can I do?
Girl, I'll plead

I'll be your fool
You're the one that I want
What more do I have to do?

He lifts his hands. The keys slowly rise, dead fish in water.

"I wish I could play."

"You can always learn."

I pick at my nail. "Maybe. Then people might respect me more. If I could play an instrument, you know?"

He leans his elbow on the keys and turns to me. "I didn't play any instruments before I began producing. I met a band at a club one night and somehow convinced them to let me produce and mix for them. I saved up all my money for equipment and taught myself how to use Logic on my father's computer. It was very mediocre stuff at first. Yusuf can play seven or eight instruments, so he's taught me a bit, but I wish I had more formal study. Still, you already have your instrument, Amber. It's built-in, and the rest of us can't ever use it." He points to my throat.

I run my hand along it, flushing.

"How do you think of this album? Your third album."

"The execs at Lolli want to build on my success."

He shakes his head. "No, what do you want it to sound like? You. The artist."

The artist. Most of the time, I don't dare to consider myself one. Don't artists have ink-stained fingers? They bend over something significant, a work that will one day hang in a museum. They sing sweeping, intense ballads like Savannah does.

"Because I think," he continues, noting my hesitation, "we need to know what we are trying to say."

"Is it strange that I just have a color in mind? I have a color. A feeling. It's what my life feels like right now."

"What is it?"

"It's golden. It's like everything is golden. I'll throw out more words. Maybe a sunrise. Dew. Nectar. Honey. Desire. Lust. Stuff like that."

"I see what you mean."

"The first track should be an intro. Super choral. We have the main vocal. Backgrounds. It's minimal and gorgeous, like you're in a medieval church. And then there's a swell, and it all crashes. We immediately come in with 'Pain,' so that illusion of, I don't know—chastity, maybe? Morality? Whatever it is, we shatter it right off the bat. That's what I want."

"That's nice. I like that idea. Very much."

We continue talking, a conversation like windshield wipers in a downpour. Me to him to me. "No one gets where they are alone," he is saying. My eyes are weighed down by his voice. "I just want to help artists see who they yearn to be, to help them become it."

Who do I yearn to be, Axel? I know you can see, and maybe now I can see. I want more again. Just before I fall asleep, I realize this is what Axel and Gwen have in common: they see the potential burning in other people, and they can free it, like a thumb striking a lighter.

We work on the intro together for a few hours, then decide to take a walk at first light. He guides me to an outdoor sculpture museum in Frogner Park. Granite statues cast long shadows. I stare at them, and they stare back: naked women transforming into trees, a mother carrying two children on her back. There is a crunch underfoot. Frost spikes between patches of soil. We stand below an obelisk of human bodies, crushed together like the contours of a brain. Nearby, an old, naked woman, lying in the lap of a man with a long beard. She covers her body with her hands. He cups her neck, her waist. I feel the years held between them.

"I like this one," I say, pointing to it.

"I do, too." Axel stands beside me, his face tilted up toward the couple. "A former girlfriend called them Magnus and Maud. She liked to name the statues."

"I thought your partner was your work. That's what you always say."

He turns back to the pathway, hands in his pockets. "My partner is my work. According to her, that was the problem in the end."

Axel's stride is so much longer than mine; a cramp develops in my side as I keep pace with him. "I'm sorry, Axel, but you have to tell me more than that."

"She is back in Stockholm. When I moved the studio to Oslo, she came with me. She was lonely here, but I had to take care of my father. I wanted to make music. All her friends and family were in Sweden. She was unhappy, so it ended. In truth, I didn't expand my life so she could find a place in it. That was my mistake."

I shake a little as I ask, "Do you still love her?"

He laughs. "I don't think so, no. Do you still love your actor? Mr. Land?"

I laugh, too. "No. That was nothing."

"It does not have to be nothing."

He is right. It wasn't nothing. No experience can be. "I do feel like it's very tied to emotion," I say. "Sex is, I mean. At least it is for me. Women should have sex whenever they want. That's important. Stop me if I'm rambling. But, for me, it is very emotional, and I can't help but feel something for that person in that moment, and hope they feel something for me. After a while, they know what you like, they can turn you inside out, and sometimes it feels like they can read your mind. What feels good, what doesn't. Maybe this is too much information or something, but do you know the moment when you're having sex and you're just repeating 'I love you' to each other over and over? That's the best." I look up at him and I know my face is red. "Sorry."

His hands are deep in his coat pockets. "No, no," he says, shuffling in place. "You're right. I do find—I have been thinking about what you said on Venice Beach. You said something to the effect of, 'Music feels like falling in love with someone.' I do think that's true."

I want to tell him I've changed my mind. Now music feels like sex. When we're making it, we listen to each other, we adjust and experiment, and then after—what elation. "You're admitting I'm right about something, Axel?"

He looks puzzled. "Do I not do that?"

"Never," I say, and we walk on. The rest of the world wakes, casts us in light. A few joggers pass us. I can see the moment the recognition hits—their eyes widen, all their concentration collapses. They look back at me over their shoulders. I probably shouldn't have left Dale behind at the studio, but I wanted to fold myself away with Axel, just for a little while. And people are far more reserved here, even unimpressed. There is always a smattering of fans outside the hotel and the studio, but rarely does anyone approach me on the street.

"How's your dad?" I ask Axel. The joggers' footsteps have faded in the distance, and we are alone again.

"He's . . ." His hand trails through the air. "He knows he's dying, and that frustrates him deeply. He has taken to reading all the books he never could. He's convinced he won't finish them all in time, so he spends all day with them. In this way, he is able to travel and live many lives in a short span of time. It's a comfort. I think when I arrive, he is disappointed because he has to pull himself away from whatever story he is absorbed in. His real life is unsettling to face. We are very alike, though. I think he secretly appreciates it when I'm there. He just never says so. We are like this." He creates two parallel lines with his hands. "I do think he's a little sick of me. And I have trouble forgetting my childhood, how he treated me then."

"How do you take care of someone you resent?"

He shakes his head. "I just take my ego out of it."

"As if that's so easy."

He shrugs. "It is for me. I feel I can— How do I explain this? I feel I can step back from myself, in a way. There are impulses I have, but I just don't follow them anymore."

I stare at him in astonishment. I wish I could take his brain in my hands and rummage through it. "Is that why you don't drink?"

"No."

"What do you mean?"

"I think parents can affect us without intending to. By being bad examples, they end up helping us. They show us what not to do. Eventually,

I saw my father in myself, and that's what I was most afraid of. I saw how he lived with no purpose, and I didn't want to live that way. I was out all night, every night in Stockholm, and I was becoming like him." He laughs to himself, then glances at me. "I can't allow myself anything. Because in here"—he points to his head—"it's absolute. If I have a little, I want it all."

"Maybe I'm the same way." For a while, the only sound is the crunch of our shoes. "Is he getting better?"

Axel shakes his head.

"When do you go to him?"

He shrugs. "When I can. Usually late morning or early afternoon, around this time."

"So, when do you sleep?"

He watches a squirrel scramble up a thick trunk. "When do *you* sleep?"

"Hardly ever. It has been nonstop for me. For six years."

He scratches his head. "Do you think you'll take a break after this next album?"

I shake my head. "Sonny wants to do another tour. A national leg, then a European one. Maybe Australia. I've never been to Australia." I pause. "But I can't sleep most nights anyway. I just lie there. I think about all the things I wish were different."

"What do you wish were different?"

"Lots of things. The way my mind works. The way people see me. My mom."

"And how is she doing?"

How is she doing? Now she lives in a house on a cul-de-sac, the kind of house we used to pass by, saying, "Those people have more money than God." She gets her hair dyed professionally. She is in a book club. I have given her the kind of life she once watched from her desk, thumbing through appointment schedules.

"She's fine. We aren't close."

He changes direction, sensing I don't want to talk about her. "Amber, you don't have to lie in bed and wish things were different. There is something inside you—you have it, whatever it is. That's why you're an artist. I've said this before, but I don't think you see yourself very clearly." His eyebrows knit together. "Your mind is a wonderful, complex place. It's not difficult to see."

Blood rushes into my cheeks. He is looking at a statue, running his hand along its cheek, so slowly, as if he might bring it to life.

Softly, he asks, "Will you come with me today?"

"Where?"

He lifts his hand off the stone, turning back to me. "To the hospital. He'll appreciate meeting someone new."

The nurse knows who I am. That knowledge is held between us, but she decides to treat me like a stranger, even asking for my name so she can write it down on the guest log. When I say it, her mouth twitches with the confirmation.

To Axel: "He's up."

We follow her through sleek white hallways, softened by large windows and sunlight. Axel reaches to open the door, and this action is so slow, almost suspended, I wonder if he's delaying it. Or maybe this is just how he moves, and I've never taken the time to notice— methodically, every moment relished instead of sped through.

His father, Per, is in a cot with a tray of food in front of him. He's grimacing as he picks at his plate with a fork, the same expression I've seen so often on Axel's face. He glances up. This is the first person I've ever seen who is clearly going to die. His face has a yellow cast with deep-blue grooves under his eyes, and his limbs are thin and feeble.

Per asks Axel a question in Norwegian, and Axel answers with my name. Then, in English, he says, "A friend."

Axel sits on the side of his father's bed, and I take the chair. They speak softly back and forth until Axel sighs, switching to English to include me.

"We are working on Amber's third album," he says.

Per's eyes narrow, and he turns to me. "And do you like it? Working with Axel?"

"Oh, I—he's very . . ." I pause, smiling to myself. "He's a bit of an asshole."

Per bursts out laughing, setting down his cup of chocolate pudding.

"But very brilliant," I place my hand on Axel's arm, then immediately remove it. "Most people say he's a genius."

Per says something else in Norwegian, which makes Axel roll his eyes.

"What was that?" I ask.

"He says I must have paid you to say this."

I lean forward in my chair and meet Per's gray eyes, a shade darker than Axel's. "No, really. He is. Not the kind who expects to be treated differently because of it. Axel is very humble, so he probably hates that I'm saying this to you right now." I turn to Axel, and his face is red. "Look at you! You are. You're hating this so much."

Axel scratches behind his ear. "I'm not hating it so much, strangely. You can go on."

We exchange a look, caught by his father. Per observes us silently, then says, "You are very different today, Axel."

I turn to Per. "Is he?"

"He usually comes in asking all these dull questions. Am I okay, do I have water, do I have a book, do I need the doctor? Today he is laughing."

I choose to ignore this, because if I touch it, I know the surface will be hot. "What are you reading?" I ask Per. He holds up a thick tome I can't understand the name of, but I nod as if I can.

"Do you read?" he asks.

"Surprisingly, yes, I do know how to read. It shocks a lot of people."

Axel smiles.

I continue, "Mostly I read the books that Oprah picks. Do you know Oprah?"

Per nods. He doesn't say anything else, but he reaches over and presses a button. Axel helps him sit up.

"He needs to use the bathroom," he explains.

The attending nurse takes Per's other arm, and together they pull him out of bed. Now I can see how frail he really is. And I can see that he is deeply embarrassed to need help in this way. The flaps of his hospital gown are loose, so I turn away until he's in the bathroom with the nurse.

Axel sighs and sits on the bed. "Thank you for coming with me. He's very happy you're here. He doesn't get to meet many of my friends."

"I really like him. He reminds me of you."

"He does?"

"Yeah. I think it's his eyes. There's so much that he's not saying, but you can see how quickly he's thinking. It's like all these options get discarded before he finally chooses something."

Axel makes a thoughtful sound. "He is right, though."

"About what?"

"I am different today."

Per wants privacy for his exercises, so I pace around the hospital lounge. I lift my cell phone to my ear. It rings for a long time, and then I get her answering machine. "Hi, Mom. I'm in Oslo now. I don't know if I told you that. I was thinking it would be nice to see each other when I'm back in New York. Let me know. Bye."

There's someone behind me—a solidity that pulls at my attention. The nurse. Her smile is shy. I know what she's going to ask before she does. Of course, I say, of course I'll sign something. She hands me a sheet of paper and I write, *Thank you for your work here. Per is lucky to have you. Love, Amber,* then hand it back to her, and it's one of those instances in life where there are probably more words to say, but I don't know her, and she doesn't know me, so we don't say them.

We slip inside the club. Axel says, "I'm afraid you might be too famous for this now."

I agree. We had to sneak out through a service door of my hotel and into a waiting car to get here. As a disguise, I'm wearing a platinum wig. He folds a stray hair back into the cap, biting his tongue as he concentrates.

"Okay. Now I would have no idea."

He greets a bouncer he knows, and we're led down a flight of stairs into a sticky little club that looks like a catacomb, with exposed crumbling brick, a decorative skull on every wall. The strobe lights are a violent shade of red. "Wait here," Axel says, and then he is consumed by the crowd. My heartbeat quickens. Sweat swipes against me, a continual baptism by other bodies.

I am thrilled by the total anonymity, by the looseness of movement, by all these swollen lips that have been kissed and kissed until they had to come up for air. Here I am no one, here I could be anyone.

Axel brushes my shoulder. He is taller than most people in the crowd, his head a submarine scope above water. He points to an alcove, where we can stand and observe. Neither of us is drinking. No gauze to cover up embarrassment. Still, I want to dance—and why not? I'm in Oslo for only two weeks, then I'm gone, off recording with different producers in Los Angeles, then on a brief tour leg in South America, then, then, then, a litany of then, and in between it all, maybe a single breath. A night like this. I pull on his arm, leading him deeper into the crowd.

He groans. "Amber."

"Please?"

The strobe lights are jumping off his face, like rain hitting a puddle. He takes a few steps toward me to adjust my wig. The music shifts, and so do his eyes. I see that it's caught him.

"What are they saying?" I yell.

"What?"

"What's the song saying?"

He listens to the rapid Norwegian, then laughs. "I'm not sure I should tell you." But he leans close anyway, his breath warm against my neck. *"Do you want to get fucked? I could really use a fuck."*

"Nice. Never thought I'd hear something like that come out of your mouth."

He's pushed into me by a stranger and grabs one of my shoulders to steady himself. Now that we've touched so casually, we both loosen up a bit. His hand finds mine, and he spins me. One of our new songs, "Lying to Myself Under U," sweeps across the floor. The production is pristine—synths, a kick drum, all kinds of subtleties that are sugary to the ear and take days for him to mix. The beat accelerates, becomes breathy. It builds and builds upon itself, just as he intended it. How will it end?

"It's beautiful," I shout.

"What?"

I stretch up to scream in his ear. "It sounds really beautiful."

He smiles, and his face is a blur of flame. I'm tempted to run my fingers through it, just to see if I'll get burned. When did I begin restricting myself? Don't lean into him. Pull yourself back. When did a new color get dragged into the one I had always known with him? Now I can't help but wonder if he's slow and deliberate with women. If he's thoughtful. Precise. This is how I imagine he would be. Can he see these thoughts pass over my face, along with the light?

Sonny is in the studio with a camcorder. He pans in on Axel. "Say hello!"

Axel glances over his shoulder. "What is this for?"

"Her video album DVD."

"Hello," Axel says. A lackluster wave. "Amber, how can I work with this here?"

"Give Sonny five minutes. He'll just film me singing in the booth. Can you tell me I'm doing a very good job, so my fans don't think you're mean to me?"

He rolls his eyes, but there's light in them. In the footage, he is mostly curled into his hoodie, radiating barbs of exasperation.

At one point, I hoist the camcorder away from Sonny. "Here we have my producer, Axel Holm. He's lovely to work with. Axel likes to say he can beat me in chess, but I kicked his ass last night."

He shakes his head, tucking away his smile before I can capture it.

Gwen on the phone. Her eager, rapid breath. I balance my cell between my ear and shoulder. "I need to take this," I mouth to Axel.

I'm surprised when he nods. His head is bent close to Oskar's and they are focused on the screen in front of them. A young producer I haven't met before is watching them intently, eagerly, his face blossoming with peach fuzz.

I push open the door. On the other end, I realize Gwen is crying. I immediately think the worst. "Gwen, slow down, what's wrong?"

Muffled, scraping sounds. Something sucked up. "I emailed her."

"Are you okay? You sound awful. What if you came here, to Oslo? We could—"

That's when I understand: she's crying with happiness.

She tells me she met Tammy at the Beverly Hills Hotel. She was waiting for a long time, stirring her drink. Then she looked up. There she was, Tammy, pushing the doors open to welcome streaming sunlight. They sat at the bar and talked. Only pleasantries at first, then they dug in. They decided to go for a drive together, somewhere secluded. They drove all the way out to Joshua Tree while the sun beat down. Tammy was concerned; she had seen all the unflattering tabloid photos, the allegations of hard drug use. Gwen told her it was all exaggerated. Sure, there was cocaine and Adderall, a few others. Just to try it. Just to feel.

They held hands for the first time in open space, among the alien rocks, the strange scrub. Weaving their fingers together felt like an exhalation. Gwen turned to her, this person she had leaned on for years, this eye in a storm of press and judgment and endless traveling, this raft in a wide ocean of currents. Tammy said it was so painful being close to her. Gwen understood. She knows she is a hard person to love.

She can be distant, ambitious, cold. She hid inside herself after the contracts SMG put in front of her, after they told her it could all be over, just like that. She was sixteen years old. But maybe we can break the promises we make at sixteen. Maybe we should. She wants to shed that skin, to shed the hours in salon chairs, dyeing her hair that signature pink. Shed the need to accept only perfection from herself. The need to mold her own body until it never tires. What does it matter? Even after all her discipline, she damaged her vocal cords on tour. There was a quick operation, only three days of rest before she forced herself to endure it. That's when her memories blur, when stages and cities begin to overlap. Somewhere she fired Tammy. Somewhere she started to die and die and die in her own dreams. The only engine moving her forward is her fans, who stand in queues for hours, waiting to meet her. Do they love her? She wondered this years ago, on the beach. If they do, truly, wouldn't they want joy for her? If they knew, wouldn't they want this for her? She hopes they do. Wants to believe they do.

And now? What now? I bite my lip, waiting for her to tell me.

"I'm so happy," she says. "I've never been so happy."

I lean my head against the wall, crying and smiling all at once. Because even after all we've accomplished, all we hope to still accomplish, love is the bedrock of all our want. We can't build anything steady without it.

"Obviously, you have to keep this quiet."

"I will." I'm smiling so hard my jaw starts to tighten, jumping up and down so forcefully that Axel sticks his head out of the studio. He silently mouths, "Are you okay?" Once I nod, he vanishes.

"What happened after?" I ask.

"We camped out in Joshua Tree, my first vacation in, like, three years. I told Mike I was off the grid. He flipped. Said my career was over. Whatever. Tammy and I just talked for hours, we hiked a bit, we had a ton of sex." Here, I gasp. She ignores this, since she knows I'll ask for more detail. "I woke up each morning and thought, This can't be my life. How is this mine? You know?"

"Oh my god."

"Was this how it felt?" Gwen asks. "With Wes?"

From the slant in the doorway, I can see only the top of Axel's head. The rest of him is hidden behind his chair. He's nodding along to something I can't hear.

"Maybe at first. But I don't think so, no. I don't think it could even compare."

It is my final night in Oslo and we are at Axel's favorite restaurant. It feels like something he would like—a local spot, very understated. Still, a woman starts screaming and weeping when she sees me, and after I sign her napkin, a few others venture over to our table and ask for photos or autographs. Eventually Sonny starts saying no for me, so we can eat.

"It's a strange tradition you have, Axel," Pat says, snapping the shell of a king crab. "Why do you listen to the songs live?"

Axel gently places the tail of a shrimp on his plate. "I like to see the reaction. The expressions, the movement."

"He likes to boost his own ego," I say.

"Ha ha," he says. "Very funny, Amber."

"Am I wrong?"

Plates are lifted, set down. I feel raised and lowered alongside them. The wine has made everything light. The world trembles. Pat and Sonny are both rosy-cheeked, their laughter carrying excessive force. I watch them closely: these men who have helped and hurt me in equal measure. They have both benefited from my career, but we all pretend it's the other way around. There are questions I don't know how to answer. There are questions I haven't thought to ask yet. Small moments I collect in my pocket—times Sonny has told me no, told me I was fat, stupid, a little girl who knows nothing. Times he steered me whichever way he felt was best. Times he was compassionate: his offer to stay in his home during the media storm, and after, in Reno.

Our plates are cleared. Sonny spills wine on his lap and excuses himself to clean his shirt. Pat says he needs to give Lyle a call. I should have known what I would do next; I know my own patterns, the pull toward disorder. I ask the table if anyone wants a smoke. Oskar, as I predicted, says no. Yusuf shakes his head, says he should get home to his wife. Axel stands and wipes crumbs off his lap. Sure, he says. He follows me outside, carrying my coat because I've forgotten it.

We find a bench to sit on. I pass him the lighter and our eyes meet over the flame.

"How do you feel?" he asks.

"I feel like this is the best work I've ever done."

"You're right."

"Thank you."

"I'm sorry if I'm hard on you. I only am because I know you're good enough. I know what you can do. If it ever comes across . . ." He shakes his head. "Anyway, you know what I'm trying to say."

The space between us is suddenly a canyon. I lean on his shoulder for warmth. Heat circulates through us. Our breath collides in midair, swirls together, draws apart.

I hesitate. The friendship also hovers between us. I don't dare to breathe for a few moments. Everything is quiet, other than the sound of his heart and his breath, heavy, almost tantalizingly slow, as if it might stop at any moment.

He hands me the cigarette, just a stub now.

"If you're cold, we can go to my apartment. It's just there."

"Okay."

When we arrive, I place my jacket neatly on the back of his kitchen chair and leave my shoes at the door next to his. He throws his keys on the table, spins around. "I'll put on some music, yes?"

"Sure," I say softly. Where did my voice go? All my nerve is gone.

Music pumps through his speakers. Bossa nova. The undercurrent of acoustic guitar, strings lightly plucked. Axel sits on his couch, picks up his own guitar and begins tuning it, running his hand along the wood affectionately, as if it were flesh. "Do you want to play?" He pats the seat beside him and hands me the instrument, which is lighter than I expect. His thumb accidentally brushes mine during the exchange.

"This is a C," he says, touching the chord. It shudders, then stills. "Your first finger should be here, on the second string. Second finger, here. Third you must stretch up here. Up, up. There." His hands maneuver mine with a touch so light it makes me grit my teeth. The thrum vibrates throughout the room.

Suddenly I want to lie down very badly.

"Are you okay?" he asks, watching me.

"Maybe a glass of water?"

"Yes. I'll bring it to you."

I settle on his bed. His smell is everywhere—in the pillows, the sheets. I can't stand it.

"Here." He places the glass in my hands. "Drink." He tilts it up, watching with approval as I swallow. I place the glass back on his bedside table and dry my lips with my sleeve. His face is so close to mine. The silence grows in pressure, the way an ocean does the farther down you swim.

"Can you just kiss me?" I'm shameless, hot all over. We stare at each other for a few moments. His eyes are wide. Slowly, so slowly, he leans forward. Then his lips on mine, soft and warm. I'm trembling from the relief. I open my mouth and press into him. He moans slightly, almost absentmindedly. Then he pulls back, shaking his head.

"I'm sorry."

I open my eyes. "What are you sorry for?"

"I don't know. You've had a good amount to drink. I wanted to, I want to take care of you. This wasn't my intention when I brought you here."

"Axel, I haven't had a lot to drink. I was a little tipsy at the restaurant, maybe, but now I'm very clearheaded."

His eyes scan my face. He finds some solution in it. "Amber, I can't."

"Can't," I repeat, aware how cracked my voice sounds, how wrecked.

He seems like he might say something else, but he just nods.

"But why can't you?"

He looks at me for a long time. Then he sighs. He says something to himself in another language, and I'll never know what it is. "I think this might mean something different to each of us. We work together. What will it say?"

I shake my head. "It's not, like, inappropriate, Axel. You're not my boss."

"You're younger than me."

"I've been with someone older than you."

He stares at the ceiling, tapping his foot against the wood floor. His eyes are shiny.

"No, you're right. You're right. I'm sorry."

"I thought I'm never right," he says softly.

"In this case. I should go."

"No, don't do that. It's late. Stay here," he insists. "You can have the bed. I'll sleep on the floor."

"It's okay. We can share the bed."

So he climbs in beside me, leaving a courteous foot of space between us, an absence I can feel. His cat leaps up onto his chest, riding his breaths, and starts kneading him. A pocket of night opens and my thoughts fill it like loose change. I am reckless. Impulsive. Willing to rip through a friendship for a one-sided attraction. I think of something I said to Wes years ago: *I wonder if two people can really be happy if there's no one else to see it.* Now I know they can. I know because I have felt it; I've been truly happy alone in the studio with Axel. I had assumed these moments between us were extraordinary, but now I know this is just his life. My miracles are his mundanity.

I twist around to stare at the skyline of his face. The dark-blond hair curling around his ears. Once I know he's asleep, I cry quietly, so

I won't wake him. Beside me: his even breathing, his warmth a whole space away. His cat's pitiless yellow eyes watching me in the dark.

He's up and making coffee in the morning. A mug steams on the bedside table, two packets of sugar, a cup of cream if I want it.

"How do you feel?" he asks.

"Awful."

He laughs nervously. "Do you need food? Here." He hands me a slice of sourdough bread.

I start ripping off pieces. "What time is it?"

"Your flight leaves in two hours. Sonny called and said they have checked out of the hotel for you. Don't worry—I told them you are okay. A car is going to come get you."

He's ignoring what happened last night as a favor to me. I swirl sugar into my mug with a spoon, then glance at his cup. "You drink your coffee black?"

"Yes."

I smile. "That's not surprising. You liked it immediately, didn't you?"

"No, I actually had to force myself. It took many years."

Outside, a car waits to take me back to Los Angeles. The exhaust hovers in the street. Axel hands me my coat. Our fingers touch, and I wish I could curl my hand inside his palm.

"I'll see you soon."

He nods, leaning down to pet his cat. "Yes. I'll see you soon."

PAIN

Amber Young   Track 2 on *Honey*

Produced by
Oskar Aasland & Axel Holm

August 18, 2003

[Verse 1]
You weren't the one for him
You hurt to be with
Swallow the truth
Can't you see the passing time?
Can't you let him go, cut him loose?

[Chorus]
But what do I do, what do I do
With all this pain?
I only have myself to blame
In the dark of the night
There's no dream, there's no light
Only shame

[Verse 2]
You're just pulling up weeds
You're seeing things half-empty
You have too many needs
Can't you just collect yourself?
Can't you just forget?

[Chorus]
But what do I do, what do I do
With all this pain?
I only have myself to blame
In the dark of the night

There's no dream, there's no light
Only shame

[Bridge]
His touch, his skin
I'm imagining the relief
Will he come back or
Will he finally leave me be?

[Chorus]
What do I do, what do I do
With all this pain?
I only have myself to blame
In the dark of the night
There's no dream, there's no light
Only shame

[Chorus]
What do I do, what do I do
With all this pain?
I only have myself to blame
In the dark of the night
There's no dream, there's no light
Only this pain

ABOUT

Genius Annotation   **5 contributors**

What have the artists said about the song?
"I had all these emotions, and I had no idea what to do with them. There was
a point where I was too much for everyone to deal with. I think a lot of people
can probably relate to that. I really see the verses as in conversation with
the chorus, a sort of back-and-forth between me and my inner monologue."
                                        —MTV's *Total Request Live*, 2003

Subject: It's been a long time
From: peaceluvgrrl81@yahoo.com
Date: 4/3/03 3:05 AM
To: tammyd@aol.com

Tamara—I remember one night after a show. We had to sleep on the bus, and I brought you back to my bunk because I wanted to show you something. What was it? It might have been my Tamagotchi. I was two years late to Tamagotchis. I wanted my Tamagotchi to hook up with yours, but it turned out you didn't have one. Anyway, you came, and you told me you had noticed how tired I was lately. You were the only person (other than Amber) who asked if I was okay during that entire tour. You saw that I was closed off. I never spoke. I shut down after every show. It made you think I hated you all. But I didn't hate you, I was just afraid.

I know the whole thing with Wes hurt you. It hurt me, too. I tried lying and it didn't feel good, even if it brought me attention. Back then, all I wanted was to be successful. When Mike took my arm and pinned me against the wall and said, "You think I don't know what's going on? You think I'm an idiot?," I truly believed he would take it all away. But what is success worth if you are alone?

It's funny how we all thought progress was made in the '90s. Sometimes I wonder if decades are tides, and the sand is men like Mike who get all stirred up and worried they won't matter anymore. The water pulls back, and it all begins again. When Mike told me I had to take you off the tour or I would lose everything, my mind went in all directions. You know how it does that.

I'm so sorry. I was wrong. I miss you so much. Are you in LA?
G

CHORUS (REPRISE)

2003

2003

Los Angeles

Photographers cluster around the car at the airport, pressing their lenses up against the windows. We push through them and into dense traffic. An hour later, I'm at the gates of Gwen's house in the hills. Tall stands of bamboo block her driveway from prying eyes. Her house is far nicer than my apartment, since I mostly live out of hotels these days. But this is home, too: the sun-warmed terra-cotta tiling, her floral scent drifting in the hallways, the beige stucco walls and wooden chicken coop. The rescue dogs that scamper behind her.

Gwen is in the backyard by the pool. She wears a T-shirt that says "KISS MY SASS" and rimless tinted sunglasses. Her roots are growing in, dark hairs pushing against the bright pink. I run over to her, and we hug, swaying back and forth in the same spot. She lowers her sunglasses, says I look tired.

"I'm jet-lagged."

"Let's grab some coffee, then. You need coffee."

Two bodyguards trail us in an SUV, while she drives me herself in her convertible. The gates open, and we are thrust out. She speeds around curves. I tell her I would prefer not to die, but she doesn't slow, keeps checking her rearview mirror for paparazzi.

The midday sun is stabbing. I forgot how ruthless Los Angeles can feel—it is much more forgiving from a distance. We end up on a main drag punctuated by stoplights every few hundred feet. Shoppers poke in and out of shops, gaudy bags swinging on their arms.

She turns to me, drumming her thumb on the steering wheel. "So how was Oslo?"

"It was fine. I made a fool of myself."

"How?"

I tell her what happened.

She's plainly shocked. "You and Axel?"

"No, because he rejected me."

"Axel is beautiful, of course. But he's so . . ." She scrunches her face up. "He's so serious and quiet. He's the last person I ever thought you'd be with."

"Yeah, well, he doesn't want to be with me." Even if he did, there's my upcoming tour, album promotion, a life that intersects with his for only a few weeks each year.

"What did he say *exactly*?"

I tell her. I've practically memorized it. After, she frowns. "So he loves you."

She slams the pedal at a red light. Behind us, her bodyguard skids to a stop, too. I glance at her in total disbelief.

"No, he doesn't. That's not it at all. Where the hell did you get that from?"

"He thinks you just wanted to have sex."

"He wasn't attracted to me, and he was being polite."

"Amber, he literally said—*you* said that he said, 'I think this might mean something different to you' or whatever. He can't just casually sleep with one of his artists. I mean, most of this industry is fucked. There are loads of slimy dudes. But not Axel. He's not like that. He's extremely reserved. He thinks through everything he does a million times over. Have you ever been to a restaurant with him? He takes, like, an hour to order. I think you've got this completely wrong."

I shake my head as we pull into the Starbucks parking lot. When she twists her key out and pushes her door open, the waiting cameras swarm. We're not particularly stunned by their appearance; their presence is a given in Los Angeles. "Hey, guys," she says. "Can you back up a little so we can get out?"

A man in the crowd speaks up. "Back up. Hey, back up!"

"Thanks so much."

"Amber, when did you last see Nicky?"

"Gwen! Amber! How are you doing today?"

Her bodyguard presses his thick arm against their chests, pushing them to the right. We're almost to the door, only several feet away, but they are a wall in front of us.

"What are you girls up to?"

"Can you just back up a bit, please?" Gwen says pleasantly, but her eyes are television static. "Thanks."

Her bodyguard shoves them back again. "Let's just step back two feet. Two feet, guys."

The men relinquish a few inches of territory, not enough for us to reach the door, and now we're in the center of them all.

"Amber, have you seen Nicky?"

"Are you girls grabbing coffee?"

"Yeah, what are you two ladies up to today?"

"That top looks great on you, Gwen."

"Thanks, David." She finally pulls the handle, and we slide into the store. We wait to order, not speaking, rays of interest traveling our way. She leans against the counter, blocked by her two security guards. And later, back in the car, after pressing through the men again, she says, "It's almost not worth leaving the house." We're at a red light. Her forehead is on the steering wheel, and her eyes are closed.

I take a sip of my latte. It's not as sweet as I imagined. "Yeah, I know."

The light changes. She drives.

Our days take on a rhythm. We wake up and eat leftover takeout together. Her assistant Maura and my assistant Brianna go over our respective schedules. I am picked up by cars for studio sessions. When I arrive home each night, I find Gwen and Tammy making out on the couch or watching DVDs. *Sex and the City* or *Buffy* or *Felicity*, since Gwen retroactively watches popular shows when she finds the time. Greg calls from Phoenix, where he owns a garage with buddies from college. Says I should come visit him. I'd like that, I tell him. Then he asks if I can bring Gwen.

"Gwendolyn!" I call. "My brother thinks you're hot."

A shriek from down the hall.

"Can I ask you something else?"

"Yeah, what?"

"Could you send me some of your hair?"

"No."

"Could you send me something you've worn before? Something you don't need. Or maybe autographs?"

"Can you email Sonny about it?"

"What's his email again?"

I tell him, and shortly after he hangs up.

One day, Gwen returns from a meeting and immediately turns on the shower. The steam pushes through the gap at the bottom of the door. Tammy and I don't bother knocking: Gwen cries only when she thinks she's being muffled by running water. Inside the shower, she's folded in on herself like a hard shell, hair slung over her face, water running down bolts of spine and pooling by her feet.

Tammy kneels before Gwen's naked body. I sit cross-legged on the bath mat.

"What happened?" Tammy asks, cupping her face.

Gwen leans her head back. Water fills her mouth. She spits it out. "I can't wait to fire Mike. I hate him. You know what he said to me? He came up close and I could smell his foul breath. He said, 'Gwen, your last single failed to chart in the Top 40. You shouldn't be resting now. You should be working harder.' He said I'm distracted, and he knows why. As if the record sales are my fault, not, like, an industry-wide problem." To Tammy: "He told me I can't bring you to New York for the Grammys. Said no one would pay for it. Then he goes, 'I've done so much for you, and now you decide to throw it all away.'"

"He's a little creep," Tammy says. "I've always said so."

Gwen says she wants to be alone for a while, so we leave her there, gnawing on her cheek, the rest of her body still.

In the hall, Tammy takes my arm. "I'm glad you're here. I'm worried. It's been bad. I don't know if she's told you."

"Bad how?"

"So, she spoke to this lawyer about breaking her contract with Mike, and the lawyer discovered something really disgusting. Mike Esposito is not even his real name. There was apparently a child pornography case against him in North Carolina. Years and years ago. He got off, no charges or anything, but he thought people wouldn't let him manage their kids if it could be traced back to him, so he changed his first name. That's what she's dealing with. Mike will probably take her to court. It might drag on."

A little creep, indeed. Most likely worse. Mike wanted to sit so close to Gwen because it made their warmth indistinguishable. Was she the heat source, or was he? I've met a lot of these types over the years. He likes to say he discovered Gwen. If not for him, she would be nothing. But take Mike Esposito away, and Gwen is still a singular talent. Take Gwen away from Mike Esposito, and he's the nothing.

Tammy is fiddling with her septum piercing. I ask, "How are you doing? Are you okay?" I want her to know that I see her kindness and all that she holds for Gwen.

She leans against the wall. "I'm fine. I don't know. Yesterday the dancers all filmed something for Gwen's *TRL* special, and I stood, like, all the way to the side. I let everyone else talk about her. We were supposed to have an authentic 'girl chat' or whatever for the cameras. CJ was like— you know CJ, right? She's cool. She was told to ask Gwen, 'So what's your ideal type of guy?' As if she'd just casually ask her that during rehearsal."

"She loves you very much. You know that, right?"

"Yeah, I do know that."

I point to her tattoo. "Is that Gwen?"

She smiles down at the bud on her arm, the one I noticed when we met. "Yeah. So, each leaf is a life event. A big tour. Things I'm really proud of. I look down at them to remind myself that so many of my dreams have come true, that I'm still growing every year. And each bud is a person I've loved. So, this one down here, that's my ex. He's an asshole. This one is Gwen. I'm going to make it a flower soon."

That night, I can hear them having sex. I pull my headphones on to give them privacy, to layer music over the moaning, the heavy breathing. Gwen, making sounds for no one but herself.

I'm eating with her in the kitchen. She has *Us Weekly* propped open on the counter. Suddenly she bursts out laughing, shoving the magazine over to me. These photographs are of us looking our most human, our most ordinary, which is meant to be the casualty.

> *Stars—They're Just Like Us!*
> **Gwen Morris** *and good friend* **Tamara Scott** *shop for sunglasses.*
> **Adrian Lee** *pumps his gas.*
> **Carter Moore** *enjoys a bucket of fried chicken with* **Ciara Ferguson**.
> **Maria Colmenares** *walks her three dogs with husband* **Troy Bennet**.
> **Amber Young** *indulges in a scoop of ice cream.*
> **Lila Rodriguez** *gets a parking ticket.*

I rub the photograph of me, lunging for the cone in my hand, the sun filling every crevice of my body, illuminating everything I'd want hidden. On the opposite page, Tammy and Gwen stand beside a rotating sunglass display. "Ah, yes. Your good friend Tamara."

"I was trying to remember why I do this." Gwen twists her face to the side so she can take a bite of her sandwich. She chews and swallows before she continues. "There was this little girl with a pink wig, just the other day. She told me she wrote a paper about me at school. It was something like What Do You Want to Be When You Grow Up. As if I'm a profession! Ballet dancer, astronaut, teacher, Gwen Morris. I didn't even go to college, and now this kid is writing a paper on me."

"At least you graduated from high school."

"Barely. It was online."

"Still counts. You know it does."

We turn up the stereo in her kitchen. When the DJ announces her new song "Count to 10," we both freeze, unsure. She hates hearing her own voice, thinks it's her weakest asset. But I know she must feel a rush whenever she comes on the radio—I always do. It feels like the very first time again. So we curl our hands into fist-microphones and lip-synch the song, bouncing from one chair to the next, stepping up onto her counter. *One night, two people across a room / three in the morning, for you, everything I do.* Tammy appears, drawn to the noise, the furniture screeching under our feet.

"What are y'all doing?" she asks. She wraps her arms around Gwen's waist. Gwen leans back against Tammy's chest, closes her eyes.

"*Everything I do,*" she whispers, swaying back and forth.

Gwen and I are sitting at an otherwise empty table. We are at the annual pre-Grammy gala at the Beverly Hilton, but we've schmoozed with too many executives, our dishonest smiles starting to hurt.

"I heard they broke up," Gwen says. At first, I think she means Wes and his wife. But I trace her gaze to the other side of the ballroom, where a tall blond woman slices through the crowd. "Alex mentioned it to me. It's not public yet. I mean, they haven't announced it, but yeah, the engagement is off. She's still wearing her ring, though."

I ask if Alex said anything else.

Gwen reaches for a chicken wing on her plate, the sauce slithering down her chin. "He was shitting on her. I walked away. I can't stand him, how he was talking about her. I like Savannah. She is the kindest human being. Not like us. I remember, when she beat me for the Grammy, she took my hand backstage. She gave me her award to hold, and she was like, 'You should have won this.' I thought she was lying. I was so annoyed. I couldn't conceive of someone in this business being so generous. But now I think she was, she really meant it. There's also the whole thing with her mom."

I reach over and wipe the sauce from her chin. "Oh, yeah. I heard a little about that."

"She's this super-religious lady. Really pissed off about the direction Savannah's career is going in. The more mature songs." Then Gwen looks over at me. "You know, you really started all that with 'Sweat.' Now we're all following you. We all want to be seen as adults, not little girls."

I watch Savannah in her glittering silver dress, the wink of light across each diamond. She laughs with teeth the color of untouched snow. And I remember when she was fifteen or sixteen years old. A doll in a playhouse. She always concealed more than Gwen or I did, kept most of her skin out of bounds. And so, the question was: What is beneath? Let's all imagine, together. And when I think back to the beginning—to 1997—it was Savannah, not us, who was the virginal, lily-white puritan. She was the city on a hill. She was never-ending anticipation. She would confirm, again and again, *yes*, she was still a virgin. And even though Gwen and I agreed it was a nebulous, imprecise term—virgin—we were cast against her in different ways. If I was the serpent, Gwen was Eve, the beautiful girl succumbing to temptation, innocence lost in VMA performances and magazine covers.

The next night, we attend the ceremony at Madison Square Garden. Gwen ascends the stage in a pale satin dress, the fabric a shade lighter than her hair. Alex Kowalczyk stands beside her, hands in his pockets.

"You know, when I was asked to present this next award," his monitor reads, "I was surprised we were paired together at first."

"Me too," Gwen says. "I wonder if they got confused. . . . There's that other ETA member I used to date."

"And you're not Savannah. Shoot. I won't tell her I grabbed your ass on the walk out."

"Maybe they mixed us all up?"

"They can't keep us straight. But nevertheless, we are both here to present the award for Best Pop Vocal Performance. These nominees are all incredibly talented artists. Right, Savannah?"

Music is changing. Where did we begin? Flutes carved from bone thousands of years ago. A primordial ritual where the first human sang, probably to a deity. Choirs in long cathedrals, a young virtuoso who became a eunuch to stop his voice from changing. Boys who sang for kings. Men who composed symphonies. Now Axel Holm, bathed in his computer's blue light.

MP3s of songs can be downloaded for ninety-nine cents. I have a shiny third-generation iPod. And there is a sense, from our handlers at the labels, that the industry will never be the same, but no one can say what these changes will mean. Even so, I hand over my new record: thirteen songs. Nine written and produced by me, Axel, Yusuf, and Oskar in the Oslo studio, the other four by songwriters and producers back in the US.

I call it *Honey*. At first, Lyle and the other Lolli executives hate the title. Their deeper voices start to drown out mine. But I dig my feet in. Because this album sounds like a lazy sun crawling up sheets. Someone's eyes igniting a radiant feeling. Everything inside you screaming *yes*. So horny you can barely breathe. So turned on you might die. The sweet tension of waiting, finally receiving. The vulnerability of pouring yourself over, hoping you'll get something—anything—back.

2003

New York

The *Honey* release party is held at a nightclub in New York. We have an ocher carpet to match the cover artwork: my naked body lathered in honey, with strategically placed swarms of bees, hummingbirds, flowers.

From the back seat of a car, I watch the city pass by. I stare at the humanity, wondering what all these people carry with them. I offer up narratives. That couple, stumbling down the block, just met at a bar and are going to have threadbare sex, but next time it will be better. That man, crumpling his fast-food bag, is trying to remember when he last saw his mother. I don't know anything about them, but they all, presumably, know something about me, have some crescent-shaped idea of who I am. The full moon is always there, isn't it? Even if the light isn't reflecting on all of it?

The car stops. For now, the press is quiet, testing their cameras, shouldering their equipment. When I step out, they lurch forward, and a wall of sound erupts. Cara says, "Can you back up please, guys? Thank you. Just back up. We're trying to get her through. You can't get a fucking picture if we can't even get her out of the car."

I step out onto a sidewalk bruised with flattened gum. Cara leads me to each outlet she wants me to speak with and pulls me away whenever an interview runs too long. *Amber, over here! To the right, Amber. Can you turn this way, Amber? How is this album different, Amber?*

"Tonally, it's even more mature." I feel Cara's hand on my elbow. "It's me exploring what my sexuality, my femininity means to me. Thank you."

"Are you dating anyone? Who are you dating?" they ask predictably. In the end, they are always, always predictable. I laugh that question off, but my heart is blinking with unfettered, naive hope.

The carpet hosts other musicians, actors, newly minted reality stars, boss men who run the labels from their high towers. A Baldwin. Pat, his red hair slicked back with gel. Sonny, my mom, Greg. Ty, whose solo album isn't being pushed by Siren the same way Alex's is, and it's incredibly obvious why. When he releases my waist, he's replaced by an executive. More of this. I am spun around and thrust at men, who leer at me and laugh with their heads held back. Mouths snake forward to eat appetizers. Straws swirl through drinks. Gwen walks the carpet wearing a baby-blue Juicy tracksuit. When our eyes meet, just for a moment in this chaos, we are saying: no one will ever understand me like you do. No one ever could. If we face each other, clasp our hands, and lean back on our heels, neither of us will ever fall.

And finally, a man wearing a loose black T-shirt, dark jeans. Everything about his demeanor is pointed inward. He probes golden waves away from his face as he nods. A scythe of desire cuts through me, and I force myself to turn away.

My mom is standing alone at the open bar, Greg off chatting with some girl he met. Her martini wobbles in its glass as she raises it to her lips. Her eyes are swollen with dark shadow, and her lips are flaky and dry. Her beauty has withered, but the bones are still there, like a tree in winter. I can see where the fullness once was, where it could grow again.

"Hi, Momma," I say. "How have you been?"

"Oh, it's been a bit stressful. Your father called me."

Such momentous things usually happen when you don't anticipate them anymore, but I never stopped. I waited patiently. My career was smoke, and I fanned it, hoping it would set the alarm off. "He did?"

"He's called several times, Amber."

I don't know which direction to push my anger in. "You didn't tell me."

"He wants money."

"Maybe he wants to know me."

She laughs. "He's only interested because there's money on the table now. I told him, 'You tell your new wife, your new family, that the daughter I raised alone, all by myself, wants *nothing* to do with you.' But apparently, the boys have started telling everyone who will listen that you're their older sister."

"I'm not, though."

"Well." She shrugs. We survey the party, the drone of conversation. "They are too young to understand. And your dad has a right to none of this. He wasn't there when I was driving you to auditions."

I shuffle through childhood memories, wondering if I've discarded the credit she deserves. Because I do remember her driving down cluttered highways, picking me up from school early to race to the city, just as much as I remember her abandonment. Once I was successful, she retreated into the house I bought for her. Gwen's mom wanted to comanage her career. Savannah's did. Mine threw her hands up, said it was time to be an adult. Maybe she interprets this as confidence in me, but I've only ever seen it as neglect. Both versions of her exist in my head at once, battling for dominance, and neither wins in the end.

I ask: "Did you ever think of coming on tour with me?"

"I knew you could do it on your own."

"There were times when I needed someone."

She blinks. "Let me tell you something. I may not have been the best mother in the world, but I do know one thing. You had no goddamn stage parent. I drove you back and forth to the city, and it was a pain in my ass, but I did it only because you begged me to take you to auditions. You were old enough to live your life. I wasn't going to coddle you in some nest, Amber. Our nest wasn't the best place to be. You were ready to jump. I recognized that. And I can't believe you're *my* daughter. Goddamn. You are the only good thing I've ever done." She shakes her head.

This sentence, a dart to my chest. I wonder if my entire life, I've been waiting for her to say this.

"And Greg, of course," she adds. She plucks the olive from her martini glass, raising it to her lips.

After she swallows, she reaches forward and cups my cheek. "Are you seeing anyone? I've been reading about you and all these men in magazines, but I have no idea what's really going on."

"I've been taking time for myself," I say. "My career."

"No boy? That's new."

"Mom."

"Well, that might be a good thing. I have a story I was telling someone earlier. I remember, when you were seven or eight, a plumber came by to fix the sink. He was young, maybe thirty. And you blushed and followed him around, asking him questions. He gave you a flower he picked from someone's garden. You carried it around the apartment for days." She laughs and chokes, pounding at her chest. "You were always like that. Boy crazy. As you got older, they started looking at you differently. You were a beautiful girl. You had these big brown eyes. Everyone, everywhere I went, would always say, 'What a beautiful girl.' I couldn't go to the supermarket without someone saying it."

"I never felt beautiful."

"You were too busy picking at yourself. You used to pick at your skin. Scratch yourself. You got hives on your neck. Remember that? You got them the night of the school dance and you screamed at me in the car saying you couldn't go, you looked ugly, no one had asked you. I think you were thirteen."

"I remember," I say. I remember: her hand tight around my wrist when I told her I'd had sex. The empty bottles in hidden places. Nights that became wounds because she was out, doing who knows what. But maybe she felt that by taking her rot elsewhere, she wouldn't infect us.

So I take her hand and tell her I love her. She looks at me curiously: What's the catch? But there isn't one. She was younger than I am when she had me. Still becoming. There must have been days after my dad left when even the light was heavy, but she didn't have a name for the feeling.

"I love you, too," she says.

The story of my birth: I was cesarean, unwilling to turn, and so she was put under as the doctor cut her open. In another century, I might have gotten caught inside the birth canal—nails clinging to the warmth of her womb, refusing to budge. She might have bled out; I might have taken us both. But I didn't, and now I'm beyond her, a whole person.

I find myself behind the DJ booth giving a short speech. Lyle Michaels lays his arm around my shoulder. His hand travels slowly down my back, a stalled elevator. When my entire body flinches, he finally pulls away.

I thank everyone for coming and raise my glass. Cameras flash and pop. I'm swept up into the crowd, my new album panting from the speakers, and there, in a corner, I spot Axel again. I'm hoping he will come over when he's ready. It's like waiting for a cat, one that moves only when it thinks it's not being watched and only to places where you don't want it to wander. I must tuck in all my desire, all my longing, and hope it's not visible. Only then will he show up. And I'm right.

"Hello," he says shyly.

"I'm glad you've emerged from under your rock."

"You know how I like my rock."

I am so aware of him—how his presence soothes the waters surrounding me, all these swirling bodies. "I didn't know if you were coming."

He looks around, clearly uncomfortable. "You know how I dislike these things."

"I do, too. But I'm glad you're here."

"Are you?"

"Yeah. I am."

He shakes his head and laughs. "That's good."

"Let's listen," I say. "Close your eyes." Around us, the discord fades to a hush. The album is currently on "Pain," and I peel back the layers. Beneath my lead vocal, beneath the background harmonies, beneath everything, I hear him.

When I open my eyes, I ask if he'd like to talk.

"Very much. Where?"

We search for a place. The back of his hand nudges my arm, and I can't tell if it's accidental or not. He starts telling me how, when he first visited New York in his early twenties, he hated it. "It looked like the inside of a computer. Everything so close together like a circuit board." He makes a face. "Don't laugh at me."

"I'm not."

"You are."

"Axel, I would never laugh at you."

Finding a deserted hallway beyond the bathrooms, illuminated only by a pulsing neon exit sign, we lean against opposite walls, a few feet apart.

"I wanted to apologize," I say. "For my last night in Oslo. I shouldn't have done that."

He crosses his arms over his chest. "That's okay, Amber."

"No, it was irresponsible of me."

He runs his hand through his hair. Axel is good. I could lean on him like a car window, watching the world pass. But I can see the aching, too: long-distance calls, Oslo to a tour bus. Wanting to be wherever I was not. My focus drifting away. My mother's voice. No man for once, what a good thing. But what if one day, I can carry two things at once? Isn't that growing up—learning you can have moderation instead of extremity, realizing this can be just as pleasurable? Not being consumed by one person, but feeding others as they feed you?

His eyes flick to me. The feeling I have then is what I imagine electrocution must be like: one intense strike of heat. I never imagined I would feel this way for Axel—but sometimes attraction wakes up in you. Sometimes it raises its head, astonished and dazed to discover what it wants.

He will never say anything because it's not his nature. It has to be me.

"I want to clarify something. I want to make sure you didn't—I'm worried you might have misunderstood me back in Oslo."

His eyebrows draw together. "Okay."

"Once I say this, we can pretend I didn't say it, if you'd like to. I just think you should know."

His face opens up. It reminds me of the easy, uncomplicated joy I saw when we recorded the first seeds of a song in his room. "Amber, I understand."

This is how we've made songs together, isn't it? His brain to mine, back to his. Mine to his to mine. This is just a conversation we've had many times before—*Try it again. The way we did it yesterday? No, the other time*—all that's needed for us to land in the same place.

"You understand?"

He nods. "Do you?"

I laugh a little. "I didn't before. But, Axel, I have to tour again for this album. I'll be away for a year. In all honesty, back in Oslo, I didn't think this through, and I should have. I should have known what I wanted."

"So, you don't think we should," he continues for me.

I shake my head.

"Maybe it's best. I agree with you. I do. You should work with other producers, expand yourself, try new things. I want that for you."

"I know. You're all logic."

"Not always."

He's just on the other side of the hallway, and I try to rein myself in, but my desire bucks. I want to reach into the chaos inside myself, pour a little of it into him, just to see what he'll do with it. So I tip over. I'm on my side of the hallway, and then I'm on his. To really kiss him is to step into my own body. To be grateful for it. When his hand is between my legs and his tongue is in my mouth, I can't believe it can feel so good, so hungry, so vital, that it can receive all these sensations and send them on to me. I'm so wet I also feel a flash of shame, but he's making such gorgeous noises in my ear, and the world can't slap my hand in this empty hallway.

"Let me," he says, kissing his way down my body until he's on his knees. "Would you like me to?"

I say yes, and then he's folding up my jean miniskirt, pressing his mouth between my legs. I wrap my hands in his hair. His fingers and tongue are working together, circling and pressing all the right places, slow at first and then faster. He's exactly as I imagined he would be. Meticulous. Generous. All senses besides touch recede. The pressure inside me slowly builds, then cracks like a window, and he is the rock thrown.

How many people have said I'm a slut? A whore. A piece of trash. I should be burned. Maybe they are right about the burning: I am red and sizzling from the ragged breaths, from the blood rushing all over, to every single limb.

Axel kissing my neck, my lips, my collarbone. Him whispering, "I want you to feel good always."

"I want you to feel good, too," I say, but as I'm reaching for his belt, someone rounds the corner, doubling back when she sees us. We laugh, our faces so close together we are exchanging hot air.

"Are you okay waiting?"

"Of course," he says.

"I mean until after my tour."

"I know what you meant." He leans down to whisper in my ear, pinning me against the wall. "Amber." His voice is so soft when he says my name. "I want you to be happy. You know exactly where to find me if you choose to make another album with me, okay?" He wraps his arms around me, and I close my eyes. Other men were pans straining in rivers for gold: I could be what they searched for. But I don't want to be metal anymore.

I return to the dance floor. Gwen's eyes widen when she sees me. She starts combing through my hair with her fingers, rubbing my lipstick off with her napkin.

"Where the hell have you been?"

I sit on her lap, pull her close, so we are pressed cheek to cheek. "You are very emotionally intelligent. Do you know that?"

"Um, yeah. I do."

My song is playing, something Axel and I wrote together. Something I wrote. I tip my face up to meet the sound.

2003

New York

The middle of summer, a heap of trash on the curb. A rat scurrying beneath the wheels of a truck. I pace back and forth along the sidewalk, smoking the dregs of a cigarette, fanning my face with my other hand. Sonny presses his whole body against the heavy door, stumbling out onto the street. He tries to convince me to come back in.

I'm supposed to enter the stage bareback on a horse, wearing a translucent bodysuit with a seashell bra. My hair will cascade down my back, blowing behind me in manufactured wind.

"I need to ride an actual horse before the show," I tell Sonny.

"It will be the same thing as the puppet we have now."

"A horse is a real animal. That mound on a stick is not a real animal. Also, PETA is going to hate me. I don't want to hurt the horse. What if the horse jumps into the audience? What will we do then?"

"The horse won't spook. The horse will be fine."

Sonny is the kind of person who has no regard or sympathy for most animals. He avoids the dogs who pass him on the street, afraid of being bitten.

"It's a trained horse?"

"Highly trained. A professional will be onstage with you. He'll be leading it the whole time."

"I want to ride the horse before," I repeat. Sonny fiddles with the rings on his stubby fingers. Six years we have known each other. The other day, he asked me when I got so demanding. When I started complaining. The success has gone to my head. But I think men like Sonny start asking these things when the way it is for them starts souring. "Sonny," I say, "I don't want to get hurt."

"Fine."

I twist the cigarette under my shoe. We go back in. This is the third and final day of preparation for MTV. There are photo shoots to promote the awards, two dress rehearsals. At some point, cameras enter the practice room to interview me. "It'll be cool," I tell the camera crew. "This is Gloria, my choreographer. We've been working together—how many years now? A long time. She was one of my dancers, but she choreographs for me now, and she can read my mind. I'm not the best dancer. I'm no Gwen Morris. I rely on Gloria a lot. I'm always nervous, since there are a lot of elements that have to go right. Hopefully I don't fall off the horse, but I guess by the time this airs we'll know if that happens. Thanks for joining me for rehearsals, MTV, and I'll see you on Friday."

Shadows of skyscrapers slowly cross the studio floor. The sun rises, falls again.

Thirty minutes before I'm supposed to go onstage, there's a knock on my dressing room door. I'm half-undressed, the zipper of the bodysuit abandoned near my waist. I wrap a towel around myself as my assistant Brianna opens the door, just wide enough to reveal an eye.

"Can I have a sec, Amber?"

Brianna and I exchange a glance.

"Just a minute, Bri. Thank you."

She backs out of the room. My possessions are littered across the floor: makeup-removing wipes, Ambien and Tylenol PM, an old sweatshirt I stole from Gwen's house. I push my head through it, and it smells like her. Then I tell Wes to come in.

"What's up?" Wes asks this casually, as if it's only been a day or two. It's almost eerie how easily he restores our familiarity.

I bend toward the mirror, stick an earring through a hole. My hands are shaking. "It's been a while."

"Has it? We've seen each other."

"I heard your wife is pregnant." I laugh. "That's so weird. You seem too young to have a kid."

"I'm twenty-five."

"I know how old you are."

He takes a seat in the folding chair next to the clothing rack. Looking at him now, I can see why my younger self was so infatuated. Why I offered up everything. But I also see the subtle changes in him: He's lost some luster now that ETA is on hiatus and he's gearing up to release his own solo album. He's fidgety, unfocused. He has a new tattoo on his arm: a coiled snake. Greasy hair, which looks like it hasn't been washed, although this could be the intended effect. Our eyes meet, and his pupils dilate.

He scratches his head. "So, you were with Max Taylor?"

I laugh again. "We hung out once."

"I also heard Leo Rivera."

"No, that one isn't true."

"Nicky Land?"

"That was a while ago."

"Too old for you?"

"I was just always on the road."

"I always thought you'd end up with someone like that. Someone who wanted to take care of you."

"I don't want someone to take care of me."

"Don't you? I feel like—" He pauses, running his hands down his face. "I don't know."

But I do know. What if I told him all the things I know? I am twenty years old, and I have his baby inside of me. I am nineteen years old, following him through darkness to a lit-up monument. I am twelve years old, folded over myself backstage, trembling after my loss. He says I should have won. And I think, because I am young, because I am fumbling and raw, that if someone like that could love me, it will decide something about me, once and for all. In stone, it will finally say: I am good, I am worthy, I have been chosen.

He stands and the folding chair falls to the floor, abandoned.

"Don't you remember?" he asks.

"Of course."

"Will anything feel like it again?"

"No. And it shouldn't. It should feel different every time."

He stares at my lips. "I got married."

"I know. What's wrong with you?"

He sighs. Finally, he steps back, head in his hands. "I'll always be obsessed with you, I think."

No. He's a magpie. He likes shiny, faraway things.

"Don't say that when your beautiful wife is sitting next to you in the audience. She really is beautiful; I've always thought so. Go back."

"I will. Can you just hold me for a second? As a friend."

"Okay."

So, we wrap our arms around each other. I can easily slip through time if I let myself. His mouth on my hair, breathing in deep. I wonder if he's going to cry, if I'll cry, too. Maybe I pity him, maybe I'm a little victorious, but these feelings are ugly—I don't want them. I push back from his chest, removing his arms from my waist. He lets go.

I press a can of Diet Coke to my forehead to cool off. Sonny hands me my iPod and headphones so I will be distracted from my nerves. I listen to the Cranberries because I want to feel like I'm sixteen again, hanging my head out of Lindsey's car window, praying for a different life. The rim of the ocean is just visible behind the dunes, and if I hold my hand out, the wind is the only thing pushing against me.

A production assistant hands me my earpiece. I am led from the greenroom to the stage, followed closely by Dale and Sonny. In the dim light, I can make out a memory: three years ago, five figures were lined up here. I stared up from the audience, assuming I would always sit at that low angle, watching ETA's synchronized choreography from below. Since then, a woman has grown old inside of me, died, been born again.

The white horse is led to me. It has apparently taken a shit in the hall. But it watches me intelligently, stomping a powerful hoof. I run my fingers down its forehead, trying to soothe it, recognizing this creature's carnal fear as my own. The powerful body, already coated in a layer of sweat, trembles with anticipation. Maybe it wants to run.

The trainer hoists me up. "I feel sorry for him," I say, patting the horse's neck.

"He was a circus horse," says the trainer. "I promise you he's happier here than with the kids who stick their fingers up his nose."

"He needs a pasture."

"I won't argue with that." The trainer tugs on the bridle and pulls us into the wings. The crowd is hushed. Cameras tilt toward the stage. A production team has created a beach set: seabirds call, waves curl into foam. My dancers take their places. Gloria squeezes my hand, and her body sends confidence into mine.

Beneath my legs, the muscles of the horse churn. "*You weren't the one for him,*" I begin. While slow at first, each verse builds the tension until you realize the song is angry. It's devastated. I jump down from the horse to join the dancers for the hook: "*What do I do, what do I do / With all this pain?*" As I sing, I am released, as if I am circling down toward some essential instinct, something as necessary as sex, food, water. It is milk glands in the breasts, an expanding belly. My body was made for this. My body was made.

The horse's tail disappears into the dark with a flick. In the crowd, a cameraman pans in on Wes, who smiles politely. Gwen is in another section, standing and clapping until her palms are red. In front of televisions across the country, kids ask for one more minute before bed, parents are complaining—"She's not wearing anything on national TV, for Christ's sake, turn this off"—and somewhere in the world, maybe even Camila Land will watch my performance. My mother, a glass of wine on the bedstand. In Oslo, Axel might take his cup of morning coffee, sit in front of his old television, and find the show broadcast on a global station. He will see the horse. Me astride it.

But what do I *feel*, as my voice echoes through the hall?

I feel like water, slowly carving away at stone. I feel like fire— sometimes the soft flicker of a candle, sometimes a hungry, devouring flame. I feel every contradiction, every current inside myself. I want this forever. Because when I sing, I feel like I'm returning to the earth, tunneling deep into it, myself at the bottom. And I want to bound across it—feet pounding, heart bursting—until I've experienced every-thing, everything there is to ever be felt.

OUTRO
2004

2004

New York

The reporter decides to interview me and Gwen separately. It is my second *Rolling Stone* cover, her third. Our first together.

Dale leads him into Battery Studios, where I'm sprawled on the floor, surrounded by notebooks. I reach up to shake his hand.

"Nice to meet you, Amber."

"Likewise. Thanks for coming."

I offer him water, but he shakes his head. We make small talk. So hot recently. Terrible traffic. He clicks his pen. Eventually, his face sags with disinterest, and I know he wants to begin. My mind springs forward, as it always does: How deep does he want to dig inside me? How deep, this time? But he seems kind enough, maybe a little removed.

I gesture to his tape recorder. "So, I thought we could start—"

His face twists in confusion. "I actually have questions I want to ask."

Our eyes meet, and it feels like we are arm wrestling. He looks away first; I've smacked his wrist on the table.

"Oh, thank you." I reach over and pluck a berry from its plastic container on the table. Juice bursts inside my mouth, runs slowly down my throat, and it's all the sweeter for its deliberateness. "It's just, I already know exactly what I want to say."

Months later. A girl, reaching for a magazine on a newsstand. She sees our slicked-back hair. Our dewy skin. The translucent white tank tops and the strategically placed headline, "*AMBER AND GWEN: WET AND WILD.*" She flips inside to find the profile, which begins: "The bubblegum pop princesses are growing up. They want you to know they're anything but perfect—they're actually very naughty, more witch than damsel. Remove the crowns and stomp on them. Take Gwen Morris and Amber Young. Both emerged when dance-pop and boy bands were the new grunge, but tastes have changed once again. They say they are ready for a new age, and they're showing even more skin in this one."

I imagine there's something ugly in her that likes when we're kicked a little. I also imagine some part of her understands. Because she knows we contain more than the first metal we are cast in. I am the glass people press their hands against, but inside the tank, twirling in wonder, there is some other, fragile self.

Amber Melissa Young (born July 3, 1980) is an American singer, songwriter, and philanthropist. Young rose to fame in 1999, following the release of her first album, *In Your Eyes*, containing her debut single "Sweat." "Please Don't Disturb," the second single from her second album, *Amber Young*, peaked at number 7 on the *Billboard* Hot 100 and topped the charts in nine countries. Young subsequently released the albums *Honey* (2003), *Life in Eden* (2006), and *The Nine Muses* (2012). *Honey* has sold over eight million copies worldwide, produced the hit singles "Pain" and "Lying to Myself Under U," and earned Young her first Grammy nomination. The album was certified multiplatinum by the Recording Industry Association of America (RIAA). She has earned awards and accolades including two Grammy Awards, an MTV Video Music Award, and two *Billboard* Music Awards. Since 2009, Young has also written songs for a number of artists, including No. 1 hits for Gwen Morris, Lauren Li, and Jade Shaw.

Born	Amber Melissa Young July 3, 1980 (age 42) Montclair, New Jersey U.S.
Occupation	Singer Songwriter Entrepreneur Philanthropist
Years active	1997–present
Spouse(s)	Axel Holm (m. 2009)
Children	1
Awards	Full list
Musical career	
Genres	Pop pop-rock dance-pop
Instruments	Vocals
Labels	Lolli
Website	amberyoungmusic.com

Contents [hide]

Life in Eden
Album booklet

I'm bursting with thanks. I'm so grateful each time I get to make a new album. My name is on the cover, but there are so many people behind me. Here are just a few . . .

Mom & Greg, for listening to me through the walls for all those years.

To everyone at Lolli: Lyle, Pat, Dee, Grace, Tom, Marsha, thank you for this career and your belief in me.

Sonny, hon, are you sick of me yet??

Bri, Dale, and my security team, I know my schedule is nuts! You are all miracles. I hope you know how much I appreciate you.

To my dancers, my makeup team, my styling team: Thank you for putting up with me and making me laugh!!

To my band and my crew, none of this would be possible if it weren't for you. YOU are the reason the show goes on.

To all the producers and engineers who made this album so special and for seeing my vision. I love learning from you all. Axel, Yusuf, Oskar, Omar, Magnus, Nick, Matt—you are true geniuses.

To my fans for their love. Nothing is possible without it.

To Angela, I won't ever forget that you saw me first.

Ty, having you as my opener on tour was indescribable, a dream come true. Let's travel the world together again soon, please and thank you. You make me more fun, believe it or not . . .

T, your friendship means so much to me. It makes me so happy that we've gotten so close. Thank you for all the pep talks.

A, you just asked what I'm doing over here. I said writing a very important book, just as a joke, but you said, "Oh, how cool," because you really believed I could be. I love you.

G, I've got you. Always. So where are you now? Where are you going next? Wherever it is, I'll be there. Love you with my whole heart.

Acknowledgments

To me, a book doesn't end until the acknowledgments page. Maybe it's because I've worked in the publishing industry myself. Maybe it's because I know a book extends far beyond its author. So here are the folks who brought this book to life. I owe them all my thanks.

First, to Jamie Carr, my agent. Thank you for seeing something in me. You are truly the most brilliant partner to have by my side. I'm so lucky. I hope you know Amber is yours, too—your sharp editorial eye made her and this book shine. To many, many more.

To the Book Group. I'm so honored to be one of your authors.

To Jenny Meyer, who took Amber's tour worldwide. Thank you for finding such perfect homes for us abroad. And to Heidi Gall at Jenny Meyer Literary.

To Berni Vann and Dana Spector, for your support and enthusiasm and care.

To Randi Kramer, my editor, you have been the perfect teammate, always on the ball. Thank you for making this book so much better and for pushing me as a writer. I'm so grateful.

To Melissa Cox, my UK editor, and the entire team. Thank you for all the love and excitement for *Honey*.

To Ryan Doherty, editorial director, thank you for guiding us to the end and for all of your support.

To Erin Cahill, studio manager and designer of my cover. Thank you from the bottom of my heart for all of your hard work on this incredible cover.

To Faith Tomlin, editorial assistant.

To Martin Dolan, editorial intern.

To Anne Twomey, creative director.

To Deb Futter, president and publisher.

To Rachel Chou, associate publisher.

To Sandra Moore, marketing assistant.

To Anna Belle Hindenlang, senior publicist.

To Christine Mykityshyn, publicity director.

To Emily Radell, publicity assistant.

To Jennifer Jackson, executive director of marketing.

To Jaime Noven, senior marketing manager.

To Rebecca Ritchey, senior manager of social media.

To Yelizaveta Rogulina, marketing and art intern.

To Megan Draper, publicity and marketing intern.

To Jane Haxby, copy editor.

To Marinda Valenti, proofreader.

To Cassie Gutman, cold reader.

To Morgan Mitchell, production editor.

To Vincent Stanley, production manager.

To Peter Richardson, director of trade manufacturing and production.

To Michelle McMillian, interior designer.

To Emily Walters, managing editor.

To Elizabeth Hubbard, associate managing editor.

To every indie bookseller who places books in the hands of readers—you are essential, and I'm so incredibly grateful. To every sales rep. To every librarian. To every reviewer.

To Zoe, what if our moms hadn't met? All my love. To Lydia, I can't wait to read what you write for the rest of our lives. You are the best writing partner and friend I could ask for. To Catalina, for your early read and your impeccable taste. To Abby and to Julie, for always being there for me. To all my friends in every stage of life—I love you all so much.

To Julie and Robbie Couch.

To my brother, Garrett. I love you so much.

To my dad, who read my early stories and told me I could be an author one day.

To my grandpa Tom. I wish you could see this.

To my mom. You always brought me to the bookstore, and you have always put my happiness first. I love to read because you love to read. I'm so glad the cover is pink because it makes me think of you.

To Collin. You've held my hand through everything, told me I could do it, told me I was good enough and that it was all going to be okay. I'm just so grateful for our life together. And to our cats, Nimbus and Zelda, who provide endless entertainment.

To the album *Honey* by Robyn, which inspired the title. To every writer and book and song and film that has ever moved me.

To the books I read for research that helped me create and imagine this world: *Open Book* by Jessica Simpson, *How Music Works* by David Byrne, *Out of Sync* by Lance Bass, *The Song Machine* by John Seabrook, *90s Bitch* by Allison Yarrow, *Paris* by Paris Hilton, and *Britney Spears's Blackout* by Natasha Lasky.

Finally, to all the pop stars I had posters of on my bedroom wall.

About the Author

Isabel Banta is a writer, book publicist, and indie book-seller based in Brooklyn. She graduated from the University of Virginia. *Honey* is her debut novel.